Knit, Purl, a Baby and a Girl includes references to fatphobia and disordered eating, and mentions of pregnancy loss.

KNIT, PURL, A BABY AND A GIRL

Hettie Bell

carina
press

carina press®

ISBN-13: 978-1-335-68800-2

Knit, Purl, a Baby and a Girl

Copyright © 2021 by Hettie Bell

This edition published by arrangement with Harlequin Books S.A.

For questions and comments about the quality of this book, please contact us at CustomerService@Harlequin.com.

Carina Press
22 Adelaide St. West, 40th Floor
Toronto, Ontario M5H 4E3, Canada
www.CarinaPress.com

Printed in U.S.A.

KNIT, PURL, A BABY AND A GIRL

Chapter One

If this were one of those mid-00s R-rated bro comedies, my story would begin two months ago, the night I got sloppy drunk and succumbed to a 2 am from my ex. Our sex would be comical, full of the usual "realistic" comedy-sex pratfalls: bumping heads, limb-entangling clothes, and downright terrible dirty talk, but never crossing the realistic and/or comical line where I as the female party stop looking sexually appealing for even a second of screen time.

I'd also inexplicably have sex with my bra still on, and as soon as my schlubby not-nearly-hot-enough-for-me ex rolled off to instant sleep, I'd have my genitals—but never my shiny, shaved legs—covered by his artfully tousled sheet.

Like he'd ever have a flat sheet on his bed, but I digress.

Luckily for all of us but especially me, this isn't a mid-

00s R-rated bro comedy. It isn't the story of a lovable loser manchild who, in spite of how bitchy and irrational his harpy nag of an ex is about everything, still manages to barely grow up and come into himself, just in time for said harpy to renounce her nagging ways and meekly accept all his faults, negating any need on his part for personal growth. It isn't the story of a guy who not only gets the girl, but gets to keep his video game and pot habit, too. It isn't the story of a *guy* at all.

It's mine.

About—among other things—knitting, having sex without a bra on, and not only *not* having permanently shaved legs, but going several months without even *touching* a razor.

And it starts at a Planned Parenthood.

"You don't have to talk to them," the woman in the neon pink vest tells me and flashes an edgy smile. "You don't have to listen to them. You don't even have to look at them."

"Okay." I nod, already shell-shocked. We're standing sheltered by the door of my cab, but it might as well be tissue paper for all it protects me from the sounds of shouting and singing. There's one particularly throaty woman who keeps reciting a version of Hail Mary that would be more at home in a horror flick than a church.

"I'm Rhiannon. I'm gonna be with you every step. If you want me to hold your hand, I can. If you want me to make small talk, I can. If you want me to recite *Monty Python and the Holy Grail* including the moose jokes from the opening credits, I can. I also have a very large umbrella."

She gestures to the four-foot-long neon pink *staff* she's leaning on. "Sadly I'm not allowed to use it as a weapon." This time her smile seems ever so slightly more natural, and I find myself smiling back.

"Okay," I say again, a little more confidently.

"You ready?"

The question isn't funny, not in the phrasing or the delivery, but it still makes me laugh. I am the absolute opposite of ready. Not ready to face the fire and brimstone waiting for me on the sidewalk (which I assume is what Rhiannon is asking about), not ready to commit to the irreversible decision I'm somehow supposed to make today, and sure as hell not ready to be a mother. I don't even consider myself ready to be an *adult*, and yet here I am, twenty-two and on my own regardless.

Rhiannon opens her very large umbrella.

She may not be allowed to use it as a weapon, but she's still damn good with it regardless. One minute she's twisting it to hide my face from some asshole recording me with a handheld video camera. The next, she's using the pink fabric of it to block my view of a particularly gory five-foot poster before my brain can register the image. She doesn't recite Monty Python to me, but she does talk my ear off with her excitement for tea latte season.

"Tea latte season?" I ask. "You sure you don't mean that lesser-known season… What do they call it? Oh yeah, 'Fall'?"

"Nope. Tea latte season," she repeats without hesitation.

"Not *pumpkin spice* season?" I continue, hoping that even though Rhiannon and I are strangers to one another, the in-joke will be one we can still share. Surrounded by hate and harassment on all sides, I'm desperate for kinder human connection, even if it means bonding with a clinic escort over stale memes.

"Oh God no. Not that I have anything against Basic girls—some of my best friends wear Uggs!—but little known fact, pumpkin spice syrup? Not the best choice for the lactose intolerant among us."

It may be impossible for either of us to be loud enough to drown out the noise, but the light talk is still a welcome distraction.

Rhiannon even manages to get me to laugh—right as some geriatric asshole is calling me a whore, no less—by regaling me with the story of the day said lactose intolerance met a disbelieving barista and a latte that *definitely* wasn't soy.

I'm so damn glad she's here. I can't imagine running this gauntlet with Jake, assuming he didn't smoke up and flake like that time we were supposed to go to my Grammie's funeral. I certainly can't imagine being here with my mother or sister, because that would mean admitting to either of them why I need to be here in the first place.

Yeah, no thanks.

Not that anyone in my family spends their weekends wailing and handing out pamphlets like this Costco-sized pack of nutbars, and I know if I called my mom she'd be here in a flash, even pay for the procedure if I needed her to, but none of that means she'd be over the moon happy that her college-dropout youngest daughter got herself knocked up by her loser ex-boyfriend. And the thought of admitting my shame to my big sister, the 4.0 student and lawyer, isn't much better.

The last thing I need in my life is to disappoint my family even more than I already have.

But unlike when I'd very conspicuously needed my mom to come and help pack up my dorm room two months before the end of semester, she doesn't ever need to know about this. As long as I do what I'm *supposed* to do and get this abortion, she'll never have to know. None of them will ever have to know.

"Remember," Rhiannon says in parting as she drops me off safely at the door of the clinic, "Whatever choice you make, it's always the right one."

It's a nice sentiment, but is it still true when your choice isn't a choice at all?

When is a choice not a choice?

I think it over as I fill out my medical history form, drumming out a tattoo on the clipboard with the end of my pen. It's an old habit from my days of high pressure tests, even though the hardest question on this sheet is *Starting Date of Last Period.*

Six weeks, four days ago, for the record. I'd figured *that* one out the day I finally gave in and forced myself to buy a two-pack of digital tests. Because, you know, there was totally a chance of the results being inconclusive, right?

I hand my form in with the guilty smile and head-duck of someone who's just finished answering every multiple choice question with *C.*

This isn't a multiple choice test. The "choice", for me at

least, is an illusion. I should be sure about this. It's simple and straightforward. I know what I'm here for, what I'm supposed to do. So why do I feel like I've taken a wild stab in the dark and flunked?

I'm still mulling it all over when the receptionist calls out, "Poppy?" In fact, I'm *so* caught up that it takes her two tries to get my attention.

"Th-that's me!" I blurt out, raising my hand like I'm still in grade school. Every other person in the quiet waiting room turns to look at me, and even though their expressions are either smiling or neutral, I want to crawl under the carpet. Instead, I laugh nervously, put my hand back in my lap. Fix my skirt. Wish Rhiannon were still here, telling me more about her dietary restrictions. Anything to release this pressure building up inside me, this horrible impending sense of doom that comes from knowing that in the next hour I'm going to have to commit to this—*my*, dammit—choice.

My choice that nonetheless feels like it's already been made. The last time I was put in this position was when I chose my college path...or rather, agreed to the path my mother set out for me. And we all know how *that* turned out.

My mother isn't here to voice her opinion on this particular choice, but I can still hear her voice loud and clear in the back of my mind:

"Just because college didn't work out doesn't mean you don't still have your whole life ahead of you!"

"I know things aren't going according to plan for you, but that doesn't mean you have to give up!"

"*Sweetheart, do you really think you're ready for a baby? I know they say nobody's ready for a baby, but that doesn't mean there isn't such a thing as being* not *ready!*"

Thanks, Mom.

And yep, I am the definition of not ready: single, living in a studio apartment, working a cushy receptionist job I only landed because of my mother's meddling—which has health insurance at least, but isn't exactly where I pictured myself being when I was sixteen and not yet a failure.

What could I possibly have to offer a baby? By the time she planned to have me, my mom was the head of her department at the hospital where she worked, was married, owned a home and two cars, and already had a contingency fund set aside to pay for the various unexpected costs of having a baby.

What would I do, bring my baby home from the hospital on the bus?

PS, note to self: stop calling this thing "baby".

The receptionist, who introduces herself as Tammy, buzzes me through a heavy steel door to the left of the glass-fronted reception desk and leads me to a small bathroom, where she points to a specimen cup on the counter. "Go ahead and get this half full, screw the lid on, and leave it on the counter for me. Then you can head over to patient counseling room 3, where someone will be in shortly to discuss the results with you.

I already know what those results will be, but I suppose they have to do their due diligence. Although why anyone would put themselves through this unless they were *absolutely certain...*

I slip into the bathroom and close the door behind me. Squat awkwardly over the toilet with my tights around my ankles and my peecup in hand. On the wall next to the toilet is a notice that reads:

Are you being abused? Coerced? Is your partner/family control-ling your reproduction? Take a sticker and attach it to your sample for confidential counselling.

I stare at the little sheet of red dot stickers while I wait to pee and think about Jake, who's probably still asleep or, at the very most, on a wake and bake right now. Not abu-sive, not coercive, not controlling. Just…not relevant at all.

If I have this baby, I probably won't even put his name on the birth certificate.

Except I'm not having this baby.

Except it's not a baby! Fuck!

My pee makes its debut all over my hand, barely splash-ing the insides of the stupid cup. So much for half full. I'll be lucky to get my cup even a quarter full. I hope they don't have to test my blood instead.

At least my fear of needles gives me something new to agonize over when I head to the patient counselling room.

It's small and beige, with three chairs set around a desk, a bowl of hard candy, and various medical posters papering the walls comparing birth control methods or advertising the importance of breast exams. Unlike my regular family doctor's, there's no saccharine Anne Geddes print to face down. Thank God. Er, or maybe not God, considering the hymn-singing creeps outside.

I unwrap and eat three candies in the time it takes a nurse to arrive. She has my chart tucked under one arm and gives me a handshake with the other, then seats herself across the desk from me.

"All right. Poppy. Hi. I'm Janine, I'm an RN here. So I see you took a pregnancy test at home before you came in?"

My palms are suddenly sweaty. "Y-yes. That's correct. Two of them, actually. If that matters. Although I guess it probably doesn't since the result was the same both times."

Why am I acting like she's interrogating me?

"And that result…was positive?"

"Yes."

She opens my chart but doesn't really look at it. "The test we just did here today came up the same." She pauses, looks me directly in the eye. "Poppy, you're pregnant. And you've come to the right place."

I wish I could wrap myself up in her validation like a blanket, let it give me the sense of relief she obviously intends to impart.

But I don't.

I can't.

So I put my face in my hands and cry.

Chapter Two

I can't remember the last time someone told me I'd done something right.

Well, Rhiannon, of course, who'd said that thing about any choice I made being the right choice.

But before that?

My mom, back when I'd accepted the admissions offer from her and my sister's alma mater. Back before I'd flunked out.

So how come instead of validation or relief at Nurse Janine's praise, I'm sitting here hyperventilating and bawling my eyes out?

Because I don't know. I'm not sure. This decision is supposed to be obvious, but it's *not*.

I don't know if I'm in the right place.

I don't know.

Nurse Janine hands me a tissue. Lays a hand on my shoulder.

"Tell me why you're crying," she prompts, gently. "Let's talk it out."

I sniff and dab my eyes, manage to blubber, "I don't know!"

"That's okay," Nurse Janine consoles me. "That's perfectly okay. Emotions can be unpredictable."

"No." I wipe my runny nose. "I mean, I know why I'm crying. I'm crying because *I don't know.*"

"What don't you know?"

"I don't know if I'm in the right place. I feel like I should know, I feel like the answer should be obvious. I feel like, I know what I'm *supposed* to do, but I… I…"

Back to wailing again. Nurse Janine takes the seat beside me. Sits silently while I cry, her hand still on my shoulder.

When the crying turns to gasping, and the gasping to sharp but controlled breaths, Nurse Janine finally speaks. "Poppy, can I give you some advice? You're not *supposed* to do anything. 'Supposed to do' implies there's an expectation that someone else has set for you, something that's required of you by outside parties, and you don't have to bring that crap into this room. In this room, it's just you. What you want, what you need, what you think is best. Not what you're *supposed* to want, need, or think is best."

I heave a shuddering sigh.

"So you don't know. That's okay. This is your body. This is your life. For some people it's simple, but for others it's a big decision. It's okay not to know."

"But what do I *do*?" I ask. My voice is high, needy. I feel like a little girl.

"Whatever you feel is best, Poppy."

"That's kind of a bullshit copout answer, Janine." My body tries to laugh and sob at the same time, and it comes out as a hiccup.

Nurse Janine laughs with me. "Sorry. It's kind of my job to stay neutral in these kinds of questions."

"And here I was thinking I'd come in here and you'd have a banner and balloons that say 'abortion is the best, you'll love it'."

"Ummm, no. The best I can do is, 'For *some* people, abortion is the best *option*.' Which isn't what you're looking for me to say to you right now, is it?"

"And you can't pick a side, you know, just between you and me?" The tears have stopped for now, replaced by a wobbly smile. I hope she realizes I'm joking.

Trying to joke.

While also trying to decide if I want an abortion.

I am a mess.

"I *have* picked a side," Nurse Janine says. "Yours. Whatever you decide to do, I'm in your corner. That's what I'm here for. But it has to be your decision, Poppy. Yours. Not mine, not your family's, not your church's, not society's, not your partner's or your sperm donor's. So here's what we're gonna do. I'm going to give you a couple of options on ways we can move forward, and you're going to put aside the *supposed to*s, and tell me what you, Poppy, want for yourself. Is that enough direction for you?"

"I'm still holding out hope you'll just grab me by the

shoulders, give me a hard shake, and yell 'Get the abortion already' into my face like a drill sergeant, but... I guess this is okay, too."

"Okay." She smiles. "Here's the deal, then. According to the dates you've written down here, you're just about six and a half weeks along into this pregnancy. At this moment in time your options are wide open. You can carry the pregnancy to term, you can have a medical abortion with pills, or you can have a surgical abortion. The longer you wait, the fewer options you have, but you still have time. If you're local, I can give you some literature, let you go home, sleep on it. If you're leaning toward the medical abortion over the surgical, though, then we should probably do an ultrasound today to be doubly sure of your dates, and that way you know for sure how much time you have to make up your mind. That's a requirement one way or another, for medical reasons, but it's strictly for the physician's and my use. You don't have to look at or hear anything if you don't want."

"And if I want to?"

God, why did I ask that?

"If you want to, then I can do that, too."

I shouldn't want that. I shouldn't want to see the baby—the fetus. Being forced to look at an ultrasound or hear a heartbeat, that's a cheap guilt-trip tactic out of the playbook of those assholes outside.

But it's not being forced on me. I *want* it, just like I *want* to call this thing inside me baby, not fetus or mistake or parasite or clump of cells—all equally valid alternatives, depending.

And thinking about what Nurse Janine said, thinking about leaving behind the *supposed to*s and the obligations and what-would-my-mother-say, I'm not left with any compelling reason for doing what I've come here to do. Sure, I'm single. Sure, I'm a college dropout. Sure, I'm working a boring nine-to-five job that doesn't leave much for savings after I pay my rent and bills. But if I told Nurse Janine I wanted to keep the baby, she'd say "Go for it." And if *I* were Nurse Janine and someone in my exact situation came to me saying "I want to keep the baby," I'd say "Go for it," too. Heck, I'd say "Go for it," To a woman in a substantially *worse* situation than my own, if that's what she wanted.

Rhiannon's words: *Whatever choice you make, it's the right one.*

Well, for now, I choose to see this stupid ultrasound.

"I'm going to turn the monitor around now," the ultrasound tech says. "Unless you tell me not to."

I clench my teeth. "Do it."

I have no idea how this is going to feel, if it's going to change anything, if I'm going to look at the screen and cry at the sublime beauty of the life inside me and hate myself for even considering extinguishing it, or if I'm going recoil like I've been infested by an alien chestburster, or if I'm going to feel nothing at all, as detached from the image on the screen as if I would be looking at an X-ray of my arm.

The tech turns the screen to face me.

I'm looking at… I don't know what I'm looking at, actually. A blob? It kind of looks like a baby hamster.

Whatever it is I'm looking at, I feel myself smiling. I

don't feel awed, or amazed, or disgusted, or transformed. It's not profound or life-changing. I can see how people can look at it and still be solidly sure that abortion is right for them. It certainly doesn't inspire me to splash the pictures of it all over Facebook for my relatives to coo over.

I don't feel love or hate.

Only one thought, one word, runs through my mind: *Hello!*

A tentative, shy greeting to the little stranger inside me. That's all.

Just…hello.

I don't say anything aloud.

The tech fills the silence by explaining my dates were off by only one day.

Nurse Janine adds, "That means you have a solid two weeks until the cutoff for a medical abortion, which gives you time to think things over, if that's what you want. Either way, we'll have to see you sooner or later, whether it's for whatever procedure you choose or to get you set up with prenatal care."

In that moment, at least, I don't need the two weeks to make up my mind.

I don't tell Nurse Janine, not just yet, but this hamster thing of mine? This little stranger? I'm keeping it.

I'll figure out how to handle the *supposed to*s and my mother and Jake and my studio apartment…later.

I thank the ultrasound tech, then Nurse Janine, who hands me a paper envelope full of pamphlets. "Some reading," she explains, "Or there's a confidential number you can call, 24/7. Be careful googling."

Yeah, no, definitely not googling.

I smile at the people still in the waiting room as I'm escorted out. Teenage girls and middle-aged women, a couple of guys, one massively pregnant lady fanning her belly with a magazine.

Will that be me?

I wonder if she came here with a head full of *supposed tos* and a disapproving family. If she's single, too. Or if she has other reasons, explanations for why she shouldn't have a baby but she's doing it anyway.

Or maybe she didn't have any doubts at all.

Rhiannon comes to get me at the door. "Your cab's here," she says. "All set?"

I jiggle my paper envelope. "All set," I say.

The protesters are still here. A couple of them hiss and boo, a couple others "pray for my baby". I don't tell them I didn't get an abortion today, that I'm keeping my baby, even though it might take at least some of the heat off. I don't want them to use me to justify what they're doing. I don't want them to think they had any say in my decision. Sure, I'm starved for approval, but not at that cost.

Rhiannon's very large pink umbrella is angled just right for the light filtering through it to turn her pale skin the color of bubblegum.

She doesn't ask me about what choice I made. Doesn't ask about what happened inside at all, just smiles and resumes our conversation about tea lattes right from where we left off, like my life hadn't completely changed in the space between. She's probably used to that, meeting people before and after life-changing events and decisions, acting as the constant point between two worlds. Charon, safely bringing us from one world, one life, to the next.

Or maybe she just feels really strongly about people having the right to reproductive care without being harassed and intimidated for it.

I'm barely pregnant and I'm already over-sentimentalizing everything and everyone around me.

Hormones, that's why I suddenly want to take Rhiannon up on her earlier offer to hold my hand.

Closest I can get is a brief little squeeze to her palm after she tucks me safe and sound into the back seat of my cab. "Take good care of yourself," she says with an unexpected gentleness, that contrasts with but doesn't contradict her brash confidence from before.

"Thanks." I'm unable to manage anything remotely close to expressing how I'm feeling just now.

She shuts the door, drowning out the sidewalk noise in an instant. The protesters are gone, but so is she.

I'm alone.

Chapter Three

Three missed calls, two from my mother and one from my older sister. I sweep the assorted crap off my coffee table, set my phone down in the center of the newly cleared space, then dump out Nurse Janine's envelope on top of it. Brightly colored pamphlets falls like leaves, drifting to settle across the surface of the table. There's information on different methods of abortion, a card advertising non-judgmental post-procedure counselling, a few different leaflets on healthy pregnancy, adoption, birth control, government programs for mothers…

This was a lot easier when I just stuck to what was expected of me.

Of course, that same thinking was what got me enrolled in the university I ultimately flunked out of, so I do with

Janine's stack o' pamphlets what I should have done then: I go through them carefully, one by one, sorting them into stacks by category: abortion vs. keeping the pregnancy, adoption vs. motherhood. Then I find an old notebook labelled POLI-SCI 104 with half its pages messily torn out, turn to a fresh page, and make myself a pair of good old-fashioned Pros & Cons columns.

I can do this. I can think my way through this decision, logic the hell out of it, like a grown-ass adult who makes her own choices based on well-researched facts.

And then I immediately pick up the pamphlet titled *Carrying Your Pregnancy to Term.*

Nothing else on the table gets a second glance, and within twenty minutes I'm rereading it for what feels like the fiftieth time as I stuff my face with ice cream straight from the tub. Which would be *Ben & Jerry's* if this was a rom-com, but since it's not, and I have bills to pay, it's freezer-burned store brand.

Kind of appropriate, really.

First Steps, the pamphlet reads. *For the health of yourself and your pregnancy, you should be taking prenatal vitamins every day. If you drink alcohol, smoke cigarettes, or use illegal drugs, now is the time to stop. You will need to arrange prenatal care for the duration of your pregnancy, and start planning how and where you would like to give birth. Now is also the time to start making nutritious food choices. Certain government assistance programs may...*

Cookie dough ice cream is a good source of calcium, although calling it "dinner" might be a stretch.

Screw it, I've been through a lot today. I can start planning "Nutritious Balanced Meals" tomorrow.

Nurse Janine said she could help me arrange prenatal care, so for now that's sorted. I can swing by somewhere later this week to get the prenatal vitamins, and I have nine whole *months* to procrastinate on the actual childbirth aspect of all this. I don't smoke cigarettes, and I haven't lit a joint since me and Jake split up: partially because after that whole thing with Grammie's funeral I started envisioning my former pot habit turning me into a complete burnout like him, and partially because after we broke up, he got our pipe and papers in the "divorce". And "custody" of our dealer, who was his friend in the first place. And who always seemed to have some kind of thing for me, which I'd definitely be worried about him acting on now that I'm single.

And ew, no, that dude is almost thirty and still wears button-down anime shirts.

I *do* still have the remains of that bottle of vodka I'd been into the night we hooked up and made a baby, and out of some weird, symbolic compulsion, I set aside my nearly finished ice cream tub, leap from the couch, and head straight for the cupboard it's hiding in.

There's only a third of it left, but it wasn't cheap. It would probably keep just fine until after the baby's born and I'm in the clear to drink again.

I pour it down the sink.

I may be having Jake's baby, but that's the only remnant of him and our time together I plan on carrying forward.

Which means I should probably return those records of his I accidentally stole when we broke up. Eventually.

But also, hopefully, before I start to show. All the better to avoid inconvenient questions.

I'm leaving Jake, and pot, and booze, and indecision—and every other symbol of my stunted mis-growth into adulthood—behind. I may not think of myself as any kind of competent adult now, but if I'm having this baby, I'm going to have to grow the hell up, and fast. A part of me even wonders if this baby is just the kick in the ass I needed to finally get myself out of this limbo and onto my next stage of life.

Of course, there's also another part of me that insists the responsible adult I'm so determined to become would have already gotten her abortion rolling by now.

But nope, I'm not listening to that voice—my mom's voice, my has-her-shit-together big sister's. I'm listening to Nurse Janine's, to Rhiannon's. This is my decision. If I want it to work, I can make it work. I have to believe that. I have to be strong.

Whether you're single, partnered, or married, you will need lots of emotional support during your pregnancy, birth, and beyond.

I stare at my phone with its three missed messages. But no. I won't call my mother or sister, not until it's too late for either of them to talk me out of my choice.

The pamphlet is right, though. I can't do this on my own. I've cried five times just *today*, and I don't even feel pregnant yet. How am I going to handle things three, six, nine months down the line when I'm massively pregnant and sick as hell and my hormones are haywire and I'm going to go into labor any second now?

Scrolling through the contacts list on my phone, I'm

struck by how many of the people listed there are people I haven't talked to since I dropped out of school two
years ago. Former classmates, former sorority sisters, former members of the film appreciation society, high school
friends in different—but equally high pressure/prestige—
schools and programs and internships. I can't think of a single one of them who'd understand what I'm going through
right now. I'm not even sure most of them would even
sympathize. A couple of them would actually probably go
so far as to judge me.

Well, I'm already going to Planned Parenthood for prenatal care, maybe I can use them for my emotional support, too.

I could see one of the clinic counsellors to work through
these messy feelings head-on. But I can't deny that the real
appeal is the chance to pick up where we left off in the tea
latte conversation with Rhiannon.

It's strange. Overnight, my entire life has changed, but all
around me, the world is just the same.

Monday morning starts with three trips to the toilet to
vomit before I've even put a bowl of cereal into myself, but
when I get to work ten minutes late and still green around
the gills, Tracy, who works the front desk with me, just
clucks and says, "Too much vodka this weekend, babe?"

I'm definitely not ready to announce myself, so I take
the opening she's so kindly given me and nod.

She doesn't doubt the lie for even a second, which is,
y'know, *totally* flattering. Not.

She just laughs and shakes her head. "I guess I don't need to ask you what you got up to this weekend then, huh?"

Well, first I ran the religious nutjob gauntlet, then I cried in front of a stranger, and then I completely fucking lost my mind and decided I wanted to have my dipshit ex's baby. You?

"You sure don't," I say instead. "You?"

"Ugh, it was such a shitshow. This bitch at my second job called in sick *again* so I wound up working a double, and I was supposed to go out with my girls afterwards but I was so tired and sweaty I just said fuck it I'm gonna stay in and actually go to bed at a reasonable hour, but do I do that? No, I open up Netflix thinking I'm gonna just watch one episode of this show in bed and then before I know it it's like six am the next day and I'm watching the season finale and just hating myself. It wasn't even a good show! Why do we *do* these things to ourselves?"

Boy do I ever wish my problems boiled down to *watched an irresponsible amount of Netflix.*

Yikes. Scratch that thought. Do I really want to be that kind of person? After all, I imagine there are plenty of people out there thinking *Boy I wish I could complain about being pregnant while also working a steady job with paid leave and medical coverage.* I can't let myself fall into that kind of patently immature thinking. I'm supposed to be learning how to adult successfully, and an Adult wouldn't be pulling this woe-is-me-my-life-is-worse-than-yours competitive suffering bullshit.

So I suck it up and try to sympathize, like I would have before I peed on a stick and my whole life went off the rails. "Don't blame yourself. Obviously it's the show's fault for not being good enough that you could justify an all-nighter watching it."

Tracy cracks a smile. "At least somebody understands me. Stupid mediocre yet addictive K-Dramas!"

"Curse you!" I add, shaking my fist. "Did you at least get to see abs?"

She groans and rolls her eyes theatrically. "God, yes. So okay, like, the love interest Kyung-Min, he has an identical twin brother…"

She fills me in on all the sordid details in between patient check-ins and appointment calls. I've long said Tracy was the only reason I could stand this boring-ass job with its parade of entitled patients and clueless dentists and crying children. Today, she serves the bonus purpose of keeping my mind off my roiling stomach and my baseline existential dread.

Later in the morning one of the dentists brings in donuts for the staff, and my preggo hunger overrides my natural fat girl self-consciousness about eating junk food in public. I take two.

"You really *are* hungover." Tracy gives me the eyebrow. "Well, whatever, you do you. I'll just look on jealously while I calculate how many calories are in a single bite of one of these." She reaches onto my plate, takes a brazen bite out of my second donut, then sets it down again. When I flash her a scandalized look, she shrugs. "Hey, I'm doing you a favor! Just think, that's like, fifty calories less you're eating, thanks to me."

"What percentage is fifty out of 'for the last time I'm not counting that shit', do you think?" I ask her, syrupy sweet. She looks suitably chastened at the reminder, so I cut her some slack, adding, "But calories aside, you probably *did* help save me from a tummy ache, so it's all good."

"Seems like you need all the help you can get on that front. You're still looking a little pale. I'll just be sitting over here thanking God it's not contagious, because it's not like I can take a sick day like everyone else seems to be able to..."

Not contagious? Well, *I* got it from somebody, anyway, but it's true Tracy's not at risk of catching it from me. I snicker to myself as I lick a fingertip and use it to pick up sprinkles. Thank God Tracy's busy on a call and doesn't notice my expression, because if I have to specifically craft a lie to her face, this whole thing is going to fall apart.

With that at the back of my mind, the rest of the day becomes a practiced dance of keeping the conversation off my mysterious "illness" and on Tracy's K-Drama addiction and her parade of terrible coworker stories—"Not you, of course, you're great!" she assures me what must be a thousand times, though I wonder if she will feel the same way once *I* start calling in sick—subjects that require not much more than the occasional nod or "Omigod, right?" from me.

At six I stumble through the front door of my apartment feeling like I've been lifting rocks all day rather than sitting at a desk, but my secret is still safe. The pile of Planned Parenthood papers reminds me I need to cook myself a nutritious dinner and run out to the pharmacy for prenatal vitamins and start looking into the maternity leave policy at my work and, and, and...

I flop down on the couch with a sleeve of saltine crackers, pull my laptop onto my belly, and spool up some K-Drama on Netflix. If I'm gonna keep Tracy talking instead of scrutinizing my body and lifestyle changes, then I need to be brushed up on her latest binge show.

Okay, I also just want to see this thing for myself. A love triangle with twins? And one of them is evil?

I may be pregnant, but I'm not dead.

Chapter Four

My next Planned Parenthood appointment, I'm met by an elderly woman in that same clinic vest Rhiannon wore. She has an umbrella, too, but her small talk is much more typical of an old lady: she's excited for the bulbs she's going to plant tomorrow afternoon and the flowers she'll have to look forward to come spring: daffodils, which were her wedding flower forty-seven years ago. She gets me to the door feeling like a warm hug, which is impressive considering there's a definite September chill in the air, and also the fact that I'm surrounded by people whose hobby is screaming at strangers.

An hour or so later, I'm sitting face-to-face with Nurse Janine once more.

I spent a lot of last night lying awake at war with myself,

wondering if I should change my mind at the last minute again and go through with the abortion after all. Or maybe take the pills just in case—not actually swallow them or anything, but like have them on hand, the way anxious suburban housewives stock up on antibiotics before travelling internationally. Or maybe I should call my mom after all and ask her advice?

I am going *insane.*

"I'm gonna carry the pregnancy to term," I tell Nurse Janine without hesitation.

"Okay," she says. That's it. *Okay.*

"Okay," I say back.

"Have you given some thought as to what you'd like to do once you've given birth?"

"Oh. Um. Keep it." I pause, struggling for what to say next while Nurse Janine looks at me with what must be a practiced neutral expression. "And raise…it?" I add.

"All right then." She smiles at me, not a trace of doubt on her face. I must be making some kind of weird face back at her, because she adds, "I just ask because it helps me hook you up with the right people and services going forward. You're allowed to change your mind at any point, though, just say the word."

That's it? There's no test? I say I want to be this baby's mom and she just says yes? Does she not realize how completely unequipped I am for motherhood? She should *not* be letting me have this baby without a fight. It's absolutely mind boggling.

"Do you think it's a good idea?" I blurt out.

Nurse Janine sits back in her chair. I know instantly that

she's not going to give me the answer I so badly want her to give me. "Do *you*? Is there something you're specifically concerned about that I can talk you through?"

I try to distill my miasma of anxiety and bad feelings and insecurities into a single sentence for her. It comes out as: "I'm a college dropout."

"Do you think a person needs to go to college to be a good parent?"

"Of course not!" I sputter. "No. No. I'd never say that. I bet you see good parents without college degrees all the time."

"Sure do." She smiles knowingly. I know where she's leading me, but the relief that's supposed to come with that revelation never hits me.

"But like, that's not what I mean. It's like… It's not that I didn't go, it's that I went but I didn't finish. I couldn't follow through. What if I can't follow through on or commit to *this*?"

"Ah. Well. You know, a *lot* of parents feel like they're not resilient enough to stick with parenting, are afraid of the lifetime commitment of a child—name a feeling you're feeling and I guarantee you're not alone—but the vast majority of them, if they decide for themselves that abortion or adoption isn't what they want, then they find out they're way more equipped and competent than they ever knew. They still need support, of course, everyone does, but it's not nearly as much of a disaster as their insecurities make them think."

"But what if I'm not one of them? What if I'm one of those people whose insecurities are *right*?"

"Then we get you a support system in place, we give you the tools you need to be successful, and we work together to get you as well-prepared as we possibly can. If this is what you want, then we make it work."

As sure as she sounds, I still can't imagine any scenario where I make any of this work.

But it's still what I want.

I leave Nurse Janine's office with a whole new armload of pamphlets about pregnancy and childbirth and social services for pregnant people and new parents, and instructions to make an appointment for prenatal care.

I'm standing in line waiting to talk to the receptionist, thinking—okay, stressing (once again) about the whole support system piece of all this, when I see it: a hot pink photocopied flyer advertising STITCH N' BITCH TUESDAYS. My mind immediately goes to visions of elderly women knitting dishcloths and baby blankets and ugly sweaters for their grandchildren.

I could do that.

Not knit for my grandchildren, obviously, because I don't have grandchildren, although maybe someday I will, now. (*Gah!*) But baby blankets, baby booties, little tiny baby old man sweaters…

I could learn to knit!

It's perfect. Grandmas knit, yes, but, *also*, so do moms. Moms my age, even. In fact, it's probably an absolute certainty there are moms in this particular group, considering where they're advertising. What better support system could you ask for than other moms and grandmas? Especially ones without any power over your life to guilt trip you or try and talk you out of your decisions.

Not to mention, learning to knit and following through might help my confidence issues re: commitment. I've always wanted to learn, and I have the closet full of balls of yarn with three-inch-long scarves still attached to prove it. This time will be different, though. This time I have a baby to knit for and a new life to build and something to goddamn prove.

I can already picture myself sitting in a rocking chair, my belly round and a three-quarters-finished hat on my needles, my baby's change table drawers filled to the brim with lovingly handmade clothes, just waiting for a chubby little someone to make cozy. The fantasy is almost sickeningly sweet, and I love it. I wanna wrap myself up in it, like the sweaters I'll soon be able to knit. I take a quick picture of the flyer with my phone and add baby yarn to my mental shopping list right after prenatal vitamins and healthy snacks.

I have two more missed calls from my mother and a few texts from my sister. I ignore my mother's calls but quickly text my sister back, responding to her questions of what I've been up to lately with a quick and simple Netflix LOL.

Well, it's not a complete lie.

Also thinking of learning to knit
…Again.

She replies near instantly.

Yeah sure, good luck with that.

I stuff my phone angrily into my purse.

Man, fuck my family. Fuck every last judgy overachieving one of them.

Chapter Five

The Tuesday stitch n' bitch is held at a hole in the wall indie coffee shop just a couple blocks down from the Planned Parenthood. There's nobody there when I arrive except for the usual MacBook crowd, so I find a seat at one of the bigger tables and plop my newly purchased baby yarn down in full view so that when people start showing up, they know what I'm here for.

The pregnancy app on my phone—which tells me I'm eight weeks pregnant and my baby is the size of a raspberry—also advises against too much caffeine, so I begrudgingly order an herbal tea to sip on while I sit. And a scone, because I'm supposed to eat small meals to ward off my so-called "morning" sickness, which, yeah, just goes on all damn day and into the night.

Also, the scone just looks really yummy, pumpkin with a very generous drizzle of frosting, and I know I'm not actually eating for two, but honestly? I do not even care at all.

I read up on my chances of miscarrying while I wait, phone in one hand and quickly vanishing scone in the other. I look up expectantly every time the little bell over the door rings, but it seems like everyone coming in has college textbooks or laptops, not knitting.

My scone and most of my tea have vanished when at long last a plump older woman with a bulging tote bag covered in cartoon cats appears at the door. I know instantly what she's here for, and sure enough, she catches sight of my yarn and immediately bustles over, dropping her bag unceremoniously in front of me. "Yes! Not the last one here!" she crows.

"You might be." I scan around the room. No sign of any other knitters. "Looks like it's just you and me today, in which case...you are."

I can't keep the disappointment from my voice. Cat-lover lady is probably perfectly friendly, but not exactly what I was hoping to get out of this group. "Oh, I wouldn't worry about that. Everyone's always late for this thing. It's really just a matter of who's the *most* late."

"Aha," I say. "Well, I'm Poppy. I'm new."

She holds out a hand. "Louise. Nice to see a new face, especially one who's on time!"

"I wouldn't get too excited about that. I won't always be this focused on making a good first impression." I laugh, and Louise laughs, too.

Louise turns at the sound of the doorbell. "And look there, not the last one here after all! Hi, Mary!"

Another middle-aged woman walks in, this one tall and willowy with short-cropped hair and a beautiful multi-chromatic shawl draped around her elegant shoulders. She reminds me a little bit of my mother, except artsier, with handmade earrings instead of ones from Tiffany. She carries *her* knitting in a sturdy burgundy leather purse. In my world, these two women would never speak with one another, but Louise and Mary are instantly warm, patting each other's hands and gushing to each other about how beautiful Mary's lacework looks now that it's blocked, whatever that means.

"Mary, this is Poppy," Louise finally introduces. "She's new."

"Hi." I wave awkwardly.

"What a sweet little dress." Mary plucks at my sleeve.

"Thanks." I touch my peter pan collar a little self-consciously. I'm not exactly used to compliments that aren't hiding insults. Many a time a woman my mother's age has complimented my clothes while meaning the exact opposite. *What a cute skirt, you're so brave to wear one that short considering your thighs! What a nice outfit, I wish I could wear vintage without everyone at work thinking I'm a slob! I really admire you wearing a high-waisted dress and not worrying if it makes you look pregnant! Enjoy those pigtails while you can, you won't be able to get away with them for much longer!*

"I'm going to grab a latte, be back in a tick!" Mary says, pulling out her wallet.

"Wait, I'll come with you!" Louise grabs her cat bag and slings it back over her shoulder.

I'm alone for roughly forty seconds before another person comes rushing through the door. This time it's a man, a tall, bodybuilder looking guy with a bald head and a neat pink button-down shirt that strains ever so slightly over his pecs. I think he can't possibly be a part of our group, but then he strides right up to me, unzips his backpack, and pulls out a ball of bright red yarn and a crochet needle. He's partway through what looks to be a child's winter hat.

"Damian! You're in the running for latest!" Louise calls from the counter.

"Damn!" he says in exuberant faux-frustration. "Not fair, I had to bring my daughter to a dentist's appointment!"

"No excuses," someone else chides. Finally! A girl my age! She wears a belted plaid dress and hiking boots over thick wool socks, with her hair in one of those messy, effortless topknots I can never pull off no matter how much I backcomb. She turns to me. "Last one here buys cookies," she explains. "So here's hoping it's not me. I hate having to buy them when I don't even eat them." I'm about to introduce myself and ask her name when she adds on, "I'm eating keto."

Oh, great.

"Good for you." I'm probably grimacing more than smiling. "My sister was doing that for a while."

Why the hell did I give her an opening to keep talking about it?

"*Was* doing it?" effortless topknot girl says distastefully. "Personally I don't know why anyone would ever stop. I feel so much better now that I'm eating more naturally. I just have way more energy now, and I'm not gonna lie, the fact that I lost ten pounds…"

I catch Damian's eye across the table. It takes all my will-power not to mouth *Help me*.

He seems to read my expression right regardless, cutting in with a jovial, "So what are you working on, Grace?"

"Oh, just a cowl. I won a custom slot with one of my favorite handspun spinners so I got her to do me up my own colorway in this super plush chunky weight merino but it was like fifty dollars a skein so I couldn't justify doing a sweater in it. So…cowl."

Damian nods along like he actually understood what in the hell she just said. "I found this ball of acrylic in my grandma's old stash and figured it would make a cute hat for Taisha," he replies, deadpan with a shrug.

"Awww, that is *so sweet*! What a lucky girl!" she coos. "Okay, well, I'm going to go get a tea before I sit down. Be right back!"

As soon as she's gone, Damian lifts his eyebrows at me. "If I were another woman and I said I was crocheting something in second-hand acrylic, Grace would have melted me into goo with pure yarn-snobbery. But because I'm the only man in the group, she acts like every project I do is some praise-worthy revelation. Go figure."

I cast a quick glance at my own ball of yarn, a soft babyish teal that I paid four bucks for at a big-box craft store. "Is there something wrong with uh…" I try to recall his phrasing. "Second-hand…whatever?"

"No way. But not everyone would agree with me on

that." He rolls his eyes. "Yarn drama. Just wait until you hear about the war between crocheters and knitters."

A war between crocheters and knitters? That's too much. "Shut up. Get out of here with that."

He shrugs. "Don't say I didn't warn you."

Oh God, is he being serious? I think he's being serious. Maybe it's not too late for me to sneak out of here before they all realize I'm a fake who's never finished a project and what's more, doesn't know the first thing about yarn.

I reach for my ball and needles surreptitiously. Maybe I can tell Damian I'm going to the bathroom and sneak out a window, like a rom-com heroine on a bad blind date.

Damian turns his head, and I think it's my opportunity to run like the flighty, noncommittal, easily discouraged flake I am, but then I see what—or rather, who—he's looking at.

"Rhi!" he calls, and waves.

And standing in the coffee shop doorway, silhouetted by the natural light streaming through the windows, stands Rhiannon. I don't need that bright pink clinic vest to recognize her, because apparently I've committed every detail of her face to memory already.

She stands in full view just long enough for me to drink in the rolled cuffs of her jeans and the messenger bag slung across the flat chest of her plain white T-shirt, and then she calls back, "D!"

"I got bad news for you." Damian points at the pickup counter where the rest of the stitch n' bitchers have congregated.

"Ah, shit," Rhiannon says.

How come I never noticed how gravelly her voice was, before?

Maybe she uses a different tone with the people she escorts. Makes sense, actually, to use a gentler tone around someone who has every reason to be raw and fearful.

Is this going to be weird for her?

I should leave. There's no "going to be" here. This *is* weird.

I cough, clutching my yarn closer to my chest. "I should…" I mutter.

"New girl!" she addresses me, and points grandly. I feel like everyone in the damn coffee shop is looking at us. I try to shrink in my seat. "What kind of cookies you like?"

"Oh, um." I set my yarn down again. She's so slim and fit, I fight off the old urge not to eat in front of her. I should tell her I already had a scone. Prove I have willpower, that I'm not some slob without self-control who can never stop.

How about stopping this? I say firmly to that nasty inner voice.

Aloud, I reply nonchalantly, "You know, whatever. Whatever's good."

The corner of her mouth pulls up in that mean smile I remember. I say mean, but it feels playful, not predatory.

I…am blushing.

And she notices. "Would you say you're *up for anything,* then?"

Oh no. "Anything but raisins," I blurt out.

"Gotcha." She saunters up to the counter, greeting the rest of the group as she goes. When she returns, it's with a huge paper bag, already see-through in places with the grease of the cookies. Louise, Mary, and Grace all follow after her, each of them with a comically large paper cup.

"Oh, shit, I didn't introduce you two yet!" Damian says when Rhiannon drops into the seat beside me.

My heart does flip-flops, terrified she's gonna say, *"Oh, we already know each other."*

She looks directly at me, our gazes locking together. Her eyes are deep, dark brown, the color of espresso. Then she cracks a smile, turning to Damian with mock scorn all over her face. "Seriously man, I was waiting for you to notice! You're never going to rise in the ranks of the country club if you don't figure out basic social niceties." Back to me now. "I'm Rhiannon." She holds out a hand for me, and I place my hand in her own. Her shake is firm where mine is limp. I'm brought back to that moment when she closed me in my cab, and I thought I was never going to see her again.

"P-Poppy."

"Whatcha got on the go there, Poppy?" She reaches into her bag and pulls out what appears to be the beginnings of a very colorful sock, strung between half a dozen tiny needles.

I look at my ball of yarn, still in its paper wrapper. "Oh, um, nothing? Yet?"

I really shouldn't have picked something so overtly babyish. I'm not showing yet, not keen on revealing myself or explaining myself, not to these strangers and especially not to Rhiannon. What if she thinks I kept the baby because I let the protesters get to me? What kind of wishy-washy loser will I look like to her then?

Ugh, what a shitty thing to think about her. How poorly do I think of her, seriously? Damn.

"I actually don't—"

"You *need* to touch this," Grace interrupts, thrusting her half-knit cowl into Rhiannon's face.

Rhiannon grabs a fistful and makes a borderline pornographic expression. "Damn that's good," she groans.

"Right?" Grace chirps.

I have to admit, it *is* a really pretty color.

"I see you're making more socks," Louise says, gesturing to what Rhiannon's got on the go.

"I *live* for socks." Rhiannon leans back in her seat, flips her ankle to rest on one knee so that her jeans draw up her calf, revealing a pair of deliriously multicolored hand-knit socks.

"That looks complicated," I say, trying not to stare at her ankle and calf instead of the sock she's showing me.

"Yes and no. I don't do a lot of pattern because I prefer to focus on a good fit and let the colorway speak for itself, but tiny sock yarn and tiny DPNs are automatically tricky."

"That's why I crochet." Damian nudges me. "One hook instead of...*that*."

"Well if she'd just learn magic loop." Louise rolls her eyes good-naturedly, pulling what appears to be the beginnings of a knit throw out of her cat bag. No wonder the thing was bulging: the throw is a good five feet wide and two feet long, and it's obviously nowhere near finished. How does a person even knit something that big? Does she have huge novelty needles in her bag, too?

"Never learning magic loop, Louise, no matter how much you nag me."

"You're missing out," Mary scolds. "Here, Poppy, you have a look at these and tell me what you'd rather knit with." She produces a slim leather envelope case and opens it up. Inside it are neat rows of metal needle tips in sets of two, ranging in sizes from teeny tiny to nearly pinky-sized in diameter. "Go on, take one out. Feel how light and smooth it is. Addi Turbos. Poor Rhiannon needs to embrace the future."

I am so confused right now.

"So you never said what you were planning on doing, there," Rhiannon says, obviously trying to take the heat off herself. Probably not intending to put it all on me.

The entire group looks at me expectantly.

I take the plunge, letting them make whatever assumptions about me that they may. "Oh, um, you know, baby clothes, hopefully? I was thinking some booties to start?"

"Awwwww," Louise and Mary say in unison.

I take a deep breath, forcing myself not to look at Rhiannon in case I see anything other than approval on her face. The others might be convinced that I'm knitting for a friend or my sister, but there's no way Rhiannon won't put two and two together. I don't want to field their questions on that front, though, so I quickly follow up with a tentative "Except…" Oh God, I have to say it. I have to admit to it. I screw up my face in consternation. Spit it out: "*Idon'tknowhowtoknit.*"

I flinch, awaiting their judgment, but it never comes.

"Oh-em-gee, yay!" Grace says. "A new knitter, that's so exciting!"

"Come to the dark side, we have cookies," Louise adds without a hint of irony or self-consciousness at how dated that line is.

Then she reaches into the bag of cookies and hands me one.

Chapter Six

It doesn't take long for everybody in the group to set aside their own projects to focus on me and mine.

Grace has my ball of yarn in her hands, twisting the strand between her fingers critically. "If you're knitting for a baby, you should really consider a nice bamboo…"

Louise is scrutinizing my choice of project. "You know, I started with dishcloths, then graduated to scarves. It's not as glamorous, but it does let you get the fundamentals down."

"Oh, my, no." Mary flips the free pattern card I picked up in the craft store and scans the back with critical eyes. "You don't want to do this, this is for a completely different weight of yarn than what you've got here. Where did you pick this up? They *should* be putting these patterns next to the suggested yarn. This one calls for fingering. What you need to do is get an account on Ravelry and find a pattern that's been user-rated so you know it's accurate and suitable for your skill level, and do that. You can search by yarn weight on there, too. This yarn is a DK..." She pulls out her phone, trailing off as she opens her web browser.

Damian, who has been sitting silently so far, takes this chance to finally speak up. "Do you have needles?" he asks plainly, no judgment in his tone. Nobody else has bothered with that crucial detail to this point.

Now those, at least, I do have. I reach into my purse and pull out the needles I scavenged from my last failed scarf project. I hold them up for the group's inspection proudly.

"Poppy, no!" they say in unison, and even Damian joins in their exclamation of dismay. "These will never work!"

My shoulders slump. "What? Why?"

Louise clucks at me. "Much too big! Too long for a tiny baby pattern and too thick for this yarn. You're going to end up with stretched out knitting full of gaps and holes."

The familiar urge to just give up and quit hits me hard and fast, like a gut punch. I gust out a breath, slumping in my seat.

A hand closes around my shoulder. Rhiannon. "Hey, don't feel bad. First time I tried to knit, I got my needles secondhand from the thrift store and accidentally bought two different sizes." She laughs and shakes her head. "Here. If you don't mind that they're not high-tech Addi Turbos, you can borrow some needles from me."

"She needs a pattern first," Mary puts in. "And personally I think she should start by knitting mittens before she graduates to booties."

"I guess that sounds all right." I know they're just trying to help, but I feel overwhelmed and outnumbered. But what would the alternative be? For them to sit there focused on their own projects, socializing with each other and ignoring me as I struggle?

It's Rhiannon, once again, who calms the chaos, both the stuff going on around us and the stuff in my head. "Okay, okay, give the girl some space, now. Mary, can you search Ravelry for a pattern for a set of mittens *and* booties? And Grace and Louise, can you wind Poppy's skein real quick so she doesn't get stuck untangling yarn barf on her very first project?" My fellow stitch n' bitch members nod, immediately turning to their tasks. She turns to me. "I left my straight needles with the rest of my stuff back at my place. It's just a short walk from here. You wanna come and keep me company?"

"You'll need a size five needle by the looks," Mary calls, eyes glued to her phone.

Rhiannon looks at me expectantly, awaiting my answer. I get the sense that if I said no to her invitation, she'd be totally cool about it. But I don't want to say no.

"Sure, yeah. Can I leave my stuff here?"

"We're not leaving any time soon," Damian flaps a hand. "Go, go. Sooner you go the sooner you get back, sooner you get back the sooner you can get started, and the sooner you get started the more time you have knitting with people who can pick up your dropped stitches."

"Gotcha." I nod. "Thanks."

"Ready?" Rhiannon asks. She grabs a cookie for the

road, stuffing it halfway into her mouth and holding it there comically.

I fight down the sudden image of myself biting that half a cookie right out from under her nose.

Wow, do I need some air. And some semblance of hormonal balance.

Instead, I'm getting alone time with Rhiannon.

Crash and burn time, here I come.

Halfway out the door, I realize it: what if she's getting me alone so she can tell me off, tell me it's too awkward being in a club with me and that I need to find somewhere else to look for a social life?

Her expression didn't seem that harried or insistent, though, did it? Or was she just playing it cool so nobody asked her any questions when I left the club and never returned?

As soon as the door closes behind us, she turns to me, biting down on her half a cookie and crumbling the remainder for a couple pigeons lurking at our feet. "So," she says through a full mouth as we begin to walk.

"So…" I echo, stuffing my hands into the pockets of my dress.

She flinches. "Considering how we know each other previously, is this whole arrangement…comfortable for you?"

I flinch right back at her. "Is it comfortable for *you*?"

"Only if it is for you," she replies.

"Well *I'm* only uncomfortable if *you're* uncomfortable."

I don't know what it is: the way we're both flinching at

each other like we're about to get into a slap fight, or the fact that we've said some variation of the world "comfortable" like six times in the span of thirty seconds, or just the fact that we are being soooo awkward with each other right now, especially for two people who have walked through literal hell together…but one moment we're flinching and shrinking, and the next we're doubled over with laughter. I don't know who cracks first. Maybe me? But suddenly her arm is around my shoulder as she guffaws and I giggle and hiccup, and we're blocking the sidewalk like a pair of clueless tourists in Times Square and the both of us are just so damn *relieved* that as weird as this all is, it's simultaneously not weird at all.

"I was trying so hard to pretend I'd never seen you before!" Rhiannon gasps.

"I was so worried you were gonna be mad at me for keeping the baby!" I babble, clutching to her as my knees nearly give out, "Or that you'd be scared I was some kind of stalker!"

"I hung the flyer right in the clinic! And yet somehow I hadn't even considered that it might get weird if a client decided to join and recognized me?" Rhiannon shakes her head at herself, then pauses. "Wait, you were worried I was gonna be *mad* at you?"

My shoulders shrink a little and I duck my head apologetically. "Yes? Sorta?"

"Pro-*choice*!" she shouts and pinches the back of my arm for emphasis. Not hard, but I still arch my back dramatically, trying to wiggle out of her grip. Her little fingers are merciless!

"Okay! Ow! Okay, okay, okay!"

She pulls back immediately, eyes huge with concern. "Oh, shit, oh, did I hurt you for real? Oh shit, I am so sorry."

I punch her lightly in the shoulder. "Relax, relax! I'm just screwing with you!"

She sighs with relief and scrubs a hand through her short, artfully tousled hair. "I don't know what came over me! I swear, I would never normally pinch a person. Well, I would, but like, in the context of a relationship or something, not a relative stranger who I don't even know whether they're okay with that kind of thing. I swear I'm not—"

"A crab?" I put in ever so helpfully, mimicking pincers with my hands.

She buries her face in her hands. A muffled "Oh God," escapes between her fingers.

"Seriously, it's fine." Her grand show of remorse makes me feel a little better about my crappy assumptions, a little less alone in my gnawing social anxiety. "It's all fine. The pinching me thing, the fact that we know each other from the clinic. All fine by me."

She lets out a sigh. "Okay. Okay. Good. Okay. So do you wanna keep up with the 'we've never met before' act or are you okay with people knowing we saw each other at the clinic?"

Good question.

"I'm only eight weeks along and I don't know if I'm ready for people to know I'm pregnant yet, so maybe let's keep it between us for now? But if you like, slip up or something about the fact that we met at the clinic or whatever I'm not gonna be mad or go to your boss about you violating confidentiality or anything."

Rhiannon nods. "Cool. Good. That takes a bit of the pressure off."

"I really appreciate what you do, by the way," I say shyly, unable to look her in the eye as I do. "I was so upset and scared that day, I don't know if I'd have managed to walk in there by myself. Even though I wound up deciding to keep the baby anyway, it's because of you that I got to talk it over with someone in the first place. Make that choice for *myself*. And, y'know, now I have prenatal care, too. Because of you."

When I chance a look at her, her expression has softened, her eyes big and a little watery.

"I'm...wow. Thank you so much. For saying that. Glad to know I helped."

"You did." I smile, crossing my arms, and nudge her shoulder playfully. "Now c'mon."

Chapter Seven

No lie, Rhiannon's apartment really is just a few minutes' walk away. We could have been there and back in under ten minutes, if we hadn't stopped halfway to spill our guts to one another on the sidewalk. It's a cute, squat little building with an entrance tucked between a deli and an old-fashioned barber shop, all three doors sporting red awnings in various states of repair. She unlocks the door and holds it open for me as I enter, making sure it closes behind her before bounding up the narrow stairwell in front of me. She's like a little kid, taking them two and three steps at a time while I cautiously make my way up behind her, clinging to the railing the whole way. I can't wait to do this when I'm nine months along.

Three flights later, she leads me to door 21 and unlocks

it before stepping through, calling out "Anybody home?" as she does. Nobody replies, and she spins to face me again, arms outspread. "Chez me," she says.

"You have roommates?"

She leans against the wall, standing on one foot to yank her sneakers off. "Yeah, Gina and Lauren. Gina's Canadian, thus the shoe thing. They're a couple. The only thing better than splitting the rent on a two bedroom three ways would be splitting it four ways." Her mouth snaps shut and she stares at me in what appears to be horror.

"Was that an invitation?" I joke, flashing her my meanest smile. Yeah, I'm totally looking for revenge for that *up for anything* comment earlier.

Success. The tips of her ears go red.

"Anyway, uh, my knitting stuff's in my bedroom. I'll run and get it. Don't worry about your shoes. Just go ahead and have a seat on the couch while you wait—" She tosses a look over her shoulder to the laundry-covered sofa in the living room behind her. "If you can find room," she adds with a wince.

"Forget about it." I wave her off as I step out of my flats anyway.

She gives me one last apologetic look then heads down the hall, leaving me to dig out a nest for my butt on her sofa. The laundry's all clean, clearly dumped on the couch directly after hauling it back from the laundromat. Can't blame Rhiannon or her roommates for that one. I have a laundry room in my building and *still* don't manage to fold that shit ninety percent of the time. The other ten percent is my precious ModCloth dresses, which I always hang with care in my closet as soon as they've been laundered because they cost too damn much to leave balled up in the bottom of a laundry basket.

The rest of Rhiannon's living room is cluttered but well kept, with towering stacks of books in various corners, potted succulents in the windows, and stolen show posters with their stapled corners ripped off papering the walls. It's a cool, laid-back aesthetic, and I'm just settling into it, enjoying the scent of clean laundry, when Rhiannon returns with a comically large mason jar full of knitting needles.

"Okay." The jar wobbles in her hands as the needles clatter against each other. "I got the stuff. Let's get outta here."

Do we have to? I almost whine, but stop myself. There's a whole knitting group waiting for us at the coffee shop, after all, and it would be a serious jerk move to ditch them in favor of alone time with a cute girl and her giant pile of warm snuggly laundry. I force myself to stand.

Oh, wow, was this room always spinning?

No, just me. Just my dumbass pregnant self forgetting to expect when I'm expecting that standing suddenly and early pregnancy don't always mix. I list sideways, my ankles turning into extra-wobbly totally structurally unsound Jell-O.

Rhiannon's jar o' needles hits the ground with a shattering crash, fragments of glass and mismatched knitting needles scattering across the hardwood floor.

And then I'm in her arms.

"I gotcha," she says in her perfectly calm, perfectly kind clinic escort voice. I lean against her helplessly, closing and opening my eyes over and over again waiting for that one magic time when the room will be standing still and the floor will be the floor again. There's no way Rhiannon can hold my entire weight like this for much longer, but she doesn't try. She just safely lowers us both to the ground, holding me the whole way down, until we're kneeling together on the floor. Her arms wrap around my shoulders, holding me upright. "I gotcha," she repeats.

I take a deep breath. Shut my eyes one more time, focusing on the smell of clean laundry and the solid feeling of the floor beneath me and her body against mine.

"Okay," I say. "I'm okay."

She lets out a big sigh. "Jesus, thank God. I don't think I coulda held up the calm, cool and collected act much longer. What *was* that?"

"Just a dizzy spell. Pregnancy thing, I'm told. I'm okay now."

"Is your blood sugar low or something?" She pushes me back so she's holding me at arm's length, looking me over.

"Rhi. I just ate a scone *and* cookies. I highly doubt it."

"Should…should we go to the hospital? Have them check you out?"

She clambers to her feet and starts to toss laundry off the couch. Shirts and jeans and dresses and panties go flying across the room like handkerchiefs in a magic show. "You should lie down at least. Just in case."

"Really. I'm fine."

She helps me to my feet and pushes me toward the now-empty couch. It hits the back of my knees and I drop like a ragdoll, like someone who is not really fine after all.

"Maybe I *should* lie down," I acquiesce weakly as she

nudges me onto my back and stuffs a pillow under my head and two under my feet.

"I should open a window, get you some air," she mutters distractedly, buzzing across the living room. It's a little worrying to see her getting so anxious. Whatever happened to the coolheaded clinic escort from before? Is it because I'm in her space and she feels solely responsible for my well-being now that we're alone? Or because by joining her knitting group, I've become more to her than a client?

Is this...personal for her now?

Too personal?

As flattering as it is to have someone fussing over me, I can't in good conscience just lie here on my fainting couch while Rhiannon struggles. I sit up, putting on a brave face in the hopes of calming her nerves. "How about we just head back to the coffee shop? Get some fresh air on the way?"

"I got it!" Rhiannon, all determination, grabs at the edge of the living room window. She grunts; the pane is old and sticky, and it takes some effort on her part to force it open.

Cool air and city noise fills her tiny apartment. It's everything I used to daydream about when I was a teenager living with my parents in stuffy Long Island: an old shoebox apartment in the middle of it all, with sirens blaring and loud neighbors and art on the walls. So maybe Yonkers isn't quite as centrally located or metropolitan as I'd once envisioned, but the gorgeous, effortlessly cool girl with her elbows on the windowsill contemplatively facing the breeze more than makes up for it.

I give my damn head a shake, which has the side effect of sending my dizziness back into full swing. I soldier through it and press on: "Aren't they gonna wonder where we went? They're gonna think we got mugged."

"I'll text Grace. Let her know something came up."

I sit up, propping myself on my elbows, and shoot her an incredulous look, raising one eyebrow. "'*Something that came up*' with the both of us when we walked alone together to your apartment?"

She somehow manages to blanch and blush at the same time. "Okay, maybe not so…vague. Medical emergency?"

"You're going to drive them crazy with worry. They really will think we got mugged."

"Shit. You're right. Um." She wraps her arms around herself, pacing across the floor.

Right into her minefield of shattered glass and knitting needles.

"She doesn't need a ride to the hospital." With one hand holding Rhiannon's foot steady and the other poking at the glass in her heel with a pair of tweezers, I'm left pinning her phone between my ear and shoulder. "We've got it handled here. It's just a couple pieces of glass. Barely any bleeding." At that exact moment, Rhiannon yelps. *Thanks,* I mouth to her sarcastically as Grace gushes, "Are you *sure* she's okay?"

"She's fine. Just a big baby. No need for an ambulance. Can you swing by with our stuff, though? I don't think Rhiannon's gonna make it back…" So okay, I could probably run and grab our stuff myself, but then I would be missing out on more alone time with a total babe.

And I *really* need to stop thinking of Rhiannon that way. She might be cool and pro-choice enough not to care about me having this baby, but that doesn't mean she's going to jump at the chance to sleep with a pregnant girl. Or God forbid, actually get *involved* with me knowing I have a kid on the way. And do I really want to be telling my mom I'm pregnant *and* that I'm bi all in the same year? Anyway, wouldn't us being friends be great all on its own? "She said you know where she lives?"

"Of course I know where she lives. I'm just glad you two didn't get mugged!"

"You hear that?" I ask. "She says they thought we got mugged."

Rhiannon covers her eyes with her hands.

For as cool under pressure as I know she can be, she really is a mess. The sight of her own blood makes her pale. I half want to shake my head at her in derision, half want to wrap her in a blanket and hug her face to my chest. I settle for picking glass out of her feet and dropping it onto a piece of blood-spattered paper towel. Luckily the fragments are large enough to spot pretty easily, and the wounds they leave are shallow. I'm just picking out the last piece of glass when the intercom on her wall buzzes.

"Just hit the button." Rhiannon flaps her arm at the wall.

I buzz Grace into the building and head into Rhiannon's cramped galley kitchen to grab a broom. I'm sweeping up glass and stooping to gather her knitting needles when the front door opens.

"Did you two start a fight club in here?" Grace asks, taking in the chaos with wide eyes.

"If we did, you know we couldn't talk about it," Rhiannon replies, voice croaky, from her place lying flat out on the couch.

"I bought Band-Aids." Grace sets down our bags at the door, and heads straight for the couch, where she plops down at Rhiannon's feet. "You really are a baby," she scolds, taking Rhiannon's injured left foot into her lap. She digs through her pharmacy shopping bag and pulls out some antiseptic wipes, giving Rhiannon's sole a thorough cleaning before bandaging the worst of her cuts. "What would you have done if…um…sorry, what was your name again?"

She turns to me, her expression blank, and I wither.

"Poppy," Rhiannon says before I get a chance.

"Right. What would you have done if Poppy hadn't been here? Fainted, probably." She gives Rhiannon's calf a gentle, affectionately-condescending-or-maybe-friendly-and-I'm-just-jealous-and-bitter pat. "There you go. This one's all patched up. Gimme your right."

I watch her nurse Rhiannon while I hunker over the dustpan, chasing the last few fragments in. My back aches. I feel light-headed again.

And like a total third wheel.

No, scratch that, I'm not even attached to the same bike as these two!

I've been sitting here agonizing over whether or not Rhiannon and I should sleep together, whether or not she's worth coming out for, whether or not I should pursue a relationship when I have a baby on the way, when the truth is, I don't even know these people!

Grace didn't even remember my name, and Rhiannon called me New Girl.

Because that's what I am to them: the new girl in the club. *Their* club.

My face burns. I look away, pretending like I have to focus on a particularly small, stubborn piece of glass that refuses to be swept up. I can force myself not to look at them, but I can't stop myself from seeing that they have history, maybe even as more than stitch n' bitch seatmates. And why not? Grace is slim and tall and gorgeous, just like my sister, and as effortlessly put together as Rhiannon. They'd make the kind of lesbian couple whose posts get ten thousand likes on Insta every time.

And even if they aren't that photogenic couple, it wouldn't stop me from feeling like I don't belong. In the stitch n' bitch, in their longstanding friendship…but most importantly, in the spotlight of Rhiannon's attention. That last, stubborn piece of glass finally makes it into the dustpan.

I'm really not needed here anymore.

"I should get going," I say, using the broom to help me stand, bitterly forcing myself not to think about how last time Rhiannon had been the one helping me to my feet.

"No!" Rhiannon cries.

"At least let us call you a cab!" Grace puts in.

Twist the knife, why don't you?

I grimace a smile. "See you two next week?"

Grace smiles sweetly. "For sure!"

I'm so flustered and distracted by my spiraling insecurities that it takes until I'm out on the street before I realize: I forgot to borrow any damn needles.

Chapter Eight

I'm lying facedown on my couch, wallowing in the misery of my ongoing self-doubt with the lights off and the TV on mute, when my phone buzzes. I blearily reach for it, and I'm 50/50 split between checking my texts or just throwing the damn thing at the wall. I barely manage to keep it in my hands.

How's the knitting going?

My sister, of course. Right on cue. An innocuous enough question on the face of it, one could even mistake it for genuine caring, but not from a member of *my* family.

I swipe my phone's screen, staring listlessly at the neatly wound ball of yarn that sits untouched on my coffee table next to my sample-sized bottle of prenatal vitamins and Planned Parenthood brochures, all reminders of how I'm all good intentions and no follow-through.

It's been a week since I left Rhiannon's place with my tail between my legs. I've vomited at work eight times. If Tracy has noticed, she's been delicate enough not to say anything about it.

Which means she probably hasn't noticed. It goes, I finally type back.

You gave up again, didn't you?

Ugggghhhhh.

I know she doesn't mean anything by it, not really, but friendly teasing about my various failures just doesn't land the same way coming from someone as accomplished as she is.

No, I reply forcefully and sit up, snatching my ball of not-good-enough yarn and stuffing it into my bag.

It was almost a lie: I'd completely planned on begging out sick of today's stitch n' bitch meeting, but my sister's text has gotten my back up. Just because she's technically right doesn't mean she has to say it, but now that she has, I'm overcome with the urge to prove her wrong.

So overcome, in fact, that I suddenly can't find it in me to care about playing third wheel to Rhiannon and Grace.

It's a stitch n' bitch, not a romantic date. Can't be a third wheel in a group of six. I can just stick close to Damian until I get my hormones in check and stop acting like a dramatic teenager about Rhiannon.

I need to grow the hell up. Wasn't that the plan? Getting jealous over a girl I'm crushing on but barely know, getting competitive and resentful of a girl I think is higher on the social hierarchy because she's prettier and skinnier than me? Not growing up. Quitting knitting in a huff before I've even started? Not growing up. Sulking and hiding from my problems? Not! Growing! Up!

I need to get my fucking act together.

Heading out to my knitting group now, actually! I type triumphantly, following it with a few suitably smug and proud of myself emojis: the OK hand, the double-underlined 100, the smiley face with grinning teeth, and three thumbs-up.

I'm going to grow the hell up. I'm going to brush my teeth and put on a bra, I'm going to put myself out there, I'm going to stop moping about my stupid crush, I'm going to follow through on learning to knit, I'm going to make friends, and most importantly of all, I'm going to be the mature capital-A-Adult parent my baby needs.

I'm also going to buy the right size of knitting needles.

After putting a bra and makeup on, brushing my hair, searching online for a local knitting shop, actually *going* to said knitting shop, getting help from the shopkeeper to find the needles I need and then finally catching public transit to the coffee shop where the stitch n' bitch is held... I'm the last one to arrive. I give the group as a whole a syrupy sweet, cheerful wave like nothing at all is wrong with me whatsoever, then head straight to the counter to buy the cookies. Double chocolate today, with big melty hunks of white chocolate.

I set the bag down and drop into the seat next to Damian.

"I printed out that pattern I found for you!" Mary produces—I swear to God—a fucking laminated, hole-punched copy.

"Wow, thanks!" I say. "You really went all out, huh?"

"It's a good habit to get into. Helps you return to patterns you've used over and over again, especially when it's something you know you're knitting two of, like mitts or booties. You can also use a highlighter to keep your place in the pattern without marking up the original permanently."

That is way more thought out and organized than I could ever dream of being. I flash her a smile, set the pattern down on the table in front of me and reach into my bag for my knitting.

"Um, hey." Rhiannon reaches into her own bag. "You left last week without getting those needles you needed—"

"No worries," I interrupt her, smiling as brilliantly as I can muster. "I went and bought my own." I dig out my brand-new needles. Right size, right length, and made of wood, too, because the girl at the knitting store told me wood is good for beginning knitters because you're less likely to drop stitches. I've got stitchmarkers and a row counter, too.

It's subtle, but I still catch it: Rhiannon winces. "Look at you, all set up, huh?"

I bat my eyelashes at her. "Yep!" I tear the needles out of their package, take the yarn from my bag…

Wait, how do I get the yarn on the needles again?

I must look like a deer caught in headlights, because Damian shrugs at me. "Don't look at me." He gestures to his crochet hook in illustration.

I'm about to ask Mary to share more of her expertise when Grace pipes up. "How many stitches do you need to cast on?"

I squint at my pattern. "Uhhh…"

Louise grabs it from across the table. "Twenty-nine," she tells Grace, then slides the pattern back to me. "Teach her long tail cast on to start, that's what my mother taught me."

"All right," Grace says. "Start by taking the end of your yarn there and measure out, oh, around eighteen inches or so? Then you need to tie a slipknot around your needle."

"A what?"

"A slipknot. Here." She takes my yarn, measures out the eighteen inches, then quickly flips the yarn and tugs it, slipping the loop she's created over one of my needles and pulling it tight.

I have no idea what she just did.

"Now you just twist the yarn around your thumb…"

"The yarn…" I repeat, holding it up cluelessly. I wind it around my thumb.

"No, no, no, not like that." Grace sounds impatient now. I don't know why she's taken it upon herself to help me when it's obvious Mary or Louise are much more keen on taking a newbie under their wing. Maybe she just wants to lord her skills over me.

I huff, frustrated and upset and wishing I'd never come.

"Hey." Rhiannon's calm, steady voice pierces through

the miasma of bad feelings. "Don't get discouraged. Maybe you just need to see it a different way." She scrapes her chair around the table until she's sitting beside me. "Personally, I've never been able to learn just by watching. May I?"

At my nod, she edges closer, close enough that we're practically sharing a seat. She waits a beat, testing the waters to be sure I don't shy away, then reaches around me from behind, her arms wrapping around my own and her palms coming to rest on the backs of my hand. "Here," she says, gently, her cheek practically brushing against mine. "Like this. We'll do it together, okay?"

Warmth floods through me, but not from Rhiannon's body heat. "O-okay."

She puts my knitting needle in my right hand, then takes my left, draping the tail of the yarn over my forefinger and thumb to make a loop then closing my remaining fingers around it.

"Let me know if I'm going too fast at any point, okay?"

Too fast? If anything, she's going too slow for me!

Just…not in the knitting sense.

Her hands on mine, she slowly guides my needle into the loop she's created, patiently shows me how to use my thumb and finger to manipulate the yarn around the tip of my needle, creating a new stitch. She does it over and over again, warm against my back and all around me, her voice calm and steady in my ear, until suddenly I'm casting on the stitches all on my own.

And damn me, as determined as I am to maintain some distance between us, I don't want her to let me go.

But she does.

"Now you got it!" she cheers me on, and gives my shoulders a brief, friendly rub. "You must be a kinesthetic learner like me. I try to read knitting instructions or watch those tutorial videos on YouTube and I might as well be trying to learn to solve a Rubik's Cube from an octopus."

"I—I guess so," I reply. I'm blushing hard and breathing rapidly. I didn't even notice until now how much of an effect that had on me. I fan myself frantically, coming up with the weakest excuse I've ever come up with: "Is it warm in here for anybody else? I think I'm having a hot flash or something."

Louise and Mary both laugh. "You better hope not! You deserve to enjoy your youth while you can!" Louise teases.

"So um," I say, picking up my needles in either hand, holding them in my fists like a clueless white person holds chopsticks. I flash Rhiannon a helpless look, and she laughs. "Oh, all right, no need to twist my arm." She returns to my back, hands falling on top of mine again, shaping my grip around the needles. "So your pattern says to work eighteen rows in knit-one-purl-one ribbing…"

Once she's got me knitting and purling on my own, Rhiannon makes herself at home between Damian and I, watching my progress out of the corner of one eye while she works on her own sock with quick, practiced movements.

"That's a purl," she warns me. "Your working needle needs to go in through the front, not the back. Don't forget to flip your yarn to the back again when you're done. Like that, yeah. Beautiful!"

And then, later, "Watch your tension, don't hold your

knitting so tightly. Which I now maybe realize is easier said than done when you have me looming over your shoulder, huh?"

I raise an eyebrow at her teasingly. "You? Looming? I never noticed."

"Point taken. I'll loosen the reins a little, will I?"

Unlike most of the other women in my life, when she says she'll let me do my own thing she actually follows through on the promise. She turns her attention to her own knitting, her needles clacking against each other and her yarn winding elegantly through her fingers.

But as soon as I squeak for help, she jumps right back in with me.

"You just dropped a stitch at the end of your needle, there. No sweat. Does somebody have a crochet hook I can borrow?" She hooks my fallen stitch with practiced confidence, quickly carrying it back up through the rows. "There, see? Easy fix. Once you've got the basics down pat I'll show you how to do it on your own."

She's so patient with me. So attentive. The cuff of my baby mitt grows. I feel like I'm only just getting started when Damian looks at his watch. "Time for me to turn into a pumpkin," he says. "And by that, I mean, time to go pick up my kid at my mom's and get her ready for bed."

"I should get going, too," Louise says. "One of my cats is on antibiotics. Don't want to be late on his dose."

One by one, the group finishes their rows, packs their knitting, brings their coffee cups back to the counter, says their goodbyes.

"How about you, Rhi?" Grace asks. "I was going to

hit Whole Foods before I head home. You want to come with?"

I force myself not to look up from my knitting. I'm suddenly hyper focused on keeping my ribbing consistent.

"No thanks," Rhiannon replies, to my surprise. "I'm going to stick around, help the girls close up."

Huh?

"All right, your loss!" Grace replies. "I guess I'll just hog all the kombucha to myself!"

"You do that." I look up just in time to catch Rhiannon scrunch her nose in exaggerated disgust.

Grace smiles and shakes her head good-naturedly. "See you next week, then."

"See you next week," Rhiannon echoes.

"You too, Poppy," Grace adds. "Looking good there, by the way."

I look up in surprise. "Oh! Um! Thanks. See you next week, too, thanks for your help."

"Don't blow smoke up my ass, I didn't help you at all."

Surprise #2: I laugh.

When she leaves, my friendly wave goodbye is genuine.

I start to pack my stuff up, too, but Rhiannon flaps her hand at me. "You can stick around, if you want. Get a few more rows in while you've got me here to help. Just pick your feet up when I mop under the table and you're golden."

"Oh. Um. Okay. Sure." My cheeks get hot again. I scramble to pick up my needles and get them back into the position she showed me, my index fingers aligned with the needles, my working yarn safely tucked between my fingers. "I didn't realize you worked here."

"The clinic escort gig is my calling, but sadly, it doesn't pay."

I nod. "Need tuition money?" I ask, half dreading the answer. What if she's Ivy League or something, and here I am, an honor roll high schooler turned higher education dropout?

"Nah. No college for me, thanks. And considering half the people I work with here are six figures in debt to Sally Mae but still making the same wage as I do? I feel pretty smart to have cut out the middleman."

She doesn't even sound disappointed about it. I can't begin to fathom what that must feel like.

"Maybe someday I'll decide there's a degree worth going into that kind of debt for. For now all I need is something that pays enough to keep me in pink vests. What about you?"

"I, well—" *I flunked out.* "I'm taking some time off, I guess? I have a pretty good job as a receptionist at a dental clinic to tide me over. Pays the bills, and the health insurance is a lifesaver."

"And you with a bun on the oven? I bet." She casts a look over to the counter, where her coworkers are cleaning out the baked good case and wiping down the espresso machine. "I better get to work. You stick around. I-if you want, that is. I mean, if you need to get up early for work tomorrow don't stay out late on my account."

There she is, acting all nervous and adorable again.

Almost like I'm more to her than a third wheel, or the New Girl I'd written myself off as.

Almost as if she *wants* me to be more.

The way *I* want to be more?

Well, there's only one way to find out for sure.

"I'll stick around," I say. "But only if you promise to walk *me* home this time."

Rhiannon's eyes twinkle. "I'd love to."

Chapter Nine

I reach the end of my ribbing as Rhiannon's mopping the floor. The pattern after that is pretty easy at first: just alternating rows of knits and purls to make an all-knit side and an all-purl side. Also known, apparently, as a "right" and "wrong" side. Look at your girl learning the jargon!

Then I hit a certain point where—in a pattern that has consisted entirely of *K*s and *P*s—I'm suddenly instructed to *S1* and I have no idea what that's supposed to mean. I cast a look around for Rhiannon, but she's behind the counter, counting out the till while her coworker pulls the blinds and locks the doors. All the lights except the ones behind the counter switch off suddenly, leaving me in half-darkness. Guess this is as good a time as any to quit for the night. I pull my knitting rows down to the ends of my needles, pray it doesn't work its way back up them and slip off, then stuff my knitting in my bag.

"Can I help you guys at all?" I ask.

"Put the chairs on the tables?" one of the baristas suggests.

"'Kay."

I go from table to table, flipping chairs onto tables until the cafe is a forest of upturned chair legs.

"You all set?" Rhiannon appears beside me. There's a fine sheen of sweat on her forehead, and she smells of coffee.

"Whenever you're ready," I reply. Without asking, she grabs my bag and tosses it over her shoulder. I should probably protest, remind her that I'm no helpless damsel and she isn't my knight in shining armor, but I have to admit a part of me is tickled to have someone so attentively taking care of me.

I button my trench coat and follow her out the front door of the cafe, where I stop on the sidewalk to loop my (store bought) infinity scarf around my neck, fluffing it up nice and high around my chin. There's a definite evening chill in the air and no way am I letting myself get sick when I can't even take cold medicine.

"Cozy," Rhiannon comments, and reaches out with both hands to tug my scarf even higher, until it tickles the tip of my nose. "There." She smiles. "Now you're perfect."

Just like that, I'm totally warm, like it isn't September after sundown.

I raise my shoulders and sink deeper into my scarf, but this time it's not because I'm cold. I suck my lips back between my teeth and smile like a twitterpated idiot, relieved she can't see my expression. If she did, would she be able to tell I'm feeling the sudden urge to pull my scarf down again and peck her right on the lips?

She reaches out with one hand, like she's going to touch a strand of hair that's fallen over my cheek, then draws it back, brushing it over her own head instead.

Her dark hair stands on end.

"Aren't you cold?" I ask, only just now noticing her tiny striped T-shirt and unzipped leather jacket.

"I retain a surprising amount of heat for my size," she replies.

"I guess I'm the opposite," I say with a laugh.

"That's okay, I happen to think it's charming when a cute girl is perpetually cold."

I'm a cute girl? I think, but instead say, "Sadist!"

She shrugs. "I just like the easy excuse to get all chivalrous. No sadism required."

"So you must have been doing mental cartwheels when I asked you to walk me home, huh?"

"Mmmaybe." She knocks her bony shoulder against my own as we begin to walk.

"I should warn you, full disclosure, it's actually about a half hour from here. If you would rather I just cab it, say the word. You won't hurt my feelings."

Please don't say you'd rather cab it, because while it wouldn't hurt my feelings, it would definitely put a damper on me inviting you inside.

What am I even thinking? Inviting her inside? To do what, knit more?

To get to know her better as friends?

Or to hear her call me "cute" and "perfect" more?

Somewhere we can be alone together, without people like Grace bringing up all my insecurities?

"I don't mind—" Rhiannon says, at the exact same time as I blurt out, "So what's the deal with you and Grace, anyway?"

"Huh?"

I manage to burrow even deeper into my scarf. "Uh, well. Um. You know." I have absolutely no explanation for myself that doesn't sound pathetic or creepy or sad or any other number of unflattering adjectives. "You two seem like...old friends."

Rhiannon doesn't ask for one, just answers plainly: "I guess you could say we are. She used to volunteer at the clinic with me, before she started seeing her boyfriend and they wound up working opposite shifts during the week and she wanted to take her weekends off to spend with him."

A girl like *her* used to volunteer at the clinic?
Wait.

"She has a boyfriend?"

"Uh-huh. Cool guy, actually. Totally laid-back. Kind of mellows her out a little, not that you can tell. I know she kind of grates on you or whatever, but she's actually pretty nice, once you get past her snooty keto exterior. Just weird and a little obsessive about stuff. You get used to it."

Shame gnaws at my stomach. I wring my hands. "She doesn't grate on me, per se."

"Oh no?"

"She just reminds me of my overachiever sister. All tall and beautiful and skinny and with her life in order."

"I'm sensing resentment," Rhiannon teases.

I crack a smile. "Just a little."

"I imagine it doesn't feel that way right now, but your life seems pretty in order to me. And as for the rest, you may not be tall or skinny but those aren't the be-all and end-all of beauty."

"Give me a break."

"It's true!"

"So you and Grace...*just* friends?"

Rhiannon stops. Folds her arms. "What made you think any differently?"

At first I'm taken aback, embarrassed at my own insecurity, horrified that it'd have me jumping to conclusions so readily—

And then I see that mean smile of hers playing at the corner of her mouth.

I smack her shoulder.

"Okay, fine! You're not entirely off base. I did have the hots for her when we were volunteering together. But I'm over it. I have to be over it. Unlike me, she *is* straight."

"Well, if it makes you feel better about your love life, consider the following: you could have hooked up with your loser ex on a drunken booty call and wound up with his baby in you."

We both grimace.

Why did I even tell her that? What is my goal here? Do I want her to come back to my place? Because I'm not gonna get her there by letting her assume I'm straight with an extra side of reminding her I'm knocked up and have baggage for miles.

Or maybe I'm just talking to her honestly, as a friend, the same way she's talking to me.

That *was* what I wanted out of this experience, after all: a friend. Someone to confide in, to support and be supported by in return.

Which is the only sensible relationship for me to want right now. In less than nine months, I'm going to have a little person to look out for, and I'm going to need to put that little person's needs first.

Mom having supportive friends? A-ok when it comes to providing a stable home life for baby. Mom sleeping with random girls? Not so much.

Except she's not some random girl, and you know it.

Okay, point, but still. It's hardly the ideal time to bring a new girlfriend into my life, either. Babies need stability. What if Rhiannon and I are dating but then after the baby's born we break up? What if Rhiannon doesn't want to commit in the first place, especially considering just how big that commitment becomes when a baby is involved? That can't be good for the baby, to have her in and then out of my life again, or only halfway in in the first place. I'm reminded of all those Lifetime Dramas with single moms who have revolving doors of boyfriends, and how they play into their screwed up kid's tragic backstory.

Do I want that to be me? Do I want to be my child's tragic backstory?

I need to face facts. I am in no position to be thinking about no strings attached sex *or* starting a new relationship.

Friendship, on the other hand? Friendship I need.

I reach out, linking arms with Rhiannon companion-

ably as we walk together down the sidewalk. "No reassuring comeback for that one? My life's not so orderly after
all, huh? Luckily you can distract me from my train wreck
of a pregnancy by telling me more about your sad, unre-
quited love for your straight friend."

In the end, we don't talk about Grace.

Why would we, when there's so much else to talk about?
Our conversation meanders from K-Dramas to our jobs to
how pretty Getty Square looks at night before circling in-
evitably back to knitting.

"So how long have you been a knitter?"

"Oh, man, I don't know, I think I was eleven, maybe
twelve?" Rhiannon stares into the distance wistfully. "My
grandmother taught me. Idle hands are the devil's play-
thing, and all that."

"She was religious?"

"No, just Irish. My mom and dad both worked so much
she kind of took over parenting duties. I think teaching
me to knit was just her way of finding me an after school
hobby that wouldn't take her away from her stories. I take
it you didn't have any knitters in your family?"

I shake my head. "My grandparents retired to Florida so
I didn't really see much of them growing up unless they
were taking us to Disney World. And my mother wasn't
interested in any hobby that didn't have an elected com-
mittee attached. I think even her book club had meeting
minutes and a treasurer."

"Oh, so you're *rich*-rich."

"I mean, I don't think so?"

"You know that's exactly what a rich person would say, right?"

"Oh God, it totally is, isn't it?" I wish I could pull my scarf up to cover my entire face in shame.

Unlike Rhiannon, I never had to do the math and decide whether my education was worth going into six figures of debt for. My parents both had jobs—we weren't quite "never work a day in our lives" rich, thank you very much—but growing up I had a nanny looking after me, not an unpaid grandparent.

Just as the chasm of class threatens to divide us, Rhiannon's arm around mine clamps down, yanking me close in defiance.

I stumble against her, enjoying the feeling of her pulling me off balance perhaps slightly too much.

I valiantly try to laugh it off with a quippy, "Damn, you're pocket-sized but mighty, huh?"

"It's all the bags of coffee beans I have to toss around on a daily basis." Even through the layers of our jackets, I could swear I can feel the hardness of her bicep where it presses against mine. Or maybe I'm just fantasizing way too hard. Before we know it, we're coming up fast on my apartment building. We've walked arm-in-arm the whole way here, and although it started out on my part as gossipy friends gesture, it's definitely morphed into something else by this point.

"This is me," I say regretfully, coming to a stop at my apartment door. I know it's time to let her go—holding on now would definitely be weird, right?—but I can't seem to extricate myself from her elbow.

When we finally separate, Rhiannon's hand lingers on forearm. The tips of her fingers brush my sleeve as she pulls away.

Is it too much to hope that she doesn't want to separate, either?

"You have roommates?" She stuffs her hands into the pockets of her leather jacket and cranes her neck to take in my building's six stories looming above us.

I shake my head. "I have a studio. Just don't ask me what percentage of my monthly expenses goes to rent."

"Just so long as you don't ask how much of *my* spending goes to tea and yarn." She chuckles and rocks on the balls of her feet. "Anyway. No roommates. Good to know."

"*Is* it good to know?" I tilt my head at her inquisitively.

Her eyes widen. "Uh, I mean. Good to know because… because…" She circles her hand in the air. It's like she's spinning the tires of her car, unable to get traction. "You know, because now I know it can be done. You can live without roommates in the state of New York."

I should really let that explanation fly. My decision that we should be just friends depends on me not cracking this conversation open to expose the obvious subtext inside. On the other hand, Rhiannon and I combining flirting and teasing is kind of becoming our *thing* and she's given me the perfect opening. It's just teasing, I tell myself. Just because I don't intend on going anywhere serious or not-so-serious with Rhiannon doesn't mean I have to give that up. I don't want things to be weird by suddenly acting all different around her. "For sure. That *is* good to know. No other possible reason for you to be happy I live alone now that we're standing at my door and it's late…"

"Oh God!" She pulls back her coat, checking her over-sized man's watch. She's not blushing or laughing. She looks genuinely awkward. "It *is* late, isn't it? And shit, you have a day job! You probably have to be up super early in the morning, right?"

Looking at her all hangdog, something in me snaps. "It's not *that* late." The words are out of my mouth before I can talk myself out of saying them.

Just like that, something about Rhiannon's body language changes. She tilts her head, cocks her hip, lists sideways until she's bracing herself by one hand on the glass front door of my building. I fall back against the door, letting her hem me in. My breath comes in little white puffs. What have I done? And why am I not feeling nearly as regretful about leading her on this way as I logically should? Is it because I'm not leading her on at all?

The corner of her mouth quirks. Not the expression of a girl who thinks she's being teased or led on, that's for sure. No, definitely not: she looks like a girl who thinks maybe she has a chance. "Hmm. Well. It's *kind of* late," she says. "And getting cold, too. Not sure I should be walking home now. Of course, I *could* take a cab…"

My hands open and close in the sleeves of my coat. Her proposition is confident, but she still gives me an out. I can still send her home. She won't get mad or pressure me. She won't resent me for my rejection, I know that for certain. Her continuing friendship with Grace is living proof.

She waits wordlessly.

As the seconds stretch between us, one of her heels starts to bounce against the pavement, less an impatient tap of her foot than it is a nervous twitch.

I press my lips together. Swallow. Lift my chin and ball my hands into fists. Yeah, Rhiannon and Grace are fine despite what happened between them. Rhiannon and I could be fine, too.

Except I want us to be more than fine.

I bite the corner of my lower lip, pressing my body flatter to the door behind me. "You *could* take a cab, but that would eat into your tea and yarn budget. Seems kind of unnecessary when you've got a free place to crash for the night right here, don'tcha think?"

Her endearingly anxious expression brightens into a grin. "Right? Yeah!" She nods rapidly.

I reach into my bag and produce my keychain. Give it a little illustrative shake before I turn around, my back to her, and put my key in the lock. Thank God I didn't fumble or pick the wrong key, because that would totally ruin this smooth flirty thing I've got going on. I toss a look over my shoulder, casually brushing my free hand under my hair. "Wanna come in?" I ask, like we haven't spent the last fifteen minutes agonizing and dancing around this very question.

She cops on to the game I'm playing. "Yeah, girl," she says with a smirk, all cool practiced confidence.

I let her in.

Chapter Ten

"This place is fantastic!" Rhiannon exclaims as soon as she gets through the door, taking a wide-eyed look around as she kicks out of her sneakers. Rather than tell her she doesn't need to do that here, I just shrug and step out of my flats, as well.

"*Fantastic?* Really? Um, I guess?" I reply, undoing the belt and buttons of my coat while taking in my cramped little studio with new eyes. I don't have near the art collection Rhiannon does, but my wall of collected postcards isn't half bad, either, and my selection of thrifted furniture is the work of many months waiting and watching and sitting on pillows on the floor until I spotted my perfect pieces: a gorgeous 1970s marigold yellow couch in perfect comfy and dilapidated yet sturdy condition, an oval-shaped coffee table with several decades' worth of mug rings, and a cute midcentury sideboard for a TV stand. A curtain strung with Christmas lights hides my completely ordinary IKEA bed from view of the rest of the room. The thought that Rhiannon might get to see that, too, has me wiping my palms on my skirt. "You want a drink or something?"

"Do I dare ask for tea?" she replies. She unzips her jacket, tossing it over the back of my couch.

"Um, that depends. Are you going to turn up your nose at anything you don't need an infuser for?"

"Are you going to kick me out if I do?"

I give her a mock offended look, putting my hands on my hips. "No, but I might just pour you a glass of tap water. Without letting it run cold first."

She laughs. "Seriously, I'm kidding. Whatever tea you have is fine. I'm actually not a snob about it at all, I just play the part because I think it makes me look cool."

"You're not just saying that because you want to get on my good side?"

"Maybe a little. But then again, maybe not."

I'm going to kick her in the shin, and then maybe kiss her. I hang my coat on the overburdened board of hooks by my front door, then turn to the kitchen.

I watch her picking around my "living room" while I fill the kettle.

She takes a seat on my couch, immediately leaning forward to fan out the PP brochures still littering my coffee table. "You took every piece of literature we had, huh?"

"I think the counsellor could pick out how wishy-washy I was on the whole thing from fifty paces. To be honest, though, the decision was really easy to make once I stopped trying to convince myself I didn't have a choice."

"It was easy for me, too. I honestly think half the time we only agonize over it because we think we're supposed to."

"You had an abortion?" I ask. The kettle is taking forever to boil. I want to go and sit with her, not just with her but *close* to her, but I know if I do, I'll end up letting it boil dry and set fire to the place.

"When I was sixteen, so I guess—oof!—I guess that makes it ten years ago now. Feel as confident about it now as I did then. No regrets."

I touch my belly below my navel, where my baby is now the size of a green olive (the thought of which immediately turns my stomach). I open my cupboard and grab the ginger tea. "I hope I'm that content ten years from now. What kind of tea do you want? I have black, green and a couple different herbals."

"All the research worth reading says that the vast majority of people, when given the *chance* to choose, wind up feeling okay about their choice, no matter what that choice is. And green's fine." She neatly stacks my pamphlets and brochures, taps them on the coffee table to straighten them, then sets them down in a pile. "Have you decided what you're gonna do after you give birth?"

"I want to keep it. Raise it. Is that…" Twitchy and full of nervous energy all of a sudden, I grab two mugs and drop tea bags into them both. "Is that a dealbreaker for you?"

She doesn't answer right away. I refuse to turn around until she does, turning our mugs this way and that on the counter and compulsively checking and rechecking the kettle, which still hasn't fucking boiled.

Which is why I'm surprised when I feel her hand on my shoulder, turning me around. She takes my elbows in her hands, cradling them as she levels me a serious look. She looks so ridiculously gorgeous and calm. "Just so long as it's not a dealbreaker for *you* that whatever happens between us doesn't automatically mean I'm gonna be this baby's mama."

I huff, half in relief, half in fear. "I was okay, uh, in theory, with being a single mom before I got to know you. I think I'm still okay with it now."

"You think you are?"

"Well, having never had a kid before, I'm not sure how good I'm gonna be at it. But I mean, I'm not actively seeking a co-parent or anything."

However, I am a little terrified I'm gonna screw my kid up irrevocably somehow.

I'm about to ask her what she thinks of that possibility when the kettle starts to scream.

Of course.

I pull out of her grip and rush to take it off the burner, switching the stove off before I slosh steaming hot water into both our mugs.

I hand her her mug, unable to meet her eyes.

"Is there something else?" she asks, and I pretend not to hear, focusing instead on dunking my poor tea bag like I'm trying to get information out of it. "Poppy. Is there something else?"

I wince and turn at last. "I'm worried I'm gonna screw the kid up with my sleeping around."

She raises an eyebrow. "*Are* you sleeping around? I mean, no judgment from me if you are."

"No! No." I dunk my tea bag a few more times. "I haven't slept with *anyone* since, well…" I gesture to my stomach in illustration.

"Okay, well, assuming you sleep with me tonight—which isn't in any way a thing that has to happen if you don't want it to I might add—sleeping with one woman is not sleeping around, and even if you do wind up sleeping with, I dunno, an entire women's soccer team or something, your baby is a fetus. You can't screw *that* up, not psychologically anyway."

"And after the baby's born?" I ask, my voice weak and nervous.

She shrugs. "If this…thing even lasts that long, we'll figure it out. It's not like an infant is gonna miss me if I leave, anyway."

I heave a huge sigh. I don't know whether her answer has comforted me, or just left me humiliated.

"Hey," she says, and takes the tip of my chin in her hand, her thumbnail brushing irresistibly close to my lower lip. "Worrying about screwing up your kids is normal. But don't let it stop you from enjoying your life. Uh, within reason of course." She chuckles. Releases my chin. "But if it's really bothering you, we don't have to take this anywhere you don't want it to go. We can have a cup of tea, watch some of that K-Drama you were telling me about, and I can crash on your couch."

Okay, so she's talking sense. I let myself breathe, then

give her a playful nudge. "An entire women's soccer team, huh? That's an oddly specific fantasy."

She looks as relieved as I feel now that I've changed the subject.

"Mmmaybe," she replies with a sly look. She shimmies her shoulders at me. "C'mon, let's take this to the sofa." She snatches the bag out of her tea, unabashedly drops it in my sink and saunters, mug in hand, over to the couch.

I tug out my poor tortured tea bag, drop it into the drain alongside hers and hurry after her.

She's leaned wayyyy back, mug in one hand, her other arm slung over the back of the couch and her legs sprawled. I lower myself into the seat beside her, automatically pressing my thighs together to maintain the space between us, but she just widens her stance even more, her knee knocking against my own playfully. She flashes me a smug look and takes a noisy slurp of her tea.

I raise my own mug to my lips with both hands, hiding my smile inside it.

I feel warm from the inside out, and I know it's not just the tea.

"Sooo…" she says.

"Sooo…" I echo.

She leans forward, setting her mug down on the coffee table.

"Do you mind if I—?"

"Please!" I blurt out, not even waiting to hear what she has in mind.

Oh God, what if she was just asking if she could turn on the TV?

I flash her a horrified, wide-eyed look, my face hotter than my tea.

She just laughs softly and turns, resting a hand on my lower thigh to prop herself on as she leans in and kisses the side of my mouth. More my cheek than anything, but I can feel the barest brush of her lips against my own, and her kiss is so soft, so gentle, so undemanding, that my eyes fall instantly closed.

I feel her pry my mug out of my hands, hear the soft thud and clatter of it setting down on the wood of the coffee table. One of her hands clasps my shoulder, half turning my body toward her own. The other runs through my hair, her splayed fingers gently combing my scalp.

She kisses me again. I want to melt into the couch, but since I can't, I just sink deeper into the cushions, my limbs going completely limp, and in response she just lowers herself against me, pressing close. Her breathy laugh gusts over my skin as she kisses me again, openmouthed this time, deeper, the backs of her knuckles brushing the skin behind my ear as her tongue dips into my mouth.

Nobody has ever kissed me like this. So unhurried, with lips so soft and plush.

I reach out, taking her small waist in my hands. Give her a gentle tug, which prompts her to shift, straddling my lap.

Yes, this. My hands sweep down her hips, past her ass to cup the backs of her upper thighs. The sensation of the denim of her jeans under my hands is nearly as erotic as the feeling of her mouth. She gasps, laughs again, takes two handfuls of my hair and tugs my head back slightly, until my face is tilted up and she's kissing me from above, rising up on her knees to do so.

Not that I don't love feeling her fists in my hair, the gentle insistent pull along my scalp, but I want her hands on me *everywhere*. I reach up, never breaking our kiss, and grasp both her wrists. She immediately releases my hair, but I'm not about to let her apologize. I just move her hands wordlessly lower, until her palms press into my breasts. It only takes a half a second for her to give both overflowing handfuls a squeeze. We moan in unison, mine high and urgent, hers low and growly, exactly like I'd hoped it would be.

I knead the firm muscles of her legs in time with her fingers on my chest. Slide my hands inward under her ass until my fingertips are between her legs, skimming the hot place where her pelvis and inner thighs meet. She thrusts her hips, causing my hands to drag back and forth between her legs.

She breaks our kiss, panting out, "I want to unbutton your dress."

"Yes please," I reply. I let my hands fall to my sides, giving her access. How lucky am I to have picked tonight to wear my belted shirtdress, the one with the buttons that extend from the collar right down to my belly button? *So* lucky.

She works at them one by one, pausing between buttons to part the fabric that little bit more, kiss every inch of my skin as it's exposed. When she's made her way to the last button, she brushes the sides of my dress as far apart as they'll go, until it's falling off my shoulders and slipping down my arms. "God yeah," she growls, unabashedly staring down at my chest.

Today really *is* my lucky day: I'm wearing one of my actually cute bras, the purple one with the unicorns and rainbows print.

When Rhiannon notices it, she looks up at me and grins. "How do you manage to be so adorable and sexy at the same time? You know, sexydorable?"

"Easy. Combine cutesy print bra with huge tits." I cup them in my hands, lifting them and squeezing them together in illustration.

Her pupils dilate. Her chest heaves. "Well, I love it."

"Do you love it too much to take it off me?" I pout playfully at her.

"Okay, not that much." She laughs, lowering her ass to my lap, and bends to kiss my neck and collarbone while her hands sweep into my bra, scooping my breasts right out of the cups in one smooth motion. I'm exposed, but she doesn't look, not right away at least. She's too busy sucking marks down my neck and shoulder, never quite lingering long enough or sucking strong enough to actually give me a hickey. Her thumbs circle my nipples, working them until they pucker and tighten. They're too round and flat and puffy to ever be considered hard, but I'm turned on just the same.

I want her mouth on me, but I can't bring myself to say it aloud. So I reach out with shaky, half-limp hands, cup the back of her head, and nudge her downward.

"All right! *All right!*" she scolds gently, tsking me. "Little Miss Impatient."

She bends at the waist, and uses one hand to lift my breast to her mouth.

But she doesn't put her lips on me.

My hips lift off the couch in frustration. "Please!" I whine.

"Damn right, 'Please'!" She turns her dark eyes up at me and smirks.

Maintains eye contact as she finally—finally!—closes her mouth around my nipple.

I cling to her hair, riding the obscene wave of pleasure she's bringing me. I don't know if it's her or the early pregnancy tenderness or both, but it only takes the gentlest suction for me to be just this side of crying, my eyes squeezed shut as I whimper through clenched teeth.

Her hot breath huffs across my damp, cooling skin: she's laughing.

"Enjoy...your power trip...while...it lasts..." I gasp back, sounding like I've just run up two flights of stairs. Yeah, real tough, Poppy.

She gives my other breast a thoughtful rub. "I'd enjoy it more if we took this to your bed. Kinda getting a crick in my neck here."

I blush. "Oh! Um! Yeah, of course!" I don't know whether I'm more embarrassed by the fact that I've completely ignored her comfort in the pursuit of my own pleasure, or if I'm just worried there might be something incriminating on my bed. At least this far into my pregnancy I know there won't be any stained panties lying around for her to see.

Small mercies.

Chapter Eleven

She gives the top of my breast one last, affectionate kiss, then hops off my lap. Turns. Grasps the bottom of her tight, striped tee and pulls it, inside out, over her head.

Oof. Feels like I've had the wind knocked out of me.

She wears a simple black lace bralette, its straps bisecting her prominent shoulder blades. Unlike my own generous hourglass, she's all shoulders and no hips. The pale white skin of her back is scattered with a sparse constellation of little black moles. I want to kiss every single one of them.

I also want to see her from the front.

I'm still a little fuck-dazed as I clumsily rise from my couch and follow after her. My dress, falling off my body, tangles my arms and trips up my legs. I struggle to get out of it, forgetting until the last second that I'm totally wearing my beige shapewear shorts over my more situationally appropriate lacy panties. I try to get the shorts off me before she sees them, but she turns just in time to catch me with them around my knees.

I'm going to die. I'm going to die of embarrassment before ever getting to have sex with this girl, and the paramedics are going to find my body in control-top shorts.

Rhiannon doesn't laugh or comment, though, just wordlessly unbuttons her own skinny jeans, revealing...

"Oh my God, is that—"

She nods. "*Duck Dynasty.*" Her boxer briefs are green camo, a little oversized, and when she lowers her jeans to midthigh and gives me a little turn, her ass reads HAPPY HAPPY HAPPY in hi-vis yellow letters. "They were a gag gift from my dad," she tells me over her shoulder. Scrunches up her nose, adding, "And today was laundry day."

She didn't laugh at me, so I don't laugh at her, either, but—no point trying to lie—it isn't easy.

I feel a little better about my choice of undergarments now, at least. I strip the rest of the way out of the shorts, then switch my attentions to my over-the-knee grey socks.

"Leave those," she instructs, her voice gone gravelly and serious again.

I leave them.

Strike a pose in them tiptoed and sweep my hands up my thick thighs and over the roundness of my hips instead.

Her eyelids half lower. She peels herself the rest of the way out of her jeans and rainbow socks, never breaking eye contact. Once she's down to her bra and undies, she grabs my hand, leading me urgently to the curtain that hides the last third of my apartment from view. She yanks it aside so hard several of the clothespins attaching it to my string of lights pop.

"It doesn't actually…draw back…" I murmur, too late.

Honestly, I don't even care. She can tear my entire place apart in her desperation to get me into this bed.

Because she wants me.

She wants me *bad*.

This stunning butch babe in her novelty boxers…wants *me*.

Not for a pity fuck, not because she's horny and I'm just who's available, neither "generously" despite my size nor fetishistically because of it.

She tugs my hand, pulling me close, and I think she's about to kiss me, but instead she grabs me by both shoulders and shoves me back onto my bed.

I laugh in surprise, bouncing on the mattress and spreading my arms, knocking aside pillows and stuffed animals. She laughs, too, then lunges onto all fours over top me. We both bounce on impact.

"Is this a bed or a trampoline?" she asks, testing the firmness of my mattress with both hands.

Is now a good time to admit it's kind of both, and that I've spent more than one night with my music loud, jumping on my bed and singing at the top of my lungs like a preteen girl, trying to ward away my feelings of hopelessness and dissatisfaction?

I stare up at her, drawing my knuckles over the skin of her left collarbone back and forth. I toy with the strap of her bra with the tip of one finger. She reaches up, folding her hand around my own, and then pins it to the mattress over my head. The other one, too. Once she's got me where she wants me, she dips her hips in one fluid motion, low and slow, just barely drawing her mound across my own before rising again.

Like the spoiled little girl I am, I whine.

She smirks. Leans in for a kiss, but stops just short of my lips. I try to lift my head off the mattress, chasing her mouth, but she just draws back, away.

"What's wrong, baby?" she taunts. I squirm in her grip, lifting my ass off the mattress uselessly. She gives my forehead an affectionate little kiss, then she releases my hands. "Don't move," she says, just as I'm about to. God damn her.

I do as I'm told, balling my hands in my quilt and biting my lip in sublime frustration as she crawls down my body.

First stop, my tits again. This time she takes them both in hand, pressing them together, and moves wetly from nipple to nipple, sucking on them in turns and leaving a trail of saliva. It was nowhere near this wet before; that's how I know she's done playing with me.

"Please," I try again.

Keeping both hands on my breasts for now, she kisses her way lower until her arms are over her head. She kisses across the lower ridge of my rib cage, then continues on, her mouth lingering on the seam that cuts across my belly over my navel. She's not shy about my body in the slightest, shamelessly pushing in deep on every kiss, seeming to revel in the softness of my body against her face. Then she's between my legs, the fingers of one hand curled in the waistband of my panties while the other rolls my socks down an inch or so, first one then the other, and kissing the skin she's revealed.

If she doesn't quit avoiding the one place I want her most, I swear…

She sits up again, doing exactly that.

I'm not disappointed for long, though, because then she tugs her bra up over her head and tosses it away.

I am…in love with her nipples. They're coral pink and small around but *long*, and hard like they are, irresistibly pinchable looking.

But she told me not to move my hands.

"Um," I say, biting my lower lip and staring up at her with my best begging eyes.

I still don't move.

"Good girl," she praises me, then she leans down again, elbows on either side of my head. A lingering kiss on the lips, first—one that has me desperately thrusting my tongue against her own and making needy noises—and then she shifts upward, perfectly positioning herself for her left breast to fall against my lips. I open wide and take as much of her in as I can manage, sucking in slow, reverent pulses that draw her nipple up the flat of my tongue. She cries out, a perfectly broken sound. Soon she's thrusting her hips in time to my sucking. The position's all wrong for her to get any kind of real contact, but I can still feel the dampness and heat coming through her stupid hideous boxers.

I'm quite suddenly done being her good girl.

I'm also pretty sure she'll forgive me. Especially when I release my blankets and reach around her back, sliding my hand right down the seat of her boxers and between her legs. She's so wet. My three first fingers glide in deep, parting her labia around them. The angle makes it a little hard to reach, what with her chest in my face, but I still manage to nudge her clit with the very tip of my long middle finger.

"Ff-fuck!" she cries out, her whole body jolting like I've electrocuted her.

If I had carpets in my place, I might assume I had.

I turn my eyes up, trying to catch sight of her as I hungrily mouth at her tit and rub her pussy, circling my finger around her clit in ever tightening circles, never quite touching her *there*.

She's not the only one who can be a tease.

I pull off her nipple, biting the inside of her small breast gently as my fingers finally dip inside her, three of them at once not meeting the slightest bit of resistance she's so wet.

She doesn't leave me with the advantage for long. As I'm thrusting my fingers inside her, she's shifting her position over top me until she's pressing me between the legs *hard* with her knee.

It's my turn to shiver.

"Go on," she urges me gruffly. "Get yourself off, baby."

If she keeps calling me baby like that, I'm not going to need any physical stimulation to get myself there.

I ride her leg shamelessly, way more rough with myself than I'd ever consider being with her. My fingers on her clit are gentle, light, delicate and precise. In contrast, I use her knee as a blunt instrument, grinding my clit and labia all at once, the shock waves of every impact against her radiating deeper. It's not long until the sensation has me losing my mind and my coordination. My fingers, once artful, rub her rhythmlessly as my mouth latches and unlatches from the sweet soft skin of her breast at random. She thrusts against my hand. Bumps her knee against me and rubs it side to side. The two of us crash against each other, all co-ordination lost, until at last she takes two rough handfuls of my hair, yanks my face tight to her chest and lets out a yell. Fresh wetness soaks my fingers, and I plunge them inside her, wanting to feel the contractions of her orgasm.

I have just enough presence of mind to rub against her in time with each crush of my fingers, but no matter how hard I try, it's not enough to get me off. I need more. I need.

"I need—"

"Of course, baby, anything," she coos, her voice a little slurred as she comes down from her orgasm. She sits back, my numb hand slipping free of her boxers as she shifts.

A quick slap to my inner thigh has me spreading my legs, and without artifice she reaches in and pulls the crotch of my panties aside. Her thumb finds my clit quickly. She rubs it in absolutely fucking *punishing* circles—it's the meanest handjob I've ever had—but damn if I don't come in less than a minute.

When it happens, I cry out in such ridiculously over-stimulated pleasure that tears squeeze out the corners of my eyes. She leans down and kisses me through it, her mouth smothering my helpless yell.

Her thumb doesn't relent until she's taken me to the peak twice more, until I'm physically screaming from the horrible wonderful intensity of it and she has to cover the lower half of my face with her palm so my neighbors don't call the cops.

At last her touch slows, withdraws from my clit, circles and circles outward and away, gradually coasting me down.

When it's over, finally over, she lets go of her grip on my face, leans in and kisses me, deeply, one last time.

I'm too dazed to really register what happens after that. When I manage to come to, we're both naked—our wet underwear and my scratchy too-tight bra all gone—and we're snuggled under my covers the right way round, with our heads on the pillows and everything. Rhiannon spoons me from behind, one small hand drifting sleepily across my belly as the other brushes my hair off my nape so she can place a series of achingly tender kisses there.

It's so perfect, so gentle, so intimate.

So why do I want so badly for her to cup the part of my belly where my baby will soon be?

Chapter Twelve

When my alarm goes off the next morning, she pulls my pillow over her head, mumbling "Makeitstop!"

I hit snooze on my phone's screen and burrow back under the covers with her, face-to-face in a tangle of limbs like we're two teen girls sharing secrets on a sleepover.

"Morning," I say, toying with her floppy bangs.

I don't want to stop looking at her. She's so gorgeous, even with dark circles under her eyes, yesterday's concealer nothing but a distant memory. I stroke her cheek gently, but she keeps her eyes resolutely squeezed shut. She's definitely awake; I don't know who she's trying to fool here. When I lean in close, nudging the tips of our noses together, she finally gives up pretending in the name of giving me a sweet, chaste kiss.

"Knew you were faking," I murmur against her mouth.

"Not faking, just concentrating really hard on trying to discover my latent time control abilities so we can have another few hours."

"Another few hours..." I throw a leg over her hip, using it to tug her in closer. "Is that for you to sleep more, or for you to spend with me?"

I keep the question light, but I'm still holding my breath despite myself, almost scared for her to answer.

"Can't it be both?" She snuggles in closer to me, stuffing her face right between my breasts with a loud, thoroughly relaxed, "Mmmm."

I pet her hair and hug her close. "I do make an excellent pillow."

Her reply is muffled against my skin: "God yes you do. The *best*."

I'm about to go full cheesy and suggest a few other things I'm good at in bed, but my alarm goes off again.

We both groan in misery. I really do need to go into work, though. I can't exactly call in "got laid last night" when I know I'm gonna need the sick days as my pregnancy progresses.

"I can't hit snooze again," I say, regretfully. "Not if I'm going to be on time. You wanna stay here, orrr...?"

She rolls over onto her back, covering her eyes with her forearm. "God, I want to, but I gotta work at three, and you're probably not gonna be back before that, huh?"

"No, sorry." I frown. "And I'd be okay giving you a key if I had a copy to spare, but my only extra is with my mom."

Did I just admit to being theoretically okay with her having the key to my place after one night of sex?

I cough, awkward, especially since she's kind of making a face.

Oh God, she's never gonna want to see me again. She's probably wondering when I'm gonna propose moving in together or marriage and is planning her escape as we sit here—

"Your mom has a key to your place? And how old are you, exactly?"

Oh. Oh. Phew. Okay.

This, at least, is a conversation I've had plenty of times and still maintained my relationships—romantic and otherwise—after.

"I know, I know. She's, well, she's kind of over-involved in my life. If I didn't give her one, she'd probably flip and think I had something ominous to hide. She lives like an hour away, though, so it really wasn't worth fighting over a key she's almost never gonna use."

"You told her you're knocked up?" She flips her legs out of the bed, takes a big stretch and stands.

"I think I'm gonna just put that off as long as humanly possible. Do you think it's realistic to just not say anything until the baby's already here?"

"Hmm," she replies noncommittally, which is all right because I'm not *actually* planning on not telling my mom. She picks up her HAPPY HAPPY HAPPY boxers distastefully between two fingers. "Guess I'm going commando today, huh?"

"Never have sex with your underwear on if you don't

have a spare," I agree, thankful I have a whole drawer of clean panties to wear. I'd loan her some, but she could probably put her entire waist through one leg hole. Refreshingly, I don't feel bad about that. Maybe the fact that she spent last night practically worshipping every fat inch of my body has something to do with it.

I follow her around my bed curtain and, arms crossed, watch her pick up the rest of her strewn clothes.

Definitely enjoying the view of her bending over to grab her bra. "Don't suppose I could interest you in a shower before you leave, could I?"

She turns to me like I just told her it's Christmas morning. "Holy shit, can we? Is that an option? Can we please?"

"Having time to shower in the morning *is* part of why I set an alarm in the first place," I chuckle. "Bathroom's just through that door there."

So I couldn't skip work just because I got laid last night. It sucks, but that's life.

Coming in kinda late because I had a cute girl washing my hair for me this morning is excusable, though, right?

Between rushing to catch the Bee-Line Bus, worrying about showing up late to work with wet hair, and arriving on the dot with a switchboard already lit up like a Christmas tree, there isn't much time for me to reckon emotionally with the hard left turn my life has just taken. It's only when I take out my phone on lunchbreak that it hits me:

I slept with Rhiannon.

I. *Slept*. With. Rhiannon!

I slept with her, and then we showered together, and

then she kissed me goodbye before we left my apartment together.

And now what?

I thumb my phone's screen absentmindedly, practically in shock. Normally in this fractured mental state I'd ground myself with my now-ritual of finding out what fruit my baby is currently the size of, but I can't risk opening a pregnancy app at work.

Without even realizing it, I find myself scrolling through my contacts, past my mother and sister and—ugh—Jake (knife emoji, middle finger emoji) to… Rhiannon. Of course.

She gave me her number at that fateful last stitch n' bitch meeting—"in case of knitting emergencies" she told me. But perhaps the terms of engagement have changed?

You know, considering the fact that I fucking slept with her?

I type and delete close to a dozen texts, unsure of what to say or whether to send it at all.

Would it be needy or smothering to text her now? Does the "three day" rule you're supposed to observe with guys apply? It's not like she slipped out of my bed and apartment before I even woke up. And what with us being members of the same stitch n' bitch, she can hardly expect me to disappear from her life like a typical one-night stand.

But even assuming a next day text is an okay thing to do, there's about a million different ways said text could go.

I could go with a completely noncommittal "hey" and toss the ball into her court like it's a live grenade, but that seems like a cop-out and Rhiannon deserves better.

On the opposite end of the spectrum, I could get mushy and send her a "missing you already", which would pretty much be akin to renting a U-Haul at this point and probably send her running screaming for the hills.

I could go the purely fuckbuddies route and send her a sext, drawing a hard line around the nature of our relationship.

But the truth is, I don't want to draw a hard line. Maybe I'm messy, but even after sleeping with her—which was mind-blowing, don't get me wrong—what I think I want most, need most, is to be her friend. With benefits, or no.

I'm so deep in my thoughts the sound of an incoming text nearly has me jumping out of my skin.

You make it to work on time?

Damn, I'm sitting here breaking out in a sweat devising a strategy for checkers and Rhiannon is playing three-dimensional chess.

Barely, I type back, breathless with relief. Or is that another pregnancy symptom?

Sorry about that. I'm sure you'll be relieved to know I am now wearing clean underwear, at least.

I smirk down at my phone's screen. Is that an invitation to be corny and say "Can I see?"

I'm a lot of things, Poppy, but corny isn't one of them. Typing dots. Although now that I think of it, the answer to the question would still be yes.

Maybe sometime when I'm not at work?

Good point. Okay, safe for work topics....... You still planning on coming to knitting next week?

I hesitate, focusing on that word, "still". Is it possible that Rhiannon feels as unsure about this whole thing as I do? If so, it's weirdly encouraging. In fact, it kind of makes me feel warm and fuzzy inside to be the one who gets to comfort and reassure *her* this time.

Only if you're going.

Which isn't strictly true; I like the rest of our stitch n' bitch group, too, but there's no harm in letting Rhiannon know I like her most of all.

You don't trust anyone else to teach you how to do increases and decreases? jk I'm looking forward to seeing you too.

The relief this short conversation has brought me... I don't dare spoil it by asking if we can see each other sooner.
I may need the rest of the week to gather my composure enough to speak in full sentences when I see her next anyway.

The following week, I text Rhiannon every single day.
It starts entirely justifiably: I've made an attempt at doing my first increases all on my own, and I want to make sure

I've done them right. So I send her a picture of my knitting in my lap.

Sorry, am I supposed to see anything but your thighs? she replies.

Hold on, let me cover up so you can focus.

No!!!!!!!!

I smirk a little as I count the exclamation points.

No? I type back innocently, taking another picture, this time with the knitting very much out of the frame.

Mmmm, thighs.

Things go rather predictably after that.

And then they don't, because the next afternoon Rhiannon follows up our steamy sexting session with: I have just found the most amazing new coconut yogurt, I may end up spending my entire month's grocery budget buying nothing else.

Going from sex to vegan yogurt flings the door between us wide open. I tell her about the new show Tracy has me watching. She vents about a shitty customer she had to serve at the coffee shop.

And you didn't climb over the counter and throttle her? I ask sympathetically.

I wanted to, but no, I am a consummate professional at

the top of my craft. I served her with a smile then when I was grinding espresso I pretended that I was grinding her bones.

Day three, we go from texting to calls. "I'm sorry to go against the Millennial Code of Honor by actually phoning you, but I'm up to my elbows in sticky flour and needed to go hands free." Cell wedged between my ear and shoulder, I survey the destruction that is my kitchenette. "I had a sudden craving for those double chocolate cookies you make at the coffee shop and decided it would be easier to bake them myself than walk my ass over there." Also, I wasn't sure whether it would be appropriate for me to show up at Rhiannon's work without notice, but I don't say that part aloud. "Do you use cocoa in the dough to make it chocolatey like that?"

"What else would you use? Nesquik syrup?" Rhiannon laughs on the other end of the line. "Honestly, though? The dough comes frozen premade. I'll make sure the double chocolate flavor is on the menu next stitch n' bitch, okay?"

"You're my hero," I say, narrowly avoiding blurting out *I love you.*

Not that I'm shy about saying it: I told Tracy I loved her just yesterday for taking a phone call for me so I could go pee, and then I said it to the Uber Eats guy for bringing me a burger and fries at five minutes to midnight.

But when it comes to Rhiannon, even saying it in a casual friendly way seems like it would make things weird.

And I like how things are going just as they are.

I like it a lot.

My call waiting beeps, and I don't even need to check who's calling for the sound to pop my good mood like a soap bubble.

"Shit, that's my mom." Calling for the second time today. After two more missed calls yesterday, and another the day before. I've never dared to screen my calls from her in the past, but then, I've never before had quite such a pressing reason not to.

Rhiannon must hear the dread in my voice. "Let her go to voicemail. It's not like you don't have an excuse. You'll burn your cookies!"

I bite my lip. "Except they're not in the oven yet, and if I keep ghosting her like this she's going to call the cops. Or, I don't know, the attorney general, because that's how extra she is."

"Right. Well, you know best." For a moment Rhiannon sounds disappointed, but she perks up when she adds, "Text me later and tell me how your cookies turned out!"

Why, so you can gloat at my failure? But no, that's my mother and sister. Not Rhiannon.

Even my worst insecurities can't talk me out of that simple truth, that grows in me like a seedling.

Rhiannon supports me. Whatever else our relationship is or becomes… Rhiannon is my *friend*.

I smile, even as my stomach clenches with worry over talking to my mother. "I'll do you one better. If they turn out, I'll bring you some."

I'm still smiling as I switch lines over to my mother. "Mom, hi!"

"Finally! I've called you a hundred times!" My mother huffs, and my smile crumples.

I have about six missed calls over the past few days, actually, but there's no point telling her so. "I know, I'm sorry. I've just, um, been throwing myself into my work this week," I lie.

That seems to satisfy her, at least. "Well, good. Not that there's much room for upward mobility in secretary work, but the right work ethic and drive could have you taking on a managerial position eventually."

I roll my eyes. "Sure."

"Your sister says you've taken up knitting." Is my mom making small talk right now? Does she miss me? "Again."

Orrrrrrr is she just looking for an opportunity to needle at me? Sounds like she and Iris have been having a good old gossip session about my various shortcomings.

Well, I'm having too good of a day to let them get to me, dammit. "Yeah, I am. It's going really well actually!"

"Really." My mother sounds simultaneously unconvinced and deflated by my rebuttal. "Well, I was just checking in to make sure you weren't dead. Call me when you're not so distracted."

Hanging up, I feel like I've run the gauntlet. But at least my mother's interrogation didn't break me to the point of spilling my big secret.

Make that big *secrets*.

Of course, it's not just my mother I need to be keeping secrets from; there's also the matter of how one shows one's face at one's stitch n' bitch after hooking up with a fellow knitter, a dilemma that is quickly going from abstract to urgent as the date approaches.

For as much as we've been texting (and sexting), Rhiannon and I haven't actually seen each other since *that night*, and we haven't firmed up plans for this first fateful reunion beyond agreeing to meet as usual at the coffee shop.

As I pack my knitting bag, though, I find myself thinking maybe we *should* firm up plans. Rhiannon hasn't raised the subject, but maybe this is the perfect opportunity for me to take some initiative, ask her what *she* needs from *me* instead of the other way around.

So….tonight, I text.

You didn't change your mind about coming, did you?

Wow that reply came fast. Almost like she's anxious to hear the answer. Well, I won't prolong her misery.

You're not getting rid of me that easy. Winking emoji. I'm mostly just wondering how you want to play things with the rest of the group.

Typing. Typing. Typing. The little three dots disappear and reappear. She really is agonizing over this, huh?

Time to put my plan to take initiative into action.

Before she can finally reply, I add, jsyk I'm cool with whatever makes you comfortable. You're not a dirty secret by any means but we don't need to announce to the world that we had sex, either.

There. I nod at my phone triumphantly. Congratulations, Poppy, you have reached new levels of mature adult communication.

Oh thank god. NGL I was kinda worried I was gonna break your heart, (jk unless….?) but I'd really rather we act as normal for the time being. Not that I think anyone in the group will be uncool if they found out, but yeah, I don't think we need to announce to the world that we had sex, like you said.

Which makes sense. What happened between me and Rhiannon—what's still going on between me and Rhiannon—is just sex between friends. Nothing that necessitates some kind of press release. It doesn't have to be a big thing.

None of this has to be a big thing.

Exactly. See u there?

See u there.

I'm feeling very proud of how coolheaded and reasonable I'm being…right up until the moment Rhiannon walks through the front door of the coffee shop and I lay eyes on her for the first time in a week.

At which point she has the fucking nerve, the absolute *gall*, to casually rake her hand through her hair.

Everyone else at the table greets her in a cheerful chorus, but my throat is suddenly too dry to eke out a single sound.

Surely somebody's noticed how I've frozen.

But then Louise loudly announces, "Guess whose turn it is to buy the cookies?" and the others let out a taunting "Ohhhhh," and Rhiannon does a bashful *Who, me?* shrug and I realize absolutely nobody is analyzing my reactions that closely.

"If you're taking requests," Grace says, raising both hands for emphasis, "I'm voting for the coconut macaroons. And before anybody says anything, exam days are officially keto cheat days."

"Grace," I tell her, suddenly finding my voice, "stitch n' bitch is a safe space. Nobody's going to deputize themselves as the diet police here."

"Well said, Poppy!" Mary praises me with a smile.

Rhiannon raises her eyebrows at me, impressed. "Okay, so that's one macaroon for Grace," she says, without ever taking her eyes off me. "In honor of her exam. Is everybody else okay with double chocolate? You better be, because I have already promised somebody double chocolate."

"Somebody" means me. I feel myself blush, weirdly flattered by the fact that she remembered my craving and her promise to fulfill it.

My last feelings of insecurity drift away, leaving me with a warm, unshakeable sense of belonging. "So Grace, you had an exam today? How do you think you did?"

Grace lets out a gusting sigh. "Ugh, I *think* I did well? But you never can tell with these things."

"I knit a sweater without doing a swatch first, once," Mary adds in, and everyone at the table nods like her statement has anything to do with the subject at hand. But then, maybe it does. "I thought I was doing so well, and then a hundred hours later I was casting off and I realized the only way I was wearing the damn thing was if I sent it back in time to my twelve-year-old self."

Louise quickly swivels my direction to explain, "A swatch is a test square of knitting to make sure your gauge matches the pattern, and that you're actually knitting the size you think you are."

Mary takes a pointed sip of her tea. "Because yes, you can knit an entire sweater before you realize it's the wrong size."

"Or write a whole exam without realizing you've flunked every question?" Grace moans.

"And that, children, is why we never knit a garment without swatching first," Louise summarizes, somehow completely missing the metaphor.

"If only there was such a thing as a swatch for an exam..." Grace slumps in her seat even further.

"Huh," Damian sniffs, not looking up from his crochet hook. "I think that's what we old-timers refer to as 'studying'."

I screw up my nose in false consternation, tilting my head for emphasis and putting on my best airhead voice. "What is this 'studying' you speak of? Is it an app?"

"Nah. *I* heard it was a new craft beer." Rhiannon appears beside me, dropping our bag of cookies onto the table in front of me.

Grace, as anxious as she obviously is, nevertheless perks up when she realizes it's her turn to add to the joke. "I thought it was a dance challenge?"

We snort and giggle as the stitch n' bitch's three non-millennial members look on in bemusement.

"I guess sometimes you need to laugh just to keep from crying..." Damian mutters.

True enough. And it never hurts to have someone to laugh *with*.

I reach into the paper bag sitting on the table in front of me, pulling out a gooey, fresh-baked double chocolate cookie, as promised.

Rhiannon, chin in her hand, watches me take my first bite with a satisfied little smile. "Good?"

I savor her expression almost as much as the chocolate, answering her with unexaggerated honesty: "Even better than I remember."

A couple weeks later, Tracy finally catches on that there's something different about me.

I'm coming back from one of my many, many pee breaks, phone in hand, when she spins her chair to face me with a suspicious look.

"All right, come clean," she says, and fuck it, I'm twelve weeks along now which is officially in "safe to announce" territory, so I might as well—

"Who's the guy you've been sneaking off to text all day every day the last few weeks?"

My eyes go wide. I gather my phone protectively to my chest, trying to hide the open messages screen where [Heart Emoji] Rhi [Heart Emoji] and I are being gross together counting down the hours until we get to see each other at knitting tonight.

"Um, no one." I'm totally not selling it.

"Bullshit," Tracy counters, then notices too late that there's a woman and her kid in the waiting room and amends, "Um, bull poop. Sorry."

Luckily the kid is absorbed in his iPad and the mom is cool, just chuckling and shaking her head at Tracy's slipup indulgently before returning to her out of date gossip mag.

I take my seat, drop my phone into our desk's top drawer and hope the accidental swear is enough to make Tracy forget her line of thought.

It isn't, of course. She rolls her chair close, hunkers in and whispers, "Don't try and deny it. You've been going 'to the bathroom' at least every hour for weeks. And today you finally slip up and bring your phone back out with you. Who're you texting, huh? Don't make me hack your phone."

I pull a face. "Tracy, you couldn't hack your mom's Facebook if she left it open on your computer."

She rolls her eyes. "Ugh, fine, point on that one, but still. I'm right about the bathroom breaks, I know I am."

"If you must know, I'm texting a girl from my knitting group." Not a lie, technically. But seeing as Rhiannon and I are friends with benefits rather than girlfriends, I'm not about to come out at work on her behalf. But I'm sure as hell not making up a fake boyfriend to satisfy Tracy's thirst for dirty details, either. Luckily, there's a real easy way to take this conversation off my relationship. "And as for the bathroom breaks…"

I take out my phone, switching from my messages to my cutesy pregnancy app, the one that announces *Your baby is the size of a lime!* and reminds me it's time to book an ultrasound for nuchal translucency screening (whatever that is). I hold up my phone to Tracy, flashing her a significant look.

It takes her a second of squinting to decode what she's seeing, and then her mouth falls open. "Oh. My. God."

"Shh!" I put my phone away again. "I'm not ready to tell anyone else yet, okay?"

"Oh my God," she says again. "Oh my God! Oh my God!" The phone rings. "Oh my God!" Tracy says, one last time, before she answers it. *Oh my God!* she mouths at me as she listens to the caller on the line. "I'll put you through to him. Hold please," she says aloud, hits the button, then turns to me with another, "Oh my God!"

I sit patiently waiting for her to get it out of her system. At least she doesn't seem upset for me or scared for me or angry at me. Surprised, definitely, scandalized maybe? But not judgmental, at least. Thank God.

"Do you..." She twirls a strand of hair around her finger, fidgety. Gives the resulting ringlet a little springy tug. "I mean, you know who the dad is, I'm assuming?"

"The sperm donor, you mean?" I roll my eyes. Just talking about Jake feels distasteful to me. "Yeah, my ex."

"Oh my *God!*" Tracy exclaims. "The stoner? Not the stoner!"

"The stoner," I admit.

"Oh my Gaaaawwwwwd."

"Trust me, I'm not stoked about it, either."

"Does he know?"

I shake my head.

"Does *anyone* know?"

"You." *Rhiannon.* "Planned Parenthood."

"Waitwaitwait, are you gonna...?" She lowers her voice to

the smallest, tiniest whisper I've ever heard from her mouth. I didn't even know she could *get* that quiet. "Keep it?"

"I think so. Yeah."

She heaves a sigh. "Phew. Okay. You scared me there for a second." Her eyes widen. "Wait. No. That sounded bad. I'm pro-choice all the way. But twelve weeks in I was worried you might have a hard time getting an abortion if you wanted one."

"Aww, you *do* care." My voice is extra cutesy to hide the fact that I really am touched by her concern.

"Yeah, I do, which is why I'm about say the following: Are you *gonna* tell your stoner ex about this?"

"Do I have to?" I hadn't exactly thought about that part. "Can't I just refuse to name the father on the birth certificate? Isn't that something I can do?"

"I guess, if you don't want any child support."

I kind of assumed whatever I couldn't afford for the baby, I could just beg my mom for.

Not exactly proving I can be an Actual Adult once there's a baby depending on me. This receptionist gig pays reasonably well, sure, but is it really enough to raise a kid? Without begging to my mother? Who I haven't even told about my pregnancy yet?

I flash her a despondent look. "I've made a terrible mistake, haven't I."

"Aww, what? No! No. No! Don't let me scare you out of your decision. Of course you can handle this. My sister's a single mom and *she* works at Walgreens." Her expression turns a little bit sour. "And a gas station. And a weekend cleaning job…"

It's only when she grabs me by both shoulders, concern written all over her face, that I realize I'm hyperventilating.

And that's how I wind up taking my first sick day of my pregnancy.

Chapter Thirteen

I'm lucky Rhiannon's home, because I didn't have the wherewithal to call her before I came. Tracy had just noticed I wasn't calming down no matter how many soothing meaningless platitudes she recited, then took it upon herself to tell Dr. Ha I needed to go home and call me a cab. And then the cab driver had asked me "Where to?" and I recited Rhiannon's address without even thinking.

When I buzzed up to her apartment and heard her voice in reply, I nearly fell to my knees in relief.

She enfolds me wordlessly as I sob brokenly, "I fucked up!"

"All right," she murmurs to me. "You're all right. C'mon inside, baby."

She doesn't ask me to take off my shoes this time, just leads me to her couch and sits me safely down.

"Before you say anything else, I'm making us a pot of tea. Okay? Just wait there for me. Try breathing in through your nose and out through your mouth." She steps away from the couch with one arm outstretched, like she's afraid I'm going to fall off it without her holding me up. She's gone just long enough to fill an infuser and get the kettle boiling before she returns again. Rather than sit beside me like a normal person, she climbs up onto the couch and squishes herself down *behind* me, her short skinny legs in grey sweatpants sandwiching my own. "All right," she says, wrapping her arms around me and tucking her chin onto my shoulder. "Talk."

Then she combs her hands through my hair over and over and kisses my shoulder and collarbone as I sob and hiccup and recount what happened with Tracy this morning. "What was I thinking?" I manage to get out, wheezing between words. I know there's snot running down my face, but luckily she's sitting behind me and can't see it. "I can't afford a baby on my own! I know I could ask my parents for money, they could afford to help, but what kind of child having a child would that make me? And what if I tell Jake and he wants custody or he wants to force me to have an abortion or he flips out and demands paternity testing or—or—"

The kettle whistles.

Rhiannon slinks out from behind me and returns with a big mug of steaming hot tea in each hand and a roll of paper towel under one arm. After setting down her cup of tea on the coffee table and handing me my own, she tears off a piece of the paper towel and hands it to me to blow my nose with. This time she crouches on the floor at my feet, insinuating herself between my knees. She cups her hands around mine as I cling to my mug.

"Poppy. Honey." Her voice is calm but firm. "I know it seems like the world is collapsing around you, but you've *got* this."

I know she means it to be comforting, but it doesn't feel that way. "I very clearly do *not* 'got this'. If I did, then I wouldn't be here having a panic attack with you of all people!"

She stiffens somewhat, but doesn't pull away. "Me of all people? What's that supposed to mean?"

"I mean… I don't know. It just feels so tacky to come to a…a…a friend with benefits about something like this in the first place, but to come to *you* specifically to cry about how bad it feels to have to beg Mommy and Daddy for money?"

"All right, well, to your first point, the word 'friend' is right there in the title, so I don't think talking you through an emotional crisis really falls that far outside the otherwise pretty sex-centric job description." She presses a kiss to my hand. "And as for the second…well, I admit I talk as much shit about gentrifying trust fund kiddies as any other working-class New Yorker. And yes, it's true, I'd be on team 'leave the nest' even if leaving my own wasn't such an economic necessity. But I'm also not saddled with an oops pregnancy that's going to turn into a baby who needs diapers and bottles and formula and those little tiny shirts with snaps at the crotch. If your parents can help and you feel like you need help to get by, then I think help with baby expenses is a little different from Daddy paying for your rent in the Chelsea while you pretend to be a social media influencer." She rubs her thumbs over my knuckles in slow, soothing circles. "And as for *Jake*, I don't know much else about him other than the fact that you told me he's a deadbeat stoner who ditched your grandma's funeral to get high. Do you honestly think he's the kind of guy to try and force you into an abortion or seek custody purely out of spite?"

I sniff. Okay, she has a point there. Jake may be an inconsiderate flake, but he's not a bad or vindictive person.

"I'm not saying there's any guarantee he won't act like an ass about this, because unexpected pregnancy can turn *anyone* who's not the pregnant party into a fucking ass in my experience, but you gotta figure out if it's your gut instinct about him telling you not to tell him, or if it's your what-can-go-wrong-must-go-wrong anxiety. On the other hand, I'd be remiss not to say that you still have options. You don't have to tell Jake or your family, but you also don't have to go through with the pregnancy or actually raise the baby yourself, either. You're not trapped."

I stare down at the surface of my tea. The liquid is choppy what with my trembling hands and shaking shoulders, but becoming more still as I watch.

I'm not trapped. I also still want to keep the baby. I have an ultrasound coming up on Friday this week and I'm looking forward to seeing it. I *want* this.

The details are...details.

"You really won't judge me if I ask my mom for help?"

She huffs a short laugh. "I still think it's weird she has a key to your place when you're a grown-ass woman, but am I gonna look down my nose at you if she buys you a crib or sends you diaper money because you can't make it to payday? Absolutely not. And you *know* my people at Planned Parenthood are gonna hook you up with every government program you're qualified for. It's not going to be easy, but it's possible. It's completely possible. I see so many people come in thinking they can't be a parent if they're not able to put fifty k away for their college straight off the bat, or if they use food stamps to get by, or if they have no choice but to move back in with their family, or they use their retired neighbor for cheap childcare, or they're not married or they don't know who the dad is or whatever else. And you know what? Some of them have abortions, and some choose to go the adoption route, but a lot of them? They work it out. They make do. They sacrifice things— their lifestyle, their independence, their full-time college enrolment—but they make do."

My lower lip wobbles as I stare into my tea. My reflection looks like she's been ugly crying for ten days straight. But there's a sense of calm there, too. Tentative, but there. Rhiannon's hands on my own. Her eyes staring up into mine.

It's okay to make do.

That's what she's saying to me. *Me*, the girl who was always expected to maintain straight As and excel in all my extracurriculars and get into a great school and land a prestigious job and have a BMI of twenty without yo-yo dieting.

I'm reminded of the day she told me she'd never gone to

college and had no intention of going, either. How *amazing* that had seemed to me, that she could have made that choice I was always told made you an underachieving loser who would never amount to anything, and yet I could look at her and see a person who seemed satisfied with her life, who had a steady job and made an difference in the world through her volunteering—which she did because it mattered to her, not because it would look good on a letter of recommendation or a college application.

All my rigid standards for myself…it wasn't that she'd failed to meet them, per se, but simply that they hadn't applied to her in the first place.

Freed from those constraints, what kind of mother would I be? I wouldn't have an entire mini-library of parenting books, all of them promising that they were the sole key to Not Screwing Up Your Child Forever. I wouldn't have to stress if my kid didn't get a spot in one of New York's top five preschools. I'd be able to do a diaper run without putting on a face full of makeup. I'd let my baby's face get dirty. Hell, I'd even let my kid watch TV…including the non-educational stuff.

If I could be like Rhiannon.

Well, at least I can be *with* her.

I lean forward, ostensibly to put my mug down on the coffee table behind her, but as soon as I'm in her personal space we're kissing.

"So you feel better then?" she manages to get out around my mouth as I slither to the floor with her and enclose her in my arms.

Her tone's jokey, but I still reply in earnest: "Yeah. I do."

I kiss her again, my dry lips sticking to hers as I pull away to add, "Thank you."

"Don't mention it," she says. She plants another kiss on my lips, then pushes me to arm's length with a faux-serious expression. "Seriously, don't. Because the more time you spend thanking me, the less time we spend making out."

Fair enough.

"Okay come *on*," I say, frustrated. "Your hair is like an inch long. How the hell do you know how to French braid and I don't?"

I'm being pouty, but I'm totally enjoying the feeling of her fingers combing through my hair, her short nails gently etching into my scalp. If girls could purr, I would be. Instead I close my eyes and tilt my head back into her touch, my whole body thrumming with pleasure.

And as for *why* she's currently styling my hair? Yeah, we may have gotten a little heated on her living room floor. And if we're already gonna show up to knitting group together, it'd probably be better for discretion's sake if I'm not arriving with mussed up post-sexytimes hair.

I *could* comb it myself, but why would I?

She kisses the nape of my neck, sweeping strands of hair into my braid with soft, confident movements. She's doing two of them, one down each side of my head starting at my temples. I'm not used to having my neck and shoulders exposed like this, but Rhiannon seems to be enjoying the access it gives her. She's had to restart my left braid like four times due to becoming distracted by kissing my neck.

"You keep doing that we're gonna be splitting the cost

of cookies," I warn her, but I still tilt my head to one side so she can get in nice and close.

"Correction, you're going to pay for them all on your own because this is all your fault. We were supposed to meet at the coffee shop, remember? And instead you ambush me when I'm at home alone? And you looking all gorgeous and vulnerable?"

"Are you trying to suggest that me ugly crying and having a panic attack is sexy to you?"

"Will you still be mad if I amend that and say the *aftermath* of you ugly crying and having a panic attack is what I find sexy?"

I wouldn't be mad either way, honestly. I'm the one who kissed her first, after all.

"And you really don't mind that I, y'know, came crashing in on you without warning like this?" I bite my lower lip.

"Of course not. Although I have to say I do appreciate you asking. But just because I don't want to jump into any long-term commitments just yet doesn't mean I don't want to be here for you."

Just yet? Does that mean…?

I can't help it: my mind wanders. Suddenly I'm picturing her with my future baby, spoiling them with non-organic ice cream or letting them get dirty at the playground. Inviting our toddler into bed with us, even though Dr. Whoever advises against bedsharing with children because they will get too attached and never go to college or have sex.

The image of her knitting little tiny rainbow socks has me giving my head a hard shake. She's not even my girlfriend—she didn't exactly protest the "friends with bene-fits" designation I gave her earlier—and here I am leaping right into her adopting my kid?

Rein it in, Poppy!

At any rate, we really should be getting going soon. I'm glad I brought my knitting with me to work today for my lunch break, or else we'd be forced to do the long trek to my place before we head to the coffee shop, and the like-lihood of us making *that* trip in time to not pay for cook-ies is somewhere between "highly unlikely" and "flat-out impossible".

She places one last kiss on my shoulder. "There, all done."

"You never told me why you know how to do braids like this," I say, my voice sharp but my eyes still half-lidded in response to the pleasure of her touching me.

"Ahh, well…" She clambers to her feet, then extends a hand to help me up. "I could make up some bullshit story about how I had sisters growing up or something, but to be honest? I learned it specifically in order to get girls."

"You *player!*" I exclaim.

"Excuse you. I'm not a player. I'm a giver, baby."

I could definitely argue with her on that point, especially considering *she just got through* with saying she learned it to "get girls", but on the other hand, ehhh. She can be a player and a giver at the same time, can't she? Because she's certainly been more than generous with me so far.

We walk hand in hand all the way to the intersection be-fore the coffee shop, then let go of one another. I'd love to keep my fingers laced in Rhiannon's all the way up to our table, let the whole club know how I feel about her, but I understand why she's not super keen on that. We're not even going out, technically—we've never been on a real date—and with me pregnant and about to be showing soon, us being openly together in *any* capacity is going to imply a level of commitment way beyond even girlfriends…and we haven't even made it *that* far yet.

Holding hands or not, though, we're still walking in together, as in coming from the same place, and I should really—"Doyouwantmetowaituntilyou'reinsideafewminut esthenfollowyou?" I blurt out.

She stops mid-step and tilts her head at me. "Huh?"

I take a deep breath, trying to slow the rapid thumping of my heart. It's a perfectly logical thing to suggest, so why do I feel so nervous? "Do you want me to wait until you're inside a few minutes then follow you in? You know, make it look like we didn't come here together?"

Her brow furrows. At first I think she's considering my proposition, but then I realize she's frowning. "Is that something *you* want?"

"No…? I mean, I want it if you want it!" My face is getting hot, even in this brisk late-October wind.

She winces. "Is that something you *think* I would want?"

"I don't know, I guess? I just thought, you don't want the knitting club to know about us…"

She reaches out, taking me by the hand, and yanks me off the sidewalk and down the stairs of a cellar entrance out of people's way. She holds my hands in front of her, staring down at them as she speaks. "I'm sorry."

Huh? "For what?"

"For making you think I didn't want to be seen with you." She raises her eyes, and her smile up at me is weak, pained. "That's not what I wanted for you. For *us*. Just because I don't want to announce that we're girlfriends to the world just yet doesn't mean I'm embarrassed to be seen with you. It's okay if people know we were together today."

"Well, I mean, 'embarrassed' isn't exactly the word *I'd* use. I just thought—wait, girlfriends?"

"Uhh." Her face goes red as she realizes her slipup.

My cheeks are so hot we must certainly be matching. "I'm sorry, I didn't mean to put you on the spot. It's no big deal. I just thought we were more friends with benefits, you know? And I was cool with it, obviously."

"Right. You did say that. And if that's the way you feel, then yeah I'm cool with it, too."

"No, it's not the way I feel. I'd…" I bite my lip. Rub my thumb over her knuckles compulsively. "I'd *like* to be your girlfriend. I just figured you didn't want to be mine. Right now. Or ever! Which I'm okay with! Totally okay with. I'm managing—"

She pulls me into a tight, squeezing hug.

"—my expectations," I finish, unnecessarily.

"Baby girl, I do," she murmurs into my scarf. "I do want you to be my girlfriend, and I want to be yours. Yeah, I know the situation is complicated because of the baby, and we're *both* still feeling out boundaries. And you're right, I don't want to make any big promises, especially when it comes to the baby, or announce anything *yet*, but that doesn't mean there's nothing *to* announce, you know? And I fully intend on declaring ourselves eventually, I do! It's just what with your whole life changing massively I figured it would be better to take things slow. But God, don't think for one second I don't want you as my girlfriend. I do."

"Oh." The word is so soft it sounds almost like a sigh. Maybe it *is* a sigh. A sigh of relief, specifically.

She pulls back from her tight hug, looking me in the eyes. "Will you be my girlfriend?" she asks.

I nod my head so hard and fast I think I'm gonna pull something in my neck. "Yes. Yes please." I gnaw on my lip, not sure if I should say what I'm thinking now. She looks so open and receptive, though, and haven't my assumptions about us done enough damage today already? I take a deep breath, steeling myself. "But do you think maybe we could go on a date, though? We don't have to tell anybody about it, but that would go a long way to making it feel official. To me. In my mind."

"Anything you want," she replies, breathy, and presses her lips to mine in what must be the sweetest kiss I've ever experienced.

I wonder if she'd still say that if she knew what I want—keep wanting—is *more*.

For the first time, I get the sense that her plan to not get too serious with each other is going roughly as well as my own.

And mine is really, *really* not going well.

Chapter Fourteen

We're still not holding hands, but when we tumble through the door of the coffee shop together it's on such a cloud of warm fuzzy feelings that for us to be holding hands on top of all that would just be flat-out Extra.

I'm pretty sure we could only look more comically infatuated with each other if we were clasping our hands under our chins and batting our eyelashes at each other adoringly. While cartoon hearts rise up between us and pop like bubbles.

It's that bad.

Rhiannon saunters in seemingly without a care in the world, and I follow a few paces behind, clutching my knitting bag to my chest protectively.

In a way, I feel even more exposed and vulnerable than

I did at the first stitch n' bitch after Rhiannon and I slept together.

But I just can't help but feel paranoid that they somehow *know*, that hand-holding or no, they can tell how we feel about each other, that there really are cartoon hearts floating in the air around us and they're *staring*.

Grace, in particular, is staring.

While Rhiannon's patting Damian's back in a jovial greeting, I hang back several feet from the table, my eyes locked with Grace's over their heads. Is she figuring us out? Does she know already? How would Rhiannon react if she *did* know? Should I be trying harder to throw her off the scent before she figures us out? Or should I just let the chips fall where they may because Rhiannon and I just went through a whole entire thing about her not being embarrassed of me and not being overly worried about keeping "us" a secret? In any case, I'm not doing such a good job of acting casual, considering I'm standing here like a deer in headlights, too panicked to even breathe as she watches me carefully.

And is it just me, or are Mary and Louise giving me some kind of look, too?

Okay, now I'm just being goddamn paranoid. I square my shoulders and march up to the table. "Who's going to teach me how to sew the halves of this mitten together?" I ask like it's the only thing worth discussing.

"You finished it!" Louise claps. "Show us! Show us!"

"Yes, show us!" the other members of the stitch n' bitch join in. And they're not saying it just to be nice: they seem actually invested in seeing my first (almost) finished project.

That's all it takes for me to shake off my paranoia, and I reach into my bag, fishing around blindly until I produce the mitten in question. It's a little lumpy and warped in places—there are a couple knits where purls should be and vice versa, and my tension isn't exactly consistent—but it still looks good as far as I'm concerned. If I just fold it in half in the center where the two sides are joined, it's pretty recognizable as what it's supposed to be. All that's left is to sew the open side together, weave in the still-dangling tails…and then do it all over again for the second mitt. But still, I'm proud.

Damian pulls a chair out for me as I hand my mitten over, first to Louise who oohs and ahhs then passes it on to Mary.

"You cast off by yourself?" Mary scrutinizes my handiwork, but her tone is definitely impressed and it makes me want to happy dance right there in my seat.

"Rhiannon helped," I admit. Credit where credit is due.

Rhiannon claps my shoulder. "For like the first three stitches. You're definitely getting the hang of things at this point."

Credit where credit is due.

"Good for you!" Mary's praise is genuine. She hands my mitten off to Grace, who thumbs it thoughtfully. Before, I'd have thought her expression was critical, but Rhiannon's right about her: she's a little abrasive at first, but she's not mean. She's not examining my handiwork for flaws, she's just making a point of taking the time to actually look at it rather than disinterestedly passing it on.

Damian's turn to take it in hand now. It's tiny in his

huge palm. He grins at me and gives me a thumbs-up. "Great effort!"

I'm practically glowing with the approval of it all. "Thank you," I gush, taking it back from Damian and laying it out just so on the table in front of me. I keep staring at it, unable to comprehend that I was the one who made it. Nearly finished it. Should *be* finished it after today, according to Rhiannon.

I didn't give up. I followed through. This mitt is so much more than a mitt. I'm over the moon about it, too excited for myself to play humble or downplay it like I normally would.

Rhiannon chuckles at me. "This is cute and all, girl, but don't get too excited yet. You have yet to conquer Second Sock Syndrome."

Louise makes a show of audibly shuddering.

"How many single socks do you have lying around, again?" Grace asks Rhiannon sweetly, turning her pessimism back on her.

Rhiannon makes a dying toad face, her mouth spreading in a grimace as her head shrinks back toward her shoulders. "Like…sixteen?"

"Uh-huh," Grace says with a satisfied nod. She turns to me matter-of-factly. "It happens to the best of us," she reassures me. "Anything you have to make a pair of, the second one has a habit of going unfinished. Permanently."

"Unless you use magic loop to do two at a time socks!" Louise puts in.

"Still not learning magic loop," Rhiannon grumbles, but she's smiling. "And anyway, I happen to think mismatched

socks are cool." She pulls her jeans up from her ankles, revealing one green and brown forest-y toned sock and one
pink and aqua shabby-chic looking one. They look absolutely terrible together, but somehow the effect is charming. "Just so long as you start and don't finish even numbers
of socks, you're always in the clear."

That's right. So what if you don't finish everything you
start? Making do is okay, too.

Louise talks me through seaming a project while Rhiannon
orders teas for me and her and cookies for the whole table.

I try to focus on what Louise is showing me while also
plotting ways to discreetly slip Rhiannon money without
her noticing, because I know for a fact she's not gonna let
me pay her back for any of it.

I've sewn buttons back onto coats and dresses before,
but never had to worry about maintaining any kind of
straight, consistent line. Louise keeps correcting me, trying to keep my seam neat and tight. I'm thankful for her
help, but I can't help but wish it were Rhiannon teaching
me instead, with her body wrapped around my own and
her hands guiding mine.

I really need to find my chill.

"So are these a baby shower gift?" Mary asks casually,
watching with hawk's eyes as my trembling hand dips the
oversized tapestry needle into one of my edge stitches and
through on the other side.

I freeze midway through tightening the loop. Inexplicably look to Rhiannon for help, but her face is nothing but

a practiced blank smile as she sets my huge cup of herbal tea down on the table in front of me.

Well, this could be good practice for finally talking to my mother. Avoiding all but ten percent of her phone calls isn't going to work for me forever, although I sure wish it would. I lay my knitting down. "Um," I say. I stay looking into Rhiannon's eyes—whether I'm looking to her for strength or some indication I should keep my big mouth shut, I'm not sure. "Well, that is. No. Yeah. No. No, they're for me."

My answer is so convoluted it takes a full thirty seconds for it to dawn on them. I can see the exact moment of recognition: Louise's eyes go huge and round, her mouth falling open. "Are you—?" Her voice trembles with barely reined-in delight.

I nod.

"We're having a baby!" she cries out triumphantly.

They all turn to me at once, their voices excited and congratulatory as they pat my arms and hands and ask a million questions:

"How far along are you?"

"Twelve weeks."

"Do you know if it's a boy or girl?"

"Not yet."

"Are you going to find out or keep it a surprise?"

"Um… I'm not sure? Should I?"

"What's your due date?"

"May fifteenth…ish?"

What they don't ask: *"Who's the father?"*

"How are you going to support the baby with the job you're working?"

"Have you thought through your options?"

"Are you sure you're ready to be a mother?"

I should feel happy and reassured by their support and confidence in me, but all I feel is overwhelmed, like I want to be sick. I don't want this attention, even if it's positive. I shrink in my chair, cold sweat on the back of my neck, as waves of nausea wash over me one after the other.

"I need to be sick," I announce, and hustle my pregnant ass to the washroom as fast as my stubby legs will take me.

It's only after I'm done vomiting up nothing in the toilet that I see a pair of shoes under the stall door. Not Rhiannon's oxfords; Grace's suede wedge ankle booties.

She's obviously here out of concern for me, I tell myself, and force myself to open the stall and face her with a smile.

She hands me a paper cup of cold water and a warm, wet paper towel. I take both gratefully, wiping my mouth then drinking the whole cup of water in one go. She hands me a pack of gum out of her purse as I examine my clammy pale face in the mirror.

"Thanks for this," I say, popping a piece of gum and handing the pack back to her. "You're a regular Girl Scout, huh?"

"Nursing student, actually," she says. Her reflection flashes me an awkward look.

"So much for my lipstick," I joke, trying to relieve the tension between us.

It doesn't seem to work, because her expression only gets *more* weird. She wrings her hands.

"What?" I ask pointedly.

"Is now a bad time to tell you your lipstick was already smeared when you came in today?"

I wince, but manage a self-deprecating laugh. "On my teeth?"

She winces right back. "On Rhiannon's mouth," she corrects.

Well, fuck it all.

Chapter Fifteen

I'm doubled over the sink, groaning in abject misery as Grace rubs my back.

"Does everyone know?" I ask.

"Maybe? I'm not sure. It's not like anyone here would say something until you confirm it, though." She bites her lip. "After all, Damian and I suspected you were pregnant right from the first meeting."

"Oh my God," I wail, pulling a Tracy. Am I even capable of keeping a secret? Does my sister know, too? My mom?

"Not that you look pregnant or anything!" Grace adds desperately, mistaking the reason for my dramatic outburst. "You're not, like, *round* yet or anything. You look great! Not that if you were round you wouldn't look great!" She squirms, and her complete inept anxiousness endears me to her more than anything else that's gone between us so far. She chews her lip. "It was just…your choice of project. No beginning knitter starts with something they want to give away as a gift, your first project always looks way too crappy and sloppy for that—no offense—but *plenty* get bit by the maternal nesting bug and take it up by starting with stuff for their unborn babies."

She's speaking complete sense.

"I can't believe I am the least sneaky person in the history of the universe."

"Hey, now, come on. You act like you *need* to be sneaky about these things. So you're pregnant. So you're dating a girl from your knitting group. Neither of these things are stuff you need to be ashamed of. Forget sneaky. Shout it from the rooftops, I say."

"And should I also shout from the rooftops that us being girlfriends now officially is giving me hope that we could be even more?"

Her mouth drops open.

Yeah, there's another big reveal for her.

Oh well, I could use someone to talk to about all this.

Considering they're friends and that she must know Rhiannon's caution around serious commitment, I'm expecting her to pump the brakes on that point, but instead, she gives a determined nod. "You should, actually!"

"What?"

"I'm serious! Don't you feel better now that all of us know about your pregnancy and I know about you and Rhiannon? Isn't it so much better to share stuff with people versus agonize over secrets? Rhiannon values honesty.

She might not be as serious about things as you want to be...*yet*, but she's not going to put you out on your ass just for telling the truth."

That was true. She hadn't reacted badly to me admitting to wanting to be girlfriends and go on a date with her. In fact, she'd been relieved to get it all out in the open.

I take a deep breath and turn to Grace, one hand on the bathroom counter propping up my still slightly unsteady body. "I have a screening ultrasound on Friday. I...want her to be there for it."

Grace grabs me by both shoulders and levels me an intensely serious look. "Oh-em-gee! So tell her then!"

This is actually happening. Not only am I seeking advice from Grace of all people, but what she's saying makes complete sense.

I'm going to tell Rhiannon how I feel.

It's after closing at the coffee shop. Rhiannon's coworkers have cashed out and left, but just as she's about to gather up her stuff and lead me out the door so she can lock up and set the alarm for the night, I grab her by the wrist.

"Can we talk?" I ask.

For a second, her expression looks horrified, but she quickly masks it with cool indifference. "Yeah, of course. Sure." She takes one of the upturned chairs on the table by the leg, flips it right side around again and plops into it. She takes me by both hands.

I swear to God, she looks like I'm about to break up with her.

"I didn't change my mind and I don't want to break up

with you," I say immediately, and the fact that she responds with an instant sigh of relief is reassuring. "I actually…"

Okay.

Okay.

I can do this.

She might say no, but she's not going to leave me. Like Grace said, she values honesty. I squinch my eyes up and spit it out. "Well, here's the thing. I have a screening ultrasound Friday afternoon."

"Oh! Oh. *Oh.* Um. Is there…is there something wrong? Is the doctor worried about the baby?" She squeezes my hands, and when I open my eyes again, her own are huge and soft and sympathetic.

My heartbeat goes erratic for a second, just at the suggestion, then calms. "No, God, nothing like that. I actually heard the heartbeat at my last appointment and as far as I know, I'm fine. No family history of anything these screening tests are looking for. Honestly, I'm mostly doing this screening just so I can see the baby sooner than twenty weeks. Because I'm impatient."

"Well that's good. Good for you. Are you excited?"

"Kind of, yes? But also really scared?" Honesty. Honesty. Honesty. "You know, the first time I saw the baby I didn't really feel much of anything and I'm kind of worried it's going to be like that, or I'm going to get way emotional and swoon and they're going to have to carry me out of there on a stretcher or something. And basically I'm wondering if maybe you could come along. You know, for emotional support."

And also because I want to share this with you. Because right now you're the only person I trust enough to share this with.

Because as much as we've both been talking about taking things slow, there's still a part of me deep down that's dreaming you could be a part of my baby's life, too.

Rhiannon may value honesty, but that seems to be one step too far, so I bite the words back.

"Um, sure. I have to check my schedule and make sure I'm not working during your appointment time, but sure. Absolutely." Her expression darkens, somewhat, to something just this side of a frown. "I…don't want you to get the wrong idea, though. I absolutely want to be there to support you, but in a you're-my-girlfriend-and-I-care-about-you way, not an acting-as-the-baby's-coparent way. If you know what I mean? I think it'd just be best if I maintain some boundaries on that front. Because, you know how you're worried about screwing your baby up by me being in and out of its life? Well I'm worried about screwing *you* up doing that."

"Right. Of course." There's that honesty Grace was talking about. Well, it does have to go both ways. And it's not unreasonable, what Rhiannon's saying. She's being remarkably realistic *and* sensitive about it all, actually.

"Also, not to put too fine of a point on it but…this could be an ideal time for you to invite the baby's dad into the picture…if you were at all considering that option."

I still haven't told Jake. Haven't decided if I even *want* to tell Jake, although the practical part of me is screaming I'd be an idiot to try and do this without child support. On the other hand, I can't bear the thought of having Jake wake and bake and not show up to the appointment if I do invite him.

"I want *you* there," I say, firmly. "In whatever capacity you're comfortable with."

She nods. "I can do that."

I half expect her to finish that sentence with a pet name: *babe*, or *girl*, like she usually would, but this time, she doesn't.

She lets go of my hands.

"You've had a rough day," she says instead. "Let me call you a cab, get you home safe."

It's perfectly chivalrous, but there's none of her usual self-indulgent spark at taking care of me. More like the clinic escort I first met than the girlfriend I've come to know.

I get it. She's trying to find the balance between being caring and careful, sensitive to my needs while simultaneously respecting her own boundaries. And she's doing it for us both.

So why are my feelings hurt?

I'm going to tell Jake. I'm not going to tell Jake. I'm going to tell Jake. I'm not going to tell Jake.

It's the day of the ultrasound and I'm sitting on my couch in my underwear, oversized bottle of water in one hand and my phone in the other. I turn the screen off and on compulsively, trying to decide whether to call him or send him a text or banish him from my contacts forever.

Yeah, I poured our last bottle of (expensive) booze down the drain in order to symbolically leave him out of my new life, but I didn't delete his number. Go figure. Had I been a little less sloppy in the first place, I wouldn't be having to make this agonizing decision right now, because faced with the choice of going to tell him in person at his apartment and not telling him at all, I'd obviously pick the latter.

I open my messages app, scroll down to his name and am immediately brought to none other than the midnight text that brought me to this point:

U up?

Yeah, I was up.
And weak. So weak.
I want to text and ask Rhiannon her opinion on things, but I know already that she'd just give me some noncommittal, wishy-washy answer like "Do what you think is best" or "It's your choice to make and I'll support you no matter what."
And by "noncommittal and wishy-washy" I of course mean "respectful of my autonomy and the fact that this is my choice to make".
She's so well-adjusted it's disgusting and also I hate her.
Well, if it's my choice to make, then it follows I should be allowed to make it in my own time. Not telling Jake about the baby *today* isn't the same thing as not telling him at *all*. And anyway, I've already invited Rhiannon to my ultrasound appointment with me. Do I really want him there, too? This whole situation is already precarious enough emotionally, without adding the awkwardness of having my ex and my newly official girlfriend in the same

room for the first time. The only way it could be worse would be if I invited my mother along, too.

Now there's *another* person I need to tell about all this eventually, despite my dread.

Her last text to me, which I've left on read for more than twenty-four hours at this point: Do you ever answer your phone? I need to talk to you.

She needs to talk to *me*?

Oh, Mother, you have no idea.

Also with no idea? Iris, although I'm mostly avoiding telling her because I don't want her telling Mom.

At least, that's what I'm telling myself. My hesitance letting her in on my secret is absolutely not because of my feelings of inadequacy comparing myself to her.

And to her perfect life with her perfect husband, and her perfect town house, and her perfect figure with its perfect wardrobe, and her perfect summa cum laude university record, and her perfect law career on track to probably become partner before she's forty or something similarly insufferably perfect and well-deserved.

"Uggghhh!" I toss my phone clear across the room and cover my face with my hands, resisting the urge to just scream into my palms.

The old wall phone connected to the door intercom rings.

Shit. Rhiannon. What time is it? Shit, shit, shit!

I can't check my phone because it's currently somewhere behind my TV, and like hell I own a watch. I launch myself to my feet, snatch the phone off the wall.

"Hey—" Rhiannon starts.

"*Heyc'monup,*" I reply, hit the button and slam the phone back onto the cradle, then launch myself at my dresser in search of clothes.

I can't wear a dress. Need a shirt I can pull up and a bottom I can pull down in order to be able to bare my belly but not, y'know, everything else below the waist. I tear through my drawers, searching for my lone pair of jeans, which I normally reserve for laundry day or in case of motorcycle ride (not that this has ever happened). I find them with a triumphant cry and yank them up over my legs, only to realize—

They don't fit. Not even a little. I can get them over my thighs and ass, but when it comes to the button at the fly, there's a solid four-inch gap.

I can't have a baby belly that big yet, can I? Is it normal to have a baby belly that big at thirteen weeks? Or—oh God—have I gained weight? The thought of telling my mother I've put on another pant size is actually worse than telling her I'm knocked up out of wedlock. At least the bastard baby comes with doting grandma perks. There's no such thing as fat daughter perks. Not to her.

A knock sounds at my door.

Fuck, fuckshit, fuck. I wipe my watery eyes and dash over to the door, unlocking and opening it a crack before rushing back to my torn apart dresser.

"Babe?" Rhiannon calls softly as she lets herself in.

"My stupid jeans don't fit," I announce. I don't mean to, but it comes out as a sob.

"Oh. Okay. Okay." She drops something on my couch

and comes to my side. "Do you have a skirt or something, maybe?"

"Nothing with an elasticized waist," I snap. "This is what I get for listening to all those internet trolls insisting leggings aren't pants!"

"O…kay." She backs off me a little. Looks down to my open fly. Pauses, thinks a moment, then puts up a finger. "You have a hair elastic?"

I flap a hand at her distractedly. "Yeah, somewhere, why?"

She trots off to my bathroom and returns with one of my bigger hair elastics. Before I can ask her why, again, she loops it around my fly button, through the buttonhole, and back over the button again, securing my pants together.

"Oh," I say, looking down at her handiwork in wonder.

"Don't get too proud of me. Wasn't my idea." She pauses. "Okay, you can get proud of me a little, because I'm not sure how many people who haven't been pregnant long enough to outgrow their pants would bother to learn or know this trick. All you need now is a long preferably baggy shirt so nobody can see the gap."

Together we find a big, oversized sweatshirt, the kind that hangs nearly to mid-thigh. She pulls it over my head, wrapping me up like a warm hug. Once the sweater's on, she brushes my hair out of my collar. Her hands linger on my nape long after my hair's been freed.

"There," she says softly. "Crisis averted."

"You say that like you're an old pro," I reply.

She tilts her chin proudly. "Who do you think managed all my two kid siblings' crises after Nana passed?"

Her tough butch expression and gruff tone belie the tremor in her voice.

I drape my arms over her shoulders but stop short of drawing her close, even though I want to. She's made herself vulnerable to me, and the last thing I want to do is make her regret it by over-performing pity and making it weird for her. Better to follow her lead.

As unselfish as I'm trying to be, though, I still feel relieved when she steps into the hug and rests her head on my shoulder. As we hold one another in silence, I feel the tension drain from her body little by little until at last she speaks, her voice muffled in my sweater. "Not that my kid siblings' crises were pregnancy related, just to clarify."

"I wasn't making any assumptions, but I kinda figured you were talking more generally."

"Let's just say that along with pants fitting issues, I'm also very experienced in messy teen breakups of all gender configurations, preteen skate park politics, and last-minute science fair projects. I also know that if you don't have waterproof makeup remover on hand, a spray of PAM will also do in a pinch."

I pull back from her, bug-eyed. "A *what*?"

"Onto a paper towel, I mean. Not directly in the eyes!"

I nod in sarcastic understanding. "Oh, of course. You're not completely feral."

"Look, sometimes your fourteen-year-old sister is putting waterproof mascara on in a hotel restaurant bathroom before her Irish dance competition and blinks before it dries and now she's got raccoon eyes and there's no time to get to Walgreens before she goes onstage to do her trophy reel."

Well, that explanation was a roller coaster from start to finish.

"But wait, I'm assuming since she was competing for a trophy then there must have been other dancers around? Wouldn't one of them have a makeup bag?"

"Sure, sure. But have you met dance moms?"

"Dance moms in general, no, but I do remember how my mom got when my sister was in ballet all those years so…point taken."

"Exactly. We were already the only family in the school who couldn't afford to buy even a secondhand dress. To go begging for makeup remover on top of that? No thanks. I'd much rather completely confuse my server by asking if the kitchen can spare some of their cooking spray."

Now that I'm calmed down, I finally have the presence of mind to notice the brown-paper package she tossed onto the couch before rushing to help me.

It's a bouquet of flowers.

Half a dozen pink carnations and a few sprigs of baby's breath. She must have picked them up at the grocer's down the block from me.

Nothing so extravagant as the elaborate arrangements my father used to buy me on my birthday when I was still young and had potential and wasn't the family failure, but a hundred times more thoughtful because I know they weren't ordered as just one more item on his secretary's miles-long to-do list.

"What're those for?" I ask, nodding toward them.

Rhiannon's cheeks color. "They're apology flowers," she admits, hangdog. "I think I came off as a little distant the other day after knitting group. I'm still trying to figure out how to act around your pregnancy but I really missed the mark on that one."

"You were completely justified," I reply, unable to hide the weird hurt in my voice. I pull out of her grasp and move to the couch, where I pick up the flowers, unwrap them, and go hunting for something to put them in. I have an old 1960s lemonade pitcher that does the trick, and I fill it with water, refusing to look Rhiannon in the eye as I say, "It's not like you didn't tell me going into this what your boundaries were. And if coming to this ultrasound crosses that line for you, I don't want you to force yourself to come just to avoid hurting my feelings."

When I turn around again, she's standing right in my personal space. She takes my jug of flowers and sets it on the counter behind me. Inexplicably lowers herself to her knees at my feet.

What is she *doing*?

"That's the thing," she says, barely above a whisper. Her hands come up to rest on either side of my belly, framing it.

She's touched my belly before—kissed it, nuzzled it, blown raspberries on it—but never like this, never so purposefully drawing attention to my growing pregnancy. To my baby.

"It does cross my line. From that first day when we met at the stitch n' bitch, I knew I was into you, but I also knew that with you pregnant it was going to be complicated, so I had a whole plan for how I was going to maintain my distance and if I was going to pursue you, be smart about it.

I had a script about how I was going to get involved with you, but not with your pregnancy." She laughs, briefly. A little bitterly. "And the plan was, if you asked me to do something like this, I would try and get you to bring someone else, and if that didn't pan out, I'd go along but give you that whole speech I gave you about only coming as a friend. I guess I thought I could just compartmentalize, separate you-my-girlfriend from you-this-baby's-mother. But after I actually said that stuff aloud I realized... *I* might be able to compartmentalize, but how could you? This pregnancy is a part of you, a part of your life, and me trying to make you pretend it *isn't* just to keep from scaring me off is just a complete jerk move."

I can't speak. My hands rise to cup her head between them, my thumbs sweeping up her cheekbones reverently. She's so beautiful looking up at me like this with her huge, honest brown eyes.

"So I guess what I'm saying is...it's still too soon for me to promise a lifetime commitment to you and your baby, but for as long as I'm here, I'm here for you *both*. Because you've made your choice to have this baby and raise this baby, and as long as that's your decision, who am I to try and separate you?" She leans in, looks up to me for permission, and when I give a trembling nod, she presses a soft, lingering kiss to my belly. Then she turns her face, pressing her cheek there instead. It's too early to feel the baby, too early to even feel the roundness of my uterus if I'm completely honest, but a slow smile still tugs the corners of her mouth. "Hi, baby. I'm your mom's girlfriend."

Not "mama", but not some completely separate entity with no real connection to the baby, either.

It's enough.

Chapter Sixteen

"Drink." Rhiannon holds out my bottle of water. I flinch back from it; she might as well be offering a bottle of poison.

"Seriously?" I whine. I'm already clamping my thighs together from the pressure. "Am I not suffering enough?"

We're ten minutes out from my appointment, sitting in the Planned Parenthood waiting room. There's no way I can survive another ten minutes of this. There just isn't. This is torture. I suddenly long for the sci-fi dildo they used at my first ultrasound. That may have been uncomfortable psychologically, but at least I didn't have to face down the very real possibility that I might pee myself in public. And in front of my girlfriend, no less.

"You need thirty-two ounces. C'mon, finish this bottle and you're there."

"I should have never brought you," I mutter, taking the bottle and forcing myself to have another sip. Another. Another. I squirm in my seat.

Luckily, she doesn't take it personally. "Aw, that's just the bladder talking, kitten. You don't mean that."

Note to self: get her to call me kitten again when I'm not in agony needing to pee. Definite sexy potential there.

"See, though, this is what I'm saying. You're stressed. They should put a nice soothing water fountain here in the waiting room." She gives me a sly, smug look.

"I hate you," I say through gritted teeth.

"You love me," she counters, so easily it must be automatic.

Suddenly my urgent bladder isn't the most pressing concern in my life anymore.

Does she realize what she just said? Did she mean anything by it? Is she embarrassed? Cool and laid-back like it was nothing at all? Something else? I steal a glance in her direction, but her head's turned.

Looking away from me on purpose?

"Poppy?" a young woman in scrubs calls.

I stand. "That's me."

"If you could just come with me?" She gives me a warm smile, hugging her clipboard close.

"You want me to come with?" Rhiannon asks, too casually.

Well, the girl in scrubs *is* her coworker of sorts. Not like I'd be acting all gooey with Rhiannon in front of Tracy if the situation were reversed.

I give her an equally casual nod. "You betcha."

With that, we're led through the security door and into the clinic halls, then directed to a bank of chairs next to a closed door labeled ULTRASOUND.

Funny, but I don't even remember this part from the first time I was here.

Holding my pee for dear life, I lower myself tentatively into a chair. Rhiannon plunks down beside me and picks up a pamphlet about STIs from the seat beside her.

The chair I'm sitting in directly faces a bathroom door.

"I'm going to die," I wail.

"Just wait until you're doing this at twenty weeks," someone chides me ominously.

I break my staring contest with the little faceless person in a triangle dress to look over at who's spoken, and am delighted to discover it's Nurse Janine, hands on her ample hips and wearing Spider-Man scrubs.

"Janine!" I cry out with genuine joy.

"Hi, Poppy, how're you holding up?"

I want to hug her, so bad, but instead I shake her hand. She pats me heartily on the back. Looks over my shoulder. "And… Rhiannon, right? I'm not getting my faces mixed up, am I? You're one of our clinic escorts?"

Rhiannon stands, raising a hand in a shy wave. "Yeah. Hey. Not escorting today, though, er, not officially anyway. Me n' Poppy met at my stitch n' bitch. She asked me to come along."

"Ah yes, the infamous stitch n' bitch everyone's always trying to get me to join. So, Poppy. How are you feeling?"

"I need to pee."

Nurse Janine chuckles. "Kind of takes precedence over

everything else, doesn't it? Ultrasound tech should be back from lunch soon. For now, let's get you set up in here." She opens the exam room door and ushers us both through.

Seems to me getting a patient ready for an ultrasound isn't exactly in Nurse Janine's job description, but I'm thankful for her company anyway. She gives me a hand up onto the exam table, then has me pull my shirt up and my pants wayyyy down. She can most certainly see my pubes right now, but she doesn't say anything, other than to instruct me to tuck a paper towel into the waist of my panties. "You don't want ultrasound gel on your clothes, trust me." Her mouth quirks. "So other than needing to pee, how are you feeling? How's the pregnancy going?"

"Oh! Um, good, I think? I'm taking my prenatal vitamins. And the doctor at the clinic here does deliveries at a hospital that takes my insurance."

"Excellent. So you're feeling secure in your decision?"

Ahh, there we go.

I look from Nurse Janine to Rhiannon and back again. "Yeah." I smile. "I am."

She pats my shoulder. "Good to hear! All right, I'll leave you two here then. Rhiannon, you'll have to step out for a few minutes once the tech gets here so she can do her measurements, but after that she'll call you in so you can both see the baby."

It's not long before the ultrasound tech is here. Rhiannon smiles and squeezes my hand, discreet but meaningful, before she leaves.

After that it's a lot of poking and prodding, an obscene amount of ice cold, disgustingly slimy gel, and the next level torture of an ultrasound wand jabbing me right in my full bladder. Like, goddamn, is she trying to push the thing into my uterus through my skin? In movies they just gently sweep the wand across the mom's firm belly, but with me she's pushing it against me hard, rubbing it in circles, wiggling it back and forth, and damn, if I thought I was gonna pee myself before…

I grit my teeth and squeeze my eyes shut, riding my discomfort.

And then I hear the telltale *WUBBAWUBBAWUBBA* of my baby's heartbeat. It's strong. This isn't the first time I've heard my baby's heartbeat, but the relief of it is still palpable.

"Aha! Got you, you little bugger!" the ultrasound tech exclaims. Holding the ultrasound wand painfully against me, she clicks her keyboard. Moves the wand ever so slightly. Click–click.

It probably only takes her a couple minutes to do what she needs to do, but I'm suddenly so desperate to see my baby that it feels like hours.

Just turn the damn monitor. Just turn the damn monitor. I recite in my head, the urgency of it drowning out everything else.

I need to see my baby. I need to know how I'm going to feel about it, whether the reality will live up to my fantasies, whether I'll finally know, once and for all, that I've made the right choice. I need this long, drawn out question mark of anticipation to be resolved.

"Will I call your friend in now?" the ultrasound tech asks.

Oh. Yeah. That would be a good idea.

I nod urgently, afraid to speak in case my mouth decides to say "Just turn the damn monitor" instead of what it's supposed to.

A moment later, Rhiannon is at my side. "Okay?" she asks carefully.

I nod again. Look to the ultrasound tech with pleading puppy eyes.

Please put me out of my misery.

"Drumroll please," the ultrasound tech jokes, and Rhiannon obliges, slapping her palms on her lap. A smile cracks my anxious expression.

The ultrasound tech turns the monitor around.

Rhiannon's drumming hands go still.

"Oh," I squeak. My lower lip wobbles.

I'm looking at my baby. My recognizably human baby.

My baby's face in profile. Round forehead and little button nose. Perfect little upturned chin.

This time there's no question at all. I'm in love.

Rhiannon's hand closes around my own. Her fingers lace through mine.

"So here's baby's forehead…" the ultrasound tech narrates unnecessarily, tracing the image with her finger. "There's baby's nose and lips. This is baby's spine, and right here—" she twists the ultrasound wand slightly "—this is baby's forearm."

"Hey, your baby's shaking their fist at us!" Rhiannon exclaims. She shifts in her rolly-chair, wheeling it that much closer to me and the monitor. Leans forward right over my body in her enthusiasm. She's so excited about all this, she's bouncing in her damn seat. "Probably trying to get us to turn down that racket," she suggests, speaking a hundred miles a minute. "Either that or shouting 'And I would have gotten away with it, too, if not for you meddling kids!'"

She's just so damn happy and overeager and excited.

My heart feels like it's going to burst. Or maybe my bladder.

"Gotten away with what, exactly?" I ask, giving her a sly look.

"Um, you know. Baby stuff?" She blushes.

I give her hand a reassuring squeeze. *I love you, you weirdo,* I want to say, but I don't. Not here. Not now. Not yet.

She brushes a strand of hair behind my ear and kisses my temple.

A part of me wonders if she wants to say it, too.

As we stare at my baby together in happy silence, I almost wish this moment could last forever.

On the other hand, I *seriously* need to pee.

Rhiannon gets me home safe, but when I try and ask her upstairs, she shakes her head.

Somehow, I'm not surprised at all that she's turned me down, even after everything we just went through together.

After all, she does seem a little bit distracted at the moment. We hardly talked on the cab ride back to my apartment, and now, standing face-to-face, she *still* won't meet my gaze.

"See you at the stitch n' bitch?" I try.

She finally looks at me, a relieved smile crossing her face. "Yeah," she agrees, and nudges forward to kiss me.

I close my eyes and kiss her back, draping my arms over her shoulders. She leans into me with a sigh.

I should probably care more that we're in public, that people can see us, but I'm still on cloud nine from my ultrasound and any bigots in our vicinity can fuck off with the anti-choice protesters.

I break off the kiss. "You sure you don't want to come up?" I ask, not caring if I sound needy.

This time she looks a little more torn, but she still says no.

Okay, fair enough. It was a pretty crazy intense afternoon. Maybe she needs some time to decompress.

Maybe *I* need some time to decompress.

"No problem," I reassure her. "Thanks for coming today. I really appreciate it."

"Thanks for including me." It's a genuine statement, not an expected polite answer.

I can't help but kiss her again.

This time it's quick and chaste, and I pull back with a blush. "I'm sorry. I'm letting you leave. Really."

She laughs. Doesn't let go of my waist.

"Go. Go go go." I peel out of her arms.

We're like two lovesick teenagers at the end of a six-hour-long phone call: *You hang up! No you hang up!*

"I'm going. I'm going!" She turns away from me.

Turns back around again.

Kisses me once more.

My heart is melting.

"Okay, now I'm really going," she says. "Get inside that apartment and lock the door behind you before I lose my will and follow you up there."

We're both laughing as we part.

Chapter Seventeen

I float on a cloud all the way up to my front door, but quickly crash to the ground the second after I open it.

My mother stands in my living room, sharply dressed in her tweed Chanel skirt suit.

Shit, shit, shit, shit, shit.

"Uh, hi, Mom, what's the occasion?" I ask.

She turns, her perfectly manicured hand clutched around a pill bottle.

A soft pastel pink pill bottle with a picture of a model holding a baby.

"Please tell me you're taking these because Doctor Oz recommends them to improve the strength of your hair and nails."

There's no point in lying. She's giftwrapped me an excuse for the prenatal vitamins, but I'm thirteen weeks along and while I'm fat enough to not be showing as far as strangers are concerned, my mother knows my body only slightly less intimately than I know it myself. She knows her daughter isn't apple-shaped. So unless she for some reason assumes I'm the notorious Yonkers Cantaloupe Thief (who would also like stronger hair and nails), I'm fucked.

Doesn't mean I have to admit my shame aloud, though.

I cup my belly, pulling my oversized shirt taut against the shape of it. There really is no mistaking it for ordinary fat girl VBO (that's Visible Belly Outline, to the uninitiated). Yep, I definitely look pregnant. "I'm taking them because Doctor Oz recommends them to improve the strength of my hair and nails," I deadpan.

"Poppy Joan Adams!" She scolds me like I'm a toddler who got into the cookie dough before she had a chance to bake it.

I square my shoulders, summoning up Rhiannon's distaste for how much I let my mother rule my life. "Yes, Mother?"

"Don't you *Mother* me, young lady. You have some explaining to do! Without sarcasm this time!"

I take a deep breath. "I'm having a baby. The dad isn't in the picture and I'm not sure I want him to be. I'm receiving adequate prenatal care. I've thought this through. I'm absolutely not getting an abortion. I'm not putting the baby up for adoption, either. I don't want to move back home. Yes I'm absolutely sure I want to keep the baby. I'm not thinking about going back to school right now and it's not just because I'm having a baby. Yes I'm really, really, really absolutely sure I want to be a mother."

There. That should cover it.

No, wait, one more thing. "And considering I'm entering a new stage of my life, I think it's as good a time as any to ask for the key to my apartment back."

She gapes at me.

Might as well go for gold. "Also, I'm bisexual. And I have a girlfriend."

I've done it. I've really done it. My mother is speechless.

She shakily lowers herself onto my couch.

"Is that all?" she manages to ask. She looks faint. Good. I'm enjoying having caught *her* off guard for once.

"Hmm. No. I also want to repeat my question. Why are you here?"

"Oh…" She flaps a hand. "Your sister and her husband are expecting, as well."

All my elation escapes me in one *whoosh*, like I'm a popped balloon.

Of fucking course she is.

Revelations behind us, my mother gathers her composure and insists on taking me to dinner.

Has no choice but to do so, since she made reservations for us in advance.

The restaurant she's chosen is expensive as all hell and hard to get into, of course, and she makes a big show of going through my closet in search of something "appropriate" for me to wear. I have lots of nice dresses that I can dress up for a nice night out, but of course she rejects them all for not being "flattering" enough.

Gag.

At the very back of my closet she finds a little black dress she bought me for a New Year's party a couple years ago. Little black dress is actually too kind a term for it, though, honestly. It's a hideous empire-waisted nightmare that is somehow simultaneously shapeless *and* too small for me. She stuffs me into it anyway, grunting as she tugs on my zipper.

I'm going to have to spend roughly five hundred hours on my various fatshion and fat acceptance blogs to undo this one night, I can just feel it.

When she's finally got me into the dress, she turns me around at arm's length and gives me a long, miserable look. "I think I'll take you to a maternity store after dinner."

"Mom, please. No. *My* clothes still fit—" other than my bastard jeans and this hideous dress that was the wrong size in the first place "—and when I'm ready for maternity clothes, I'll buy them for myself. I have a job."

"Of course you have a job, dear. But you need to save money for the baby now. You can't be buying a capsule wardrobe."

"I know I have to save for the baby, but I think I've got enough left to buy a couple outfits from the thrift store."

Okay, I may have just said that last bit to get a rise out of her. "Do you have any idea how much babies cost?" she admonishes me, obviously upset but not taking the bait, either. "There's the crib, the change table, the stroller, the delivery, the checkups, the hospital room, the baby clothes, the diapers, the bottles, the formula, the baby monitor, the SIDS alarm, the wipes warmer, the diaper bin, the car seat and travel system, the diaper bag, the newborn portraits, the—"

And here I was thinking I'd get myself a little IKEA crib to put beside my bed and some secondhand onesies and sleepers.

"Is *Iris* buying all that for *her* baby?" I spit out.

"Well, *she'll* have a baby shower. And *she* has friends who can afford to really shower her."

Ouch. Low blow.

"And a husband to support her for everything else."

Double ouch. *Lower* blow.

Damn, she's going for blood this time. I guess I shouldn't have taunted her about my intention to buy clothes from a secondhand store.

"You should really consider involving the baby's father. You might get away with being a single mother—"

"Not single," I correct her, and she glares.

"—But not wanting to say who the father is makes people think you don't *know* who the father is. Makes you seem easy."

"Mom!"

"I'm just being honest with you. Even if he's…not up to your standards, nobody in our circles will *know* that. But if you don't name names at all, they'll assume."

"Let them assume."

"Don't be childish, Poppy. Haven't you thought of the *baby* in all your stubbornness? Don't you think the baby deserves to know where he comes from, not to mention the child support payments that you could clearly use? That's what being a mother is all about, after all. Doing what's in your child's best interest."

Is that what *this* is?

I look into my mother's eyes. She doesn't look mean, even though it would be so much easier for me if she did. She looks…concerned. Pleading.

She cares about me in her way. Like always, she wants what's best for me. Wanted me to have a body people didn't make fun of me for. Wanted me to graduate from a good school and get a good job and be self-sufficient, then to have a happy little family and an expansive friend group. To live in a nice house in a nice neighborhood where I was safe and secure and never wanted for anything.

She wants me to give my baby a good life, too. A life where they know where they come from.

A life where their mother has enough money to support them properly. It makes sense, but it still hurts.

I'll never be good enough for her.

And what's worse, now I can't shake the fear that I won't ever be good enough for my baby, either.

Chapter Eighteen

It takes me two weeks after my mother's impromptu visit to make up my mind on the Jake issue and get up the guts to contact him, and two more for our schedules to align enough that he can come meet me in person.

That's one prenatal checkup, four stitch n' bitch sessions (I bought last person there cookies three times), twenty-seven prenatal vitamins, a solid ten dates with Rhiannon—more if you count all the times we met up a couple hours before stitch n' bitch or hung out after, more *still* if you count every time we spent all night texting—and roughly a thousand phone calls from my nagging, over-concerned mother.

I'm eighteen weeks along and *definitely* showing when we finally make it work.

When Jake walks into the coffee shop, I don't have to say a thing. His eyes go wide as saucers, and he *runs* to greet me.

"Babe!" he announces, getting his hands all up on my belly.

From her place incognito spying on us from behind the counter, Rhiannon's eyebrows lift. I flash her a helpless look.

Neither of us were quite sure how Jake would react—thus the meeting in a public space under Rhiannon's watchful eye—but neither of us expected him to suddenly decide he was my boyfriend again just because I was carrying his baby.

I gently shove his hands off me. Gesture to the table I've selected for us, as close as possible to the espresso machine so the noise of it can hopefully drown us out for any potential eavesdroppers.

"Uh, yeah," he says, bewildered, and saunters over. Pulls my chair out for me.

Is this guy for real? Rhiannon mouths at me.

I force myself to look at Jake. Look straight into his eyes.

Be honest, be kind, be firm.

Rhiannon's advice to me.

I take my seat. Wait for him to take his, as well. I've ordered us both drinks: an herbal tea for me, and a coffee with five sugars for him—just the way he's always liked it.

"So obviously you know why I wanted to meet up," I say once we're settled.

"Uh, yeah! We're having a baby!"

I recoil. "No," I correct him as gently as I can manage. "*I* am having a baby."

"It's not mine?" Jake tilts his head in an accidentally perfect imitation of a confused puppy.

"It's…" I struggle for words. "No. It is your baby, and yes, I'm sure of that. I haven't slept with any…other men. But I'm the only person that's pregnant here, okay? And I need to have some boundaries with you."

"Of course, babe, whatever you want!"

I mean, I appreciate that he's taking this so well and not flying off the handle and demanding a paternity test or whatever, but this isn't going to work for me, either. "Starting with not calling me babe. You're this baby's father, but you're not my boyfriend, okay? We broke up. For good reasons. That hasn't changed."

He sits back in his seat, crestfallen. "You don't think… considering the circumstances…we could give it another chance? For the baby?"

I need to put this in words he'll respect. "I'm seeing someone else."

"But you said you didn't sleep with any…other…*men*…"

His eyes go wide again. This time it's an expression of utter delight.

Oh for fuck's sake.

"Yeah. I have a girlfriend."

"What! That's so hot! I mean, that's so cool! Good for you, rock on, gay rights."

Is there such a thing as taking things *too* well?

"Bi," I correct him, automatically. Now that I'm with Rhiannon, I've been working on not dismissing my sexuality as just a college phase or a natural extension of my indecisive nature. Rhiannon's a lesbian, but she moves in circles with lots of bi girls, and she's been more than supportive of me really claiming my sexuality instead of trying to explain it away or downplay it for other people's satisfaction. It feels pretty good, honestly.

Except for when it doesn't, like right now, when Jake responds to my revelation with, "Well have you ever considered, like, polyamory or whatever? The three of us together?"

Over his shoulder, I catch Rhiannon making a disgusted face.

"I don't think my girlfriend would be interested, even if I was. Which I'm not. Jake, you're a nice guy—honestly, you're actually surprising me in a good way right now with how nice of a guy you can be—but I'm really genuinely not interested in us starting up again. But I am interested in you being this baby's dad, if you want."

"I want!" he says, without even thinking it over. "Man, I will be the *best* dad! I love kids. You'll never have to fight for me to take the kid on weekends or whatever. I'll be looking forward to it all week! Me and this kid are gonna have so much fun together, I'm gonna show him all the great old nineties cartoons, starting with *The Real Ghostbusters...*"

"It's not all going to be fun. I'm sure a lot of it will be, but it's work, too. If I'm gonna involve you in this baby's life, I want you to be there for more than just the fun stuff. I want you to be at the parent teacher meetings and to change diapers and..." I take a deep breath. "To pay child support."

He really is a lot better of a guy than I gave him credit for, because that last bit doesn't phase him in the slightest. "I will totally pay child support. And change diapers. Ba—Poppy, I'm gonna take such good care of you and our baby. Without getting your girlfriend mad at us, that is."

"Cool." I lean back in my seat and rub my belly. For the first time in a long time, I feel very much at peace.

"This is all so amazing," Jake says, dreamy.

He always was a dreamer.

For the moment, I feel a bit like one, too.

"You must hate Christmas," Rhiannon murmurs, still a little out of breath. We're lying side by side in my bed, sprawled out staring at the ceiling, too hot and sticky to touch each other even a second longer.

"Why...do you say...that?" I reply, a *lot* out of breath myself.

She gestures to my dividing curtain. "Your lights. Now that it's the right time of year for them it totally ruins their *aesthetic*." She says that last bit with a sarcastic drawl.

I huff a laugh. "I feel like having a gay butch girl in my bed more than makes up for it."

"It's true. I am the ultimate accessory for cute femme millennial girls hoping to live their best twee New York life, right up there with cute fall scarves and steaming hot mug selfies. If you opened an Instagram account that was just candid photos of us together, you'd be unstoppable."

"Pff." I roll my eyes. "Pictures of *you*, maybe. I've yet to see a lesbian aesthetic collage of girls like me." I grab a handful of my muffin top in illustration.

"Which is a damn shame, because your cozy femme scarf wearing game is on point." She's kidding around, but I can see the sincerity in her eyes. She hears what I'm saying and she respects it. Doesn't understand it, maybe, because how could she really? But she trusts what I'm saying, and that alone means the world.

I could open up to her right now, share more, tell her about how unwelcome I sometimes feel, how I've worked so hard to love myself but still catch myself wondering what a girl like her is doing with someone like me. Wondering, too, if I subconsciously overlooked another fat girl in favor of dating Rhiannon. I could pour my whole heart out to her, start talking and never stop until I was *done*. She'd listen.

On the other hand, her quiet acceptance of my truth is enough.

I tilt my head until my cheek nudges her shoulder.

Her hand fumbles across the mattress to find mine.

We lace our fingers together.

My phone buzzes.

"Ignore it!" Rhiannon pleads. Ever since she found out about my pregnancy, my mom has been texting me seemingly nonstop. Considering how many of those texts have interrupted our makeouts, Rhiannon is well within her rights to complain.

Doesn't mean I can fix her problem, though. "You know if I ignore my mom's texts she only texts me more, right?"

"Ugh." She shakes her head in disgust, her expression exaggerated just enough that I can't tell whether she's just giving me a hard time or is genuinely annoyed. I dig for my phone in the pile of blankets.

Surprisingly enough, the new message is from my sister.

Other than my knitting updates to prove her wrong about my follow-through abilities, we haven't communicated in months.

Her text today reads: Mom says you know.

There's only one thing that message could reasonably be about, but just in case Occam's Razor is a little dull today, I decide to play dumb.

Know about what?

Don't play dumb Poppy.

Haha, oops.

I bite my lip shamefully as I type, Ok, ok. Yes, I know.

For a few minutes there's nothing but the animated dot dot dot of her typing, then at last, Dammit! I told her not to tell anyone!

And u expected her to respect that?

True enough. She told me about you, too.

"Dammit!" I exclaim. Rhiannon sits up beside me in bed and wraps an arm around my shoulders, leaning in close so she can read.

I don't know what I expected, I reply.

When are you due?

May. You?

June.

Holy shit that's so soon!

Yeah, sorry. Another long pause while she types and deletes something over and over. It's just that...this is my third pregnancy. Was a little scared to reveal any earlier.

Her third pregnancy, yet only the first one I've heard of. Oh.

My lower lip wobbles. I can't stop myself from envisioning her catching blood in her hands, all those constant frantic fears of early pregnancy and What To Expect coming to bitter realization. I clutch at my belly in sympathy. In shared fear.

Rhiannon has stopped reading over my shoulder.

I'm sorry, I type, feeling useless. I'm so sorry.

Tears sting my eyes.

I hate how helpless I feel.

It's okay, she replies.

How typical. She's the one who went through something so horrific, and yet she's consoling *me*.

I'm about to reply with something along those lines when another message comes in.

Are you coming for Christmas?

Just like that, our moment of shared tragedy is over.

Do I have a choice? I write back with a watery little smirk.

Rhiannon kisses my shoulder and rises from the bed.

Did my mom tell Iris about *her,* too, or just my pregnancy?

I mean, technically you do, but I can't promise mom won't chew you out for the next twenty years for it.

You think she's only going to live another twenty years? That's pretty pessimistic of you.

LOL. I love that she still capitalizes it. I'm surprised she doesn't put the periods in, she's so proper. Just warning you now though that you need to get mom and dad to pay for your Christmas trip because you're going to have to come up again in February for my gender reveal party.

A gender reveal party with my sister and all her high society friends sounds like complete torture, but I can't exactly say no after everything she's shared with me.

Though maybe I can alleviate my suffering somewhat.

Sure. Can I bring a plus one?

Chapter Nineteen

My sister's baby belly is perfect. I can't stop staring at it. It's so pronounced yet small, round and cute, and accentuated by her perfectly composed maternity wardrobe. I spend my entire Christmas visit with the family silently envying her effortless glow and the way her normally reticent husband dotes on her.

My mother, too.

Sure, every incoming phone call to wish us season's greetings immediately turns to the fact that both her daughters are pregnant and isn't she *so lucky getting two little grandbabies at once?* but there's no missing the fact that once that statement is out of the way she's much more keen to talk about my sister's upcoming birth than mine.

I'm there for four days, and for every minute of every

one of them (that's five thousand seven hundred and sixty minutes in all for those of you keeping score at home), it's Iris-this and Iris-that. Iris hasn't gained any weight yet in her pregnancy. Iris's husband is spoiling her with a baby-moon in the Hamptons. Iris hired a nearly impossible to book interior designer to do her baby's nursery.

The fact that I resent her for it, even after everything she's gone through, makes me feel like absolute shit, so there's that, too.

Oh, and every time I try to bring up my relationship with Rhiannon with the rest of the family, my mother changes the subject before I can get my point across. After four unsuccessful tries to come out, I finally just say fuck it and entirely give up speaking unless spoken to.

I've never been so relieved to get the hell out of my parents' suffocating house and go back to my adult life, alone.

Except I'm not alone.

I'm barely in my apartment three hours before a delivery guy arrives with a bouquet of flowers and a novelty-sized teddy bear.

The card reads:

For you and our baby.
Love, Jake

It's completely over the top and unnecessary and unasked for, but it still gives me warm fuzzies. Maybe this baby was a wake-up call for him. Maybe he really has changed.

Isn't that what I wanted for myself? For this baby to be the kick in the ass I need to finally learn to Adult?

If Jake can manage it, there's definitely hope for me, too. After all, I've never skipped my girlfriend's grandma's funeral to get high.

And speaking of my girlfriend…

I whip my phone out of my back pocket. Hey babe I'm home! When do I get to see you?

Her reply is so fast I can't help but wonder if she was sitting there staring at her phone waiting for my text.

Gimme an hour.

She's there in forty-five minutes.

When she wraps me in her arms, that's when I know I'm home. You'd think my growing belly would get in her way, but she just bends her body around it effortlessly, like the three of us are meant to fit together. The mere thought of that has little overwhelmed, happy tears pricking at my eyes, and I laugh and sniffle and press my face into her neck.

"Awwww, I missed you, too, cupcake!" she says with a little chuckle, petting my hair. "Was Christmas at your parents that terrible?"

"The less said about it the better," I reply. "How about yours?"

"Well, Dad has a new girlfriend so that was predictably a whole *thing*, but at least it kept the heat off of me for once. The holidays have this funny way of reminding me why I don't see my family except for on the holidays. But on the upside, I got to see my nephews."

"Huh, I just realized: this time next year I'll be able to say the same thing."

Rhiannon grins. "Hell yeah you will, and trust me, Christmas with kids is a game changer. Especially as an auntie. It's all the Santa magic with none of the sugar crash the next day."

I wonder if next year I'll be able to find the silver lining of *my* family holidays the way Rhiannon has clearly found hers. Well, in the here and now, it's a comfort and a balm just to see her happy. "Did you spoil them?"

"Boy did I! They shall never want for the latest Lego, not so long as Auntie Rhi still draws breath." She pulls back from me suddenly. "And speaking of spoiling, what in the name of God is *that*?"

I turn around, following the direction of her gaze to the giant novelty teddy bear currently taking up residence on a solid half of my sofa. "Present for the baby from Jake," I say with an embarrassed bite of my lip. "How old are your nephews?"

"Three. They're twins. Has Jake not been to your place?" She scrunches her nose in disgust.

I blush, remembering the last time he was here in a little bit too much detail. "Uh, yeah, he has. Are they your brother's kids, or your sister's?"

"My sister's. So he should already know you have no damn room in this shoebox for a teddy bear the size of a compact car."

"It's not that big," I reply, but my heart's not in it. Maybe I should be getting a bit more serious about all this—what if she's jealous he's moving in on her territory? Is that something I should be asking about, addressing? But she's so over the top offended on my behalf by the presence of this damn teddy bear, it's hilarious to me.

"Like, seriously, do you not see the problem here? Do you not see what I am seeing? This teddy bear is so big it needs to be paying you rent."

"*Come on.*" I laugh.

"No, no, no, I got another one. I got another one. This teddy bear is so big he should be at Pride, marching with the leather daddies."

"That doesn't even make sense."

"This teddy bear is so big, we could use him as a new surface for us to have sex on."

I flash her a sly look. "Okay, now, that one has a certain appeal."

I'm joking.

Mostly.

"You kinky little minx," she purrs, and presses her lips to mine.

"Don't judge me," I murmur into her mouth.

"Oh, I'm judging you."

Not judging me enough to discourage her from yanking me in tight against her body, though. I laugh as our bodies crush against one another, Rhiannon's hands skirting over my lower black to get two handfuls of my ass.

That's when we feel it.

I say "we", because at the exact moment I squeak in surprise, Rhiannon leaps three feet backwards in her best imitation of a cat spotting a cucumber.

She rushes forward again, hands cupping my belly now. "Was that—?"

I bite my lip, pure joy surging through me, closing off my throat with tears I damn well *will not shed I swear to God.* "Y-yeah," I manage to get out.

My baby kicked.

And Rhiannon *felt* it.

At twenty-one weeks along I've definitely felt vague movement in there: the occasional bump or flutter and even an effervescent bubbling that may or may not have just been gas. But this was the first honest to God *kick*, and Rhiannon was here for it.

Rhiannon's palms explore my belly like she's never touched it before, fingers splayed, eyes wide and locked to my gaze.

I think she realizes the intensity of her expression just then, because she gives her head a shake and fixes my belly with a dramatic glower as she gives it a gentle but very determined poke.

"I know you're in there!" she announces, mock serious.

"Don't you *dare* say 'come out with your hands up'," I warn her with a laugh.

She laughs, too. Cups my belly in her hands as she gives me a peck on the chin.

We stay like that awhile, just holding each other, basking in one another and in this moment like there's nothing else in the world.

"Guess this means you two are now formally acquainted," I say after a while.

She tucks her face into my collarbone, saying, muffled, "I wish I were a baby and could just kick people as a greeting."

"Yeah but if you were a baby you couldn't—"

She reaches around my body, dipping her hand between my legs to grip me on my inner thigh. "Do that?" she finishes. I feel her smile against my skin.

Is it weird to go from sex to mushy baby feelings and back to sex again?

Eh, who cares.

"How was everyone's holidays?" Louise asks without looking up from her project. "Not to make anyone jealous, but Mary had me over for Christmas dinner at her house and it was *delicious*."

Mary raises a hand. "Speaking of which, does anyone want any leftovers? If I have to eat one more turkey-based meal I might turn into one."

"Oh, me! I didn't get any of my mom's Christmas turkey this year. We did Hanukkah with Nate's family in New Jersey and didn't get back until yesterday. It was lovely, don't get me wrong, but eight days of gifts and still no little blue box?" Grace holds up her ring-less left hand peevishly. "How about you, Damian? Did Taisha get everything she asked for from Santa?"

Damian clears his throat pointedly. "*Taisha* is about two more skeptical questions away from learning the terrible truth about Santa Claus. There's only so many times a parent can get away with 'Well how do *you* think Santa visits houses without chimneys?'"

"It's an interesting conundrum, isn't it?" Mary puts in. "How to balance the magic of Christmas traditions with the ethical quandary of what ultimately amounts to lying to children."

Grace turns to me. "Are you going to do the whole Santa thing with your baby, Poppy?"

I grimace. *Don't I have at least a few years left to put that question off?* "Hey, so who wants to see baby's new booties?"

"You finished them!" Louise cheers. I fish them out of my bag, unreasonably relieved my change of subject worked.

Whether or not to "do" Santa is a small decision in the grand scheme of things, but discussing it only reminds me of all the other—way more important—stuff I have yet to decide. Like, do I take Jake's grand gesture as a sign he really does want to be involved in our baby's life, even if he's going about it the wrong way? Do I keep Iris and our mother in the loop regarding my pregnancy now that the cat's out of the bag, knowing every piece of information my mother has access to may be an opening for her to try and take over proceedings?

And if I don't involve Jake or Iris or my mother, is it fair of me to ask Rhiannon to carry their weight? Even if her ultimately finding that burden too heavy means I might now lose her altogether?

I shove my worries down deep and try to focus on the here and now, the people right in front of me who are currently passing my latest knitting project down the line.

Grace turns my bootie over in her hand, as always actually taking her time to really look at it. "Cast off *and* sewn up!" she praises as she hands the bootie on.

"Didn't even need my help this time," Rhiannon adds with a proud little nod.

I blush and give an awkward shrug. Will I ever stop

being weird about positive attention? "When I cast off I still had another couple days with my parents to get through, so I figured I could use the distraction. You were right about IKnitWithCatFur's tutorial videos, Louise. Very helpful!"

Louise hefts her ubiquitous cat-print tote bag up onto the table. "Helpful, *and* a kindred spirit!"

"Kindred spirit? I'm still not convinced you and she aren't secretly the same person," Rhiannon says.

"She does have a magic loop video," I add in a conspiratorial tone.

"Well that settles it then, doesn't it?" Damian stabs the air with his crochet hook. "Conspiracy theory confirmed."

Louise's eyes twinkle. "I can neither confirm nor deny."

"So what are you working on next, Poppy? Have you decided?" Mary asks.

"Decided and already started!" I produce my next project and hold it out to the stitch n' bitch proudly. "Not that you can tell just yet, but it's going to be a sweater!"

"Ooh, ambitious!" Grace intones.

Too ambitious, perhaps?

I look over at Rhiannon, who smiles back at me without a shade of doubt in her eyes.

Nah. I'm ready to take a risk.

The tricky thing about taking risks is that in order to fly you have to accept that sometimes you're going to fall flat on your face. This is one of those times.

My sweater is going surprisingly well, actually, but I'd trade the despair and frustration of dropped stitches and yarn barf for this feeling any day.

I've just asked Rhiannon if she'd like to come to my next ultrasound.

"That's a Wednesday?" Rhiannon hisses a breath in through her teeth, and I can already tell what her answer is going to be before she has to say a word. "That's…shit. That's not a good day for me, to be honest."

She doesn't elaborate on why, but I don't press the issue. If she wanted to tell me, or offer to reschedule, she would.

"Oh. Right. Sure. Of course." I rub my arm, avoiding looking at her directly, and try my level best not to let my disappointment show.

I've asked so much of her for such a new relationship, and despite her reluctance, she's always come up with a way to make it work for the both of us.

She was bound to say no eventually.

She has the *right* to say no, I remind myself.

At the end of the day, this is my baby, not hers.

I have to respect that and give her space.

I square my shoulders, mentally pulling up my big girl maternity pants. "You know what? It's actually fine. After all I was really struggling on how to get Jake more involved with the baby, and this is kind of the perfect opportunity."

"Exactly!" Rhiannon nods along with me a little too enthusiastically; I can tell she's relieved to be given an out. Which is precisely what I was trying to do by saying all that in the first place, but for some reason her response still rubs me the wrong way. "That's a great idea. Bring him along, let him see the baby, ask any questions he has…"

"Right. Yeah. I guess I should let him know, huh? Give him some advance notice, at least."

Rhiannon reaches out and clasps me by the wrist. "If he really wants to be a part of his baby's life, Poppy, he'll make time for you."

Comforting words of affirmation, and a sincere expression to match.

But they feel sour in my ears.

Because if what she's saying about Jake is true, then what does it say about her and me?

I cover her hand with mine, refusing to let myself think that way. "You'll still text me, though, right? To see how it went or whatever?"

"Of course."

Rhiannon still cares about me.

And if I truly care about her, I won't ask more of her than what she can give.

Rhiannon and I stay in for New Years, watch the ball drop livestreaming on my laptop from the comfort of my bed. At midnight, she kisses us both: me first, and then my belly.

I try not to think of it as a promise.

Chapter Twenty

Twenty-three weeks pregnant. My app says my baby is the size of "a large mango", which sounds totally cute until you realize it comes with having feet and ankles that look like overstuffed sausages just this side of splitting open, and strangers who suddenly think it's hunky-dory to touch a fat woman's belly.

I am Done.

And the worst part is, I'm only barely past halfway.

At least I have my ultrasound to look forward to. Maybe seeing my baby's sweet little face will help me get over the fact that I can no longer fit into any of my cute shoes.

Too bad I couldn't have had my drunken booty call a little later in the year so I could be pregnant at a time that I could just wear flip-flops.

(Who am I kidding, I wouldn't be caught dead in flip-flops.)

Sitting in the back of my cab on the way to Planned Parenthood, I open my phone to Rhiannon's last texts to me:

Good luck today baby girl!

Wish I could be there

I wish that, too.

If it weren't for the fact that I had to arrange this day off a month in advance, I'd just cancel the appointment and reschedule it for a day when Rhiannon's free to come with.

But that's ridiculous. It's just an ultrasound, and she's already been to one more of those than I should be expecting of her. Besides, Jake is coming today, and it wouldn't be fair to him to cancel on short notice, not after I got him all excited about it. He also sent me that nice grocery store gift card after I texted to tell him the giant novelty teddy bear needed to go back to the store and that in the future I'd prefer practical gifts over grand gestures.

Maybe the two of us fuckups are gonna be able to handle this co-parenting and adulthood thing after all.

There must be some kind of anti-choice dickbag convention out of state, because today I'm greeted on the sidewalk by one old guy holding a yawn-worthy REPENT sign. When they're not drastically outnumbering you, it really highlights how sad and sorry the whole enterprise is. "Get a hobby," I shout fearlessly as I stride by.

Rhiannon would have high-fived me.

I really miss her.

Damn pregnancy hormones.

When I get into the waiting room, Jake isn't there to greet me. Not much of a shock: I'm early, and he's always late. I check in with the nurse and take my seat, chugging my huge bottle of water while I scroll through my phone.

At five minutes to my appointment time, I send him a Where r u at? text.

No response. Maybe that means he's on his way, in too much of a rush to answer.

I put my phone away so I can stop obsessively check-ing my messages and focus on drinking my water instead.

"Poppy?" the nurse with the clipboard calls sometime later. I give one last look around the waiting room, then head through the security door.

"My, um, friend might be coming. Is supposed to be coming. I think he's running late, though. His name's Jake. If he shows up, can you let the woman at the front desk know I'm expecting him and that he's welcome to come back?"

"Sure, honey," the nurse says. "Have a seat here. The ultrasound tech will call you when he's ready."

I finish my bottle of water.

The ultrasound tech, a scrawny six-foot-tall guy with locs in a ponytail and Doc McStuffins scrubs, comes to collect me.

I don't even return his friendly hello. I can't stop my-self from blurting out the question that's at the forefront of my mind.

"Did my friend Jake come?" I ask, and hate myself for how small and scared my voice sounds.

He shakes his head. "Sorry. If he had, they'd have brought him back."

My stomach feels like a black hole, and all my intestines are tangling themselves up as they get sucked in.

"Can I call someone quick?"

It's just an ultrasound, I say to myself. *It's just an ultrasound. It's just an ultrasound. You're not giving birth. You can do this alone. You will be okay.*

"Sure, go for it."

I take my phone out of my pocket and dial Rhiannon's number.

Straight to voicemail.

I feel like my heart is breaking.

I hang up without leaving her a message. Scroll through the rest of my list of contacts and hit dial.

She answers on the second ring.

"Hello? Mom?"

There's no way she can make it to the clinic in time for my ultrasound, but she's there waiting for me in the lobby when I come out afterwards.

"Well?" she says, opening her arms to me. "Did you find out what it is?"

I'd fully intended on finding out when I woke up this morning, but then, I'd also fully intended on Jake being there with me.

So when my ultrasound tech had asked me if I wanted

to know the sex, I'd told him no, even though I was—and am—still curious.

Jake didn't show up today, so he doesn't get to know. And since a part of me is well aware that if I'd found out for myself all it would take would be one blubbering, seemingly heartfelt apology and I'd cave and tell him, I didn't let myself ask.

Now nobody gets to know.

I hug my mother briefly, then pull away. The child in me is grateful she's here, but the rest of me wishes it could have been literally anyone else.

"Sorry, Mom," I say with a shrug, not sounding sorry at all.

She scowls. "Really, Poppy! How am I going to know what color onesies to buy you? And don't you dare suggest I buy hideous yellow and green 'gender neutral' anything."

"Okay, don't buy me yellow and green gender neutral anything. Buy me pink onesies. Or blue onesies. Or heck, buy me both. Buy me the whole rainbow of onesies. The infant will not care, and neither will I."

"Don't be so contrary. I swear, you do it just to get a rise out of me."

Is that true? I'd like to believe I'm genuinely working on expanding my binary understanding of gender, giving my baby a chance to grow up a little less constricted by the same expectations that strangled me my whole life, but what if my mother's right?

What if it's all just a knee-jerk reaction to *her*?

I'm wondering if I'm only bisexual for attention all over again.

Except I *am* bisexual, and the gender binary *is* bullshit. Those things don't stop being true just because I get a little thrill out of rubbing my mother's nose in them.

"A little thrill," Poppy? Really?

How much more immature can I get? Doing and saying stuff just to rub my mom the wrong way? What am I, fifteen?

Well, it's obvious parenthood hasn't miraculously transformed Jake into an adult, so why in the hell did I think it would work on me?

The reality of that thought is so depressing I feel numb, and I follow my mother out of the clinic and into her hired car like a zombie.

Jake hasn't changed, despite his best intentions.

I haven't changed, either.

I'm the same immature, aimless loser and excuse for a barely functioning adult as I ever was, except now I'm going to be that same person with a tiny dependent human being to look after. I can't even pay my bills on time. How the hell am I going to get my kid to doctor's appointments? I couldn't even finish a four-year degree. How can I expect myself to get my child through twelve years of schooling?

At lunch, my mother orders for me. A salad with dressing on the side, and lots of healthy fats and proteins. An honest to God glass of milk to go with it.

And out of her purse she produces a powder blue gift bag with pink tissue paper, containing another bottle of prenatal vitamins, a gift card to a maternity clothing store, and a certificate good for a ten week session of prenatal classes…

held at her usual yoga studio, which is a five minute drive from *her* house.

I'm so stunned and miserable I don't even fight her on any of it.

When she drops me off at home, I flop onto my couch and stare at the stacks of Planned Parenthood brochures I still haven't cleared off my coffee table.

Ones I hadn't read before, because I was too busy day-dreaming. Ones like *Make an Informed Choice* and *Thinking Realistically About Parenting*.

If you're having a baby to fix your relationship with your part-ner or spouse, or to solve other existing problems in your life, please know that babies put strain on interpersonal relationships, on fi-nances, on your lifestyle. They can add richness and joy to your life, but the problems you had before a baby will still be problems afterwards. Confidential counselling is available…

I'm a fucking idiot.

When my phone buzzes with a text, I almost don't pick it up in case it's Jake, grovelling or making excuses for himself.

It's only the thought that it might be Rhiannon that makes me check and see.

It's not Rhiannon, though; it's my mother. She hasn't even been gone ten minutes!

Poppy, I'm worried, the text from her reads. I think you should seriously consider moving back home.

Maybe she's right.

Maybe she's been right about me all along.

Chapter Twenty-One

I keep my phone close for the rest of the evening, obsessively checking my messages in between stewing over how—or whether—I'd even reply.

Jake? At this point I'd probably delete any text from him without bothering to open it in the first place.

But Rhiannon?

Should I pretend everything's hunky-dory, cry on her metaphorical shoulder, chew her out…or leave her on read?

I may be torn on how or whether I'll respond, but I am certain of one thing: I want—no, *need*—her to text me.

But she doesn't.

All night.

And I don't text her, either.

It's a war of attrition she doesn't even know she's fighting, and somehow I still come out of it feeling like the loser.

Because when I finally give up the ghost and sink into bed to sleep, it becomes the first time in months I've done so without a cute good-night text from her, sending me off to my sweet dreams.

Instead, I dream of nothing at all.

Two more days pass without texts to or from Rhiannon.

I feel like shit, but I simultaneously can't bring myself to do the one very simple thing that would end my suffering and *just text her already.*

It doesn't even have to be about the baby! I could text her a funny meme, or a picture of a cat I saw, or asking her to re-explain how to pick up dropped stitches *again* because yeah, there's currently eight of them just hanging out in the no-man's land between the needles on my latest project…which I'm now too afraid to touch lest it all unravel.

Anything! I could text her anything! Anything but this long, miserable silence that just feels longer and more miserable as time goes by.

And what's worse, this entire conflict could all still just be in my head! Rhiannon and I never actually fought, after all.

Maybe she's just busy, or thinks I'm busy, or is torturing herself wishing she could text me but not wanting to look clingy. Or maybe she really is upset with me for some reason, or senses that I'm upset with her and has decided I'm not worth the drama of asking why.

It's gotten to the point that every time I glance at or even think of my phone, my heart rate spikes.

You'd think it was some automatic evolutionary response, like humanity's vestigial fear of spiders.

It's ridiculous. I'm ridiculous.

Now it's stitch n' bitch day and I'm seriously considering skipping out just so I can carry on avoiding Rhiannon.

Who may not even know I'm avoiding her.

Or who may be avoiding me, too.

But no. I can't let myself even entertain that as an option.

After all, these dropped stitches won't fix themselves, I need human contact—other than my nagging mother—desperately, and if I miss a session without explanation, everyone is going to worry I've gone into early labor or something.

Fact is, I *like* the people from stitch n' bitch. I don't want to cause them undue misery.

Especially not if that undue misery comes with a side of theorizing about what happened between me and Rhiannon.

I get enough of being the subject of supposedly well-meaning rumors in my parents' circles, I don't need them with my own social circle, too.

Hell, maybe all this agony will be for nothing and Rhiannon won't even be there today!

As I'm gathering my knitting and heading out the door, I find myself wondering whether I'm hoping for that to be the case…or dreading it.

When I get to the coffee shop, I don't head in right away like I usually would. Instead, I loiter on the sidewalk outside and try to convince myself I'm not just trying to avoid Rhiannon.

Which would be sad and childish.

And totally not what I'm doing at all.

Obviously.

It's just that the brisk walk here has left me flushed and kind of light-headed, and I need some additional time in the cold to regulate my body temperature.

I stroll back and forth just out of view of the coffee shop windows, stubbornly refusing to acknowledge that I'm starting to shiver and my fingers and toes are stinging from the cold.

The colder I get, though, the more my sensible explanation starts to look like a flimsy excuse, and there's no more mental gymnastics I can perform to change things.

I have to go inside.

I have to see them all.

I can do this.

Taking a deep, fortifying breath, I reach for the door handle…then draw back at the last second. Head over to one of the plate glass windows and surreptitiously peer inside.

Once again, I try to tell myself it's not because of Rhiannon. I just want to see who all's here already, and if that happens to include Rhiannon…

"Dammit!"

How the hell am I the last one to arrive at the coffee shop *again*?

The whole group, including Rhiannon, is already gathered around our usual table, laughing and chatting with knitting in hand and a friendly cluster of mugs steaming away on the table between them.

I know I dragged ass getting here, but I honestly thought I was actually early for once.

Checking my smartwatch I realize... I *am* early! A whole freakin' ten minutes early!

The members of the stitch n' bitch can't even manage to make it on time, most weeks. For every single member to show up more than ten minutes early?

Something's up.

My curiosity about what it could be completely overrides my determination to delay the inevitable, and I finally make my way inside.

"Surprise!"

As I approach the table, everyone seated around it all bend down to retrieve something out from underneath.

Gift bags. Stuffed with pastel tissue paper and decorated with rattles and bottles and rubber duckies.

For some reason it takes me a couple seconds to clock in to the fact that they're for *me*. For *my* baby.

"You guys, seriously?"

They extend the gifts toward me in reply, all smiles.

Still not quite computing.

"*Seriously?*"

"Yes, seriously!" Grace says in a tone I'd have found insufferably condescending before I got to know her. "Do you really have that hard of a time believing your friends would throw you a baby shower?"

"My...friends? My friends! You called me your friend!"

My pregnancy hormones must be going haywire, because I actually choke back tears.

I throw my arms around Grace's shoulders in a tight hug as the rest of our knitting group laughs.

I'm so busy processing this unfamiliar feeling of genuine belonging, and trying not to cry because of it, that I almost forget about the whole Rhiannon awkwardness.

But then I pull out of my hug with Grace and see her standing there, and she's smiling at me, and maybe it's just me and my shit but it doesn't seem like her usual smile somehow. Her eyes are blank, the curve of her mouth strained.

"Open my gift first!" Louise, blessed bad-at-reading-social-cues Louise, bursts into my frame of view, holding up her gift bag with its baby bottle motif.

"Ugh," Mary exclaims, eyeballing the bag. "It disgusts me how so many baby things just *have* to be printed with bottles. It just contributes to our wider culture of breast-feeding shaming."

Louise turns to me with a comforting smile. "You don't have to worry about that with us, Poppy. Feed that little bundle of joy whenever and however you like."

"That *includes* the bottle," Damian adds. "Breastfeeding shaming, bottle feeding shaming…shit. As long as baby's loved and has a full tummy, then nothing else matters. Right, ladies?" He looks around pointedly, expression friendly but firm. Papa Bear Damian.

The stitch n' bitch all nod.

"It's *your* baby," Rhiannon says at last. "Nobody else

here has any claim or any right to say anything to you about anything."

Um, that was…quite pointed.

I try to smile at her, but I mostly grimace. I wonder if she thinks my smile looks different, too?

Grace, the opposite of sweet bumbling Louise, keys into the tension immediately and clears her throat in a deft redirection. "Except for me. *I* get to tell you that that baby deserves at least one garment knit out of something besides acrylic!" She taps her gift. "Which is why I got you this!"

I can't stop staring at Rhiannon. Studying her. Analyzing her. My anxious theories spin out of control.

Everyone else at the table smiles at me like there's nothing wrong at all and pushes their offerings toward me.

Right. Gifts.

The perfect distraction.

I open them one by one, going through the motions of cooing and holding each gift up to show it off.

Which I realize is pretty shitty of me, since they're wonderful, thoughtful gifts.

Louise's, opened first as requested, is a plush pastel baby blanket. Judging by its size alone, it must have taken her hours.

Grace gifts me an entire layette, knit out of her promised natural fiber yarn. Her stitches, of course, are leagues neater than my own, her baby booties perfectly formed, but I'm no longer letting the implied competition get under my skin.

Mary's present is a gift card to the kind of baby boutique my mom and sister would probably shop at. It's tucked into the front cover of a massive parenting book, written by the doctor Mary assures me is *the* voice of crunchy, gentler, attachment parenting…whatever the hell all that means. I'm getting the feeling the mom world is even more unnecessarily complex and in-fighty than the knitting one.

Damian gives me a workhorse of a baby carrier—*"One of these saved our lives and sanity when Taisha was born, she was so damn colicky"*—and a promise of all the hand-me-down baby things I or my baby could ever need.

Rhiannon's gift is last. I don't even want to open it, and by the sickly look she's wearing, Rhiannon doesn't want that, either.

But I can't let this awkwardness between us ruin this lovingly planned party, and despite our differences I know Rhiannon would agree.

And so, feeling like there's a thousand eyes on us, I open her gift.

It's…

Rhiannon smiles half-heartedly. "Sorry for the duplicated baby blanket. I really should have asked around and made sure no one else was giving you one."

"I don't mind," Louise announces, as if the apology is to her. "Is a baby really loved if it doesn't have at least three hand-knit baby blankets?" She blanches. "Oh, but of course your baby is still loved even though you only got two, Poppy…"

I murmur comforting platitudes without even looking up. I'm too engrossed examining the blanket Rhiannon gave me, feeling the texture of it in my hands.

Just like Rhiannon's demeanor, there's something…off about it. I can't put my finger on what.

"Is that *worsted* weight yarn, Rhiannon?" Mary asks in a friendly teasing tone. "I didn't know you knew how to knit anything heavier than fingering!"

Rhiannon coughs, uncomfortable. "Uh, about that... Before anyone gets ahead of themselves, I should be honest. I didn't knit this blanket myself. I mean, I *wanted* to knit something myself, but I just didn't have the time."

Inexplicable anger rises in my chest, making my heart pound.

I look up at her sharply.

"It's okay, Rhi. I figured you *must* be busy after you went days without texting me."

Damian looks at me in panicked question.

Grace laughs nervously. "Hey, who wants—"

I cut her off with merciless abandon. "And whatever it is, I trust it must be super important, too." I look around the table at everyone shrinking into their seats until my eyes land straight on Rhiannon. "The Rhiannon we all know would never leave her girlfriend high and dry to go to an ultrasound on her own, not without a damn good excuse."

Rhiannon looks at me expressionlessly. I can't tell if she's hurt or angry or sorry that I'm calling her out. "Didn't Jake go with you to that?"

That's it. The final fucking straw.

"No, actually, he didn't. He flaked. Which you'd have known had you texted me at *all* since my appointment." I ring Rhiannon's baby blanket in my hands furiously. It's almost hard to stay angry when I'm touching it. The fibers of it are so soft and worn, not crisp and newly blocked like

Louise's. I drop it unceremoniously onto the table, holding on to my anger instead.

"I'm sorry he did that…" Rhiannon tries. Her tone is sympathetic, but all I hear is the fact that no apology for her own behavior seems forthcoming.

"Me too, but you know, I'm cool. I kinda expected it from that loser. Flaking's his M.O." My voice suddenly sounds like someone else's, light and calm and giving no fucks. "But I really *didn't* expect it from you."

"All right, Poppy, I'm sure—" Mary, picking up peace-keeping efforts where Grace left off.

"It's fine, Mary. I'm a big girl. So what if she was too busy to come to my ultrasound? So what if she didn't text me for days afterwards to see how it went? So what if now she's giving me some thirdhand thrift store blanket…" I cast said blanket a derisive look. "That somebody's distant aunt knit them twenty years ago, probably not knowing it wouldn't be considered important enough to become a keepsake?"

"Secondhand, not thirdhand." Rhiannon corrects me without meeting my eye.

I make sure my apology is extra fake sounding. "Oh, excuse me—"

"And it wasn't somebody's aunt who knit it. It was my grandmother. For me."

The revelation hits me like a full force punch to the chest.

This time my apologetic tone is heartbreakingly genuine. "Rhiannon I—"

Rhiannon pushes out from the table, her chair legs scraping loudly.

I think she's going to storm out in a well-deserved huff, but instead she proves once again how she's the bigger person in this argument, not to mention in our relationship as a whole.

She speaks in a measured, even tone that nonetheless burns through my skin like acid.

"Everyone, sorry to cut the party short, but I think Poppy and I should head back to my place now and finish this conversation in private."

Mary takes point on being the gracious host. "Of course. Take all the time you need, girls."

"I hope you work it out between you," Louise puts in helpfully.

Neither Rhiannon nor I can bring ourselves to answer her.

Chapter Twenty-Two

The walk to Rhiannon's apartment is as short a distance as ever, but the time it takes to get there feels like a fucking eternity.

We don't walk there together. Rhiannon paces ahead of me while I trail behind, silent and sorry and unsure of what the hell just happened or what's to come.

When we finally make it, Rhiannon stabs her key into the lock and pushes through her building's door angrily. I'm horribly reminded of my first time here, the way she'd held the door open for me, chivalrous for a fleeting moment before forgetting herself bounding up the stairs ahead of me—so nervous and excited to have me here with her that she didn't realize she'd left me behind.

Then all the times after, when we'd raced each other

up these stairs hand in hand, both of us desperate to get through her door and into her bed.

Now we march up them with the simmering, practiced silence of people used to fighting in apartments where neighbors can overhear.

This is our first fight. We should be that couple who, in the heat of the moment, forget our surroundings and scream all the way through the building before we come to our senses.

But no. We fight like a couple who should have broken up years ago, like it's our thousandth fight and through dedicated practice we've perfected our technique.

We reach the privacy of Rhiannon's apartment, blissfully/horrifyingly free of interfering roommates. Rhiannon storms in and I fall over the threshold after her, tripping all over myself literally and figuratively.

As soon as the door's closed behind us: "Rhiannon, I—"

Rhiannon rounds on me, hands clenched into fists and tears in the corners of her eyes.

I've never seen her lose her cool like this. Not when we had heavy conversations, not when we had awkward misunderstandings, not even when she nearly fainted at the sight of her own blood.

Rhiannon is *angry*. At me. So angry she's shaking with it.

I'm not afraid of that anger, like I would be with some of my exes in this state.

I'm hurting for her.

So I swallow all my apologies and explanations and excuses and grievances and just…let her speak.

In that critical moment, she says: "It was nothing, okay?"

What?

She announces it like it's some earthshaking revelation, but I'm not following. As distraught as she is, she at least notices that fact.

Sighing, she tries again, more calm and clear this time.

"The day of your ultrasound. I said I was busy, but I was...doing nothing."

Somehow, I'm not surprised. It's like I instinctively knew all along. She hadn't even bothered to come up with an excuse beyond the fact that she was busy, and I didn't even *attempt* to get more information out of her than that. Subconsciously protecting myself from the humiliation of falling for deeper lies, maybe.

"When I was texting you that I wished I could be there with you, I was here sitting on my couch watching that K-Drama you got me addicted to."

I swallow thickly. "But...why?"

Rhiannon's been a little hot and cold my whole pregnancy. I get it. Our relationship is so new, and we should be free to enjoy our life-consuming infatuation, but instead there's a Big Scary Commitment hanging overhead and constantly killing our buzz.

But we've talked about all that! She's been to one of my ultrasounds already, for Christ's sake! I thought we were cool!

I cross my arms. "Well?"

"I just... I guess I thought that if I was available to come with you again, then you wouldn't have even bothered to try including your weird ex."

"Because me including him obviously worked out *so* well…"

Rhiannon flinches. "Okay, so I clearly gave him too much credit when I made my plan. But in my defense? Dude's obviously a bit of a loser and a bit too *m'lady* for my tastes, but he doesn't seem like a *bad guy*, either."

I sigh heavily, dropping onto Rhiannon's couch. I feel completely exhausted suddenly. And my feet are pulsing with the pressure of being squished into these recently-too-small shoes. "He really isn't a bad guy."

"Exactly. And maybe I should have considered the high possibility of him flaking on you, but my heart was still in the right place." She sits down on the couch next to me, far enough away that we can't accidentally touch one another. "I just thought…if the sperm donor's not some abusing shithead, why not at least try and include him? Just because you don't *like* him doesn't necessarily mean he can't or shouldn't be a part of the kid's life in some capacity."

My regret and sympathy turn to disgust in an instant. "I didn't realize you were secretly one of those 'CHILDREN NEED A MOTHER AND A FATHER' homophobic bumper sticker types."

As soon as it's out of my mouth, I regret it. It's a low blow. Completely uncalled for and unfair, especially to a lesbian.

Rhiannon's nostrils flare, her jaw set. "You don't mean that."

"You're right. I don't. Sorry."

Rhiannon smiles wanly in recognition of my apology and I realize: she didn't come here to fight dirty; she came here to clear the air. Make things right. "Kids don't *need* a mother and a father. They don't *need* the so-called traditional nuclear family at all. But if the option's there? Why not?

"Hell, not even just for the kid's benefit! But for you, too! You're going to need so much support in the next few months, way more support than you realize now, and I...

"I just don't want to be your reason for not even trying to make things work between you and the kid's dad."

She finishes with a sigh. The whole frantic speech, she hasn't looked up from her knees once.

I turn toward her, grab her by the shoulder and force her to make eye contact with me.

"So *tell* me that? Don't just lie to me and ghost me and try to manipulate me into having him there! That's not your call!"

Rhiannon winces.

"It was my *choice* to tell him about the pregnancy. It was my *choice* to invite him to the ultrasound. I just can't fucking believe you of all people would try and pull my fucking strings like that!" I'm so upset right now I'm giving myself a goddamn headache. "Whether I include him or not... I won't say it's none of your business because as far as I know you're still my girlfriend...but it's definitely not your fucking call!"

"I know it's not!" Rhiannon shouts. "I fucking know that, okay? And I felt like shit for doing what I did, but I did it anyway! I had to do *something*!" She scrubs her hands over her face in frustration. Rakes them through her hair. "You need someone to support you, Poppy, and it was either him or your mother and I went for the lesser of two evils."

"Him or my mother? No one else?" My anger washes out of me, leaving me dizzy and heartbroken.

"You have a cool auntie or something I don't know about? Fine, call her up. Literally, call anyone up!"

Here it comes.

"Anyone but me!"

I blink back the tears burning in my eyes. "Is it that bad? Am I really pressuring you that much? I know you've been a little hesitant to get too involved, and I tried to respect that. I thought I *was* respecting—"

"It's nothing you did, Poppy. It's really nothing. It's me. I just like you *so* much and I keep giving myself these pep talks about being levelheaded and cool about all this, but then I see you and I get all love-dumb and forget the promises I made myself and I…" She turns away. "I just keep getting caught up in it all. Giving up ground in a game of tug-of-war where you're not even pulling on your end of the rope.

"I say I wanna be realistic about this and maintain at least some emotional distance from this baby, support you in this pregnancy without making any rash promises, and then I go and give you my fucking heirloom baby blanket."

My mouth quirks. "That *was* a bit of a mixed signal." I reach out tentatively. Brush my fingertips across the back of her hand in question.

She takes my hand in her own with a watery laugh. "Aaaaaand now I'm feeling like I probably should have just told you all that in the first place, huh?"

"Would likely have worked out better for the both of us than you trying to orchestrate my life for me behind the scenes, yeah." I smile encouragingly at her. "But I get it. All this…it feels like it's snowballing out of control for me, too. It's scary and exciting and overwhelming all at the same time. And trust me, I know better than anyone how, um, not ideal the timing is."

Rhiannon's head drops. "I just don't know what the hell I'm doing. I try to act like I have it all together, but I'm a complete fucking mess."

I rub my belly pointedly. "I know how that feels."

"I want to be with you, Poppy. And I think I even want to be a part of your baby's life, too? But I'm afraid of making that decision from a place of infatuation when I can't actually commit to it long term. And in the meantime, I'm afraid of you growing to need me too much. I'm afraid of *making* you need me. I want to support you, but I don't want you to depend on me for that support."

"I'd never make you do something you were uncomfortable with, Rhi. You can *always* say no."

"I know that. I know, I promise I know. But what if there's a time when I know I should say no, but I don't? What if I say yes when I know I can't follow through? Look, I was raised by two well-meaning but ultimately absent parents. It wasn't their fault they had to work eighty-hour weeks just to make ends meet, but if I had a nickel for every time they promised me they'd be there for a track-and-field meet or help me with a science project then didn't show? Well, let's just say they wouldn't have *needed* to work so much."

How disappointed must she have felt? Over and over and over, all through her childhood years. But what's even worse is imagining that one fateful time she suddenly *stopped* feeling that way. No wonder she's so afraid to perpetuate that cycle. "Rhi, I'm sorry."

True to form, she flaps a hand at me dismissively. "Don't be. They love me, and they supported me as best as they could. And I did have Nana. That tough old bird showed up to *everything*, knitting bag in hand. Especially the stuff I would have rathered she didn't."

"Let me guess, you got called into the principal's office for a lot of 'parent teacher conferences'?"

"Babe, I went to Catholic school. It was pretty much daily dress code violations from freshman year on." She rubs her chin thoughtfully. "Although there was that one time I got wrote up for bringing 'pornographic literature' to school, aka the translated works of Sappho."

It's hard not to smile, picturing rebellious baby queer Rhiannon facing off with a nun over two-thousand-year-old lesbian poetry. But at the time there can't have been much for Rhiannon to smile about. "Sounds like a long few years."

"It was. But I like to think I knew what I was getting into for a lot of it. And hey, last I heard they have a GSA there now, so I'm pretty sure Sappho and I won in the end."

"I was always too micro-managed to get in any kind of trouble," I say. "Calling my mother a 'helicopter parent' would be an insult to helicopters everywhere."

Rhiannon's eyes widen in mock disbelief. "Your mother? Overbearing and controlling? I don't believe it."

"No wonder I have no idea how to do things for my-self or make it on my own." I slump in defeat. "She never gave me the chance to learn! Hell, if she had her way, she'd probably do all my prenatal care herself. Stick the epidural in my spine, too."

"Why stop there? Maybe she can breastfeed your baby."

Alas, Rhiannon's noble effort at lightening the mood has the opposite effect on me. "Ugh, maybe the reason you're so hesitant to get too involved with me is because some part of you rightfully senses that if you do, I'll expect you to take over piloting that helicopter?"

"Whoa, whoa, whoa. Poppy! Give yourself *some* credit. I've seen your apartment. You're hardly on the level of those guys who go straight from Mommy washing all their laun-dry to wifey taking over."

"Nope, that would be Jake. I honestly have no idea how he hasn't starved to death since we broke up. Guy couldn't even be trusted to microwave a frozen dinner."

Rhiannon touches my arm tentatively. "I'm really sorry he didn't show."

I let out a cleansing sigh. "Yeah, me too."

"I never wanted to make you feel abandoned like that."

"And I never wanted to make *you* feel like you had to be on call for me 24/7."

"Surely there has to be a middle ground between Jake who never shows and your mom who barges in whether you want her there or not."

"A healthy, balanced relationship? I don't know her."

We both laugh, the sound nervous and fragile and relieved. We collapse against each other, wrap ourselves up in each other, hold each other...fall still.

I stare up at the ceiling. "If there *is* a middle ground, I want us to find it...together."

"I want that, too. I really do want to be there for you, Poppy. I *like* being there for you. It's like I'm a knight and you're my princess." As soon as she says it, she buries her face in my shoulder, embarrassed.

"Wow, you really just said that aloud. I mean, I always got a chivalry kink vibe from you, but you just laid it out there, huh?" I give her a comforting pat. "But can I be serious for a second? I think I finally get where you're coming from."

"Oh?"

"Yeah. You want to be there for me, but unlike Jake you understand what that commitment really *means*. The work and sacrifice it takes to follow through. And how much it hurts when you don't. It's too much to ask of one person, especially when the relationship is so new."

"Even with a girlfriend as great and multitalented as me," Rhiannon agrees.

"You can't be expected to serve as a one-woman support system for me, but we've now learned that Jake can't be depended on to step up when you can't."

"And your mother can't be trusted to step *back*."

"Right. So how about this? I'll find someone else. Someone we can both trust to be there for me. I'd say Tracy from work, but the truth is she's my co-worker, not my friend, and she's got her own shit going on. I really don't think it'd be right to put her on the spot like that. My sister, maybe? Or Grace? I'm not sure yet, but I'll figure it out." I poke her for emphasis. "That's 'I', as in me, as in this is *my* responsibility, not just another thing I'm going to ultimately dump on you. Or let you pick up like you insist on carrying my bag."

"Thank you, Poppy. That means a lot. And I'll be sure to be up front with you the next time this all starts to feel scary and too much."

I clear my throat. "So um, speaking of asking too much of you…is this a bad time to tell you my sister's having a gender reveal party and I'd really, *really* appreciate it if you could come along?"

Chapter Twenty-Three

I stand and watch as Rhiannon holds up various ties to the collar of her floral button-up shirt, biting her lip in indecision.

Turquoise tie. Plaid tie. Eye-searing floral. Vintage knitted wool. Back to turquoise again.

I'm not sure how she's ever gonna find one that doesn't clash with her shirt's busy, garish print of tiny multicolored roses, but I'm keeping that to myself.

After all, I'm the one who used the maternity store gift card my mother gave me to purchase a one-two punch "not for fat girls" formfitting bodycon dress in horizontal stripes.

Which I look amazing in, by the way, but even if I didn't, it would be worth it just for the epic *fuck you* to my mother that it represents.

"You could always skip the tie," I finally say.

"Nuh-uh." Back to the plaid tie again. "If there's ever a time where going full butch dandy isn't optional, it's a fucking genital—I mean *gender*—reveal party."

Fucking gender reveal party. She keeps calling it that, never missing the invective.

Which, normally I'd be right there with her—doubly so if it involves deadly, wildfire-causing pyrotechnics—but now that it's my sister's party...

Maybe it's because Iris is family that I think she's the exception. Maybe it's because after two miscarriages I think she deserves to celebrate her baby in whatever hokey way she sees fit.

But whatever. That's my hang-up, not Rhiannon's, and it's not like Rhiannon doesn't have completely valid reasons to think the whole concept of a pink and blue ceremony enshrining prescriptive gender roles is, well, *the worst.*

"The fucking gender reveal party where you're meeting my family—who still refuse to believe I'm not straight by the way—for the first time. Don't forget that part."

Rhiannon's reflection smirks at me in commiseration. "Oh trust me, I haven't forgotten. And I *fully* intend on testing how deep their denial goes."

I sidle up closer behind her, notching my belly against the small of her back and pressing my face to her collar. "Mmm, I love it when you talk dirty to me." I make a reach for her selection of ties, picking one up and handing it to her. "And in that case, go with the floral on floral."

Her deft, long-fingered hands make quick work of the

tie, and I watch in appreciation as she tightens it at the base of her throat with practiced confidence.

Part of me wants to reach out and straighten it, just to touch her, but the truth is, it's in perfect alignment already.

And besides, I don't need an excuse.

I reach around to smooth my hands over the shoulder seams of her shirt, savoring the interplay of crisp straight cotton and softly rounded shoulder bone.

Rhiannon cups her hands over mine, scrutinizing her reflection. "Okay. I'm ready. For better or worse."

"You don't *have* to come."

"Thanks for the out, but yes, I do." Her tone is no less tense than before, but she still tries for a comforting smile. "The last thing you need right now is to have your promised girlfriend no-show to a family event. You'll *never* convince them you're really queer then!"

My answering laugh is still a little uneasy. "Yeah. As it is they'll probably still be calling us 'such good friends' even as we're tongue kissing right under their noses."

Rhiannon turns around to face me, draping her arms over my shoulders. "Can I be blunt for a second? Fuck your family, honestly."

I stiffen, pulling away from her. "They're not all that bad."

"Oh? You could have fooled me," Rhiannon snaps. "Let's see, your mother shames you for everything, from the choices you make right down to your body size and how you clothe it. According to your own admission, your whole damn family refuses to accept you're bi and have a girlfriend, like if they just ignore it, it'll go away. And now your sister is throwing a whole-ass party just to tell a bunch of her snooty friends whether her baby has a dick or a vagina, probably while forcing a bunch of outdated gender stereotypes on them before they're even born?"

"Okay but—"

"What is with their like…*sick need* to control everything and everyone? Is it a rich people thing? Don't you ever want to tell them to just butt the fuck out?"

"Are you even gonna be able to make nice with them today? Not that they don't deserve the shit-talking I'm sure you could give them, but I'd really rather save those particular fireworks for a time when it'll ruin my mother's day instead of my sister's."

Rhiannon smooths her hair over her head and puts out her hands in an unintentional but pitch-perfect imitation of that one Hades reaction gif. "I'm fine. I'm cool. Promise. I work in customer service, remember? I'll just spend the next few hours acting like they all just demanded to speak with my manager."

My phone buzzes. "Oh, the car's here. Last chance to back out."

Rhiannon grimly cracks her neck. "Nope, we're doing this."

"Just try and remember this is supposed to be party? And who knows. Maybe they'll surprise us by not being terrible…for once," I say, although my tone doesn't exactly sell the part where I believe it. "And if they aren't, we can always ruin Thanksgiving in revenge." *If you still want to be with me by Thanksgiving.*

* * *

When we pull into the driveway, my mother and sister are both waiting outside for us.

Ostensibly to greet us personally, but more likely running interference before we get to their guests. Making sure for themselves that we're going to be on our best behavior.

"This is it," I say to Rhiannon. "You ready?"

Rhiannon stares back at me matter-of-factly. "Are *you*?"

I fussily smooth the fabric of my belted coat over my belly. "You're not the only one with years of practice faking agreeableness."

"She says, having specifically chosen her outfit this morning to ruffle her mother's feathers…"

"Touché."

As my mother gets closer, Rhiannon leaps into action, jumping out her side of the vehicle and flat-out *running* to open my door for me before my mother gets there first.

Which she does, and—as my mother stands there looking gobsmacked—bends forward with a flourish to offer me a chivalrous hand up.

"Thank you, dear," I say, putting on my best proper little rich girl voice and catching my mother's eye over Rhiannon's shoulder as I lever myself out of the car.

"Think nothing of it, my little…berry…scone…" As she scrambles for a suitably highbrowed pet name, Rhiannon's mouth twitches in suppressed laughter.

Little berry scone?

I'm so going to have to razz her for that one.

Later.

For now, I school my face into a suitably I-mean-business

expression, pointedly take Rhiannon by the hand and turn with her to face my mother as a united front.

Deep breath. "Mom, Iris, this is Rhiannon. My *girl-friend*."

"Hey," Rhiannon says, gruffly, and holds up a hand in greeting.

Yep, definitely going extra butch for the benefit of my family. As if she's just daring them to do the mental gymnastics it will take to convince themselves she—no, *either of us*—is straight.

My mother's lip very nearly curls, but then her perfect hostess instincts kick in. "Welcome to our home, Rhiannon. We're so glad you could join us to celebrate *Iris's special day*."

Underneath the welcome, an unspoken warning: "Don't you dare pull the spotlight off her with any attention grabbing antics…like insisting on having your relationship recognized or acknowledged for what it is."

I hear her loud and clear. I'm sure Rhiannon does, too, but good fucking luck to my mom if she thinks it's gonna make any kind of difference.

Iris steps forward, breaking our standoff with a beaming smile, and hugs us both. "Rhiannon! It's so nice to meet you, finally! And Poppy, you look great!"

"You too," I say, without artifice. Fresh manicure, fresh blowout, and I bet under those chic little booties *her* ankles aren't swollen to twice their normal size.

Iris steers us back toward the house. "Let's get you two out of this cold! I want to hear about how you met!"

My mother visibly bristles, hostess etiquette be damned.

"Oh Iris, you're too gracious. I'm sure there will be plenty of time for that after our other guests have left, don't you think? They're here to celebrate you and your baby, not..."

I cut my mother off, unable to stomach whatever withering euphemism she's about to use. "It's cool, there's not much to tell anyway. Rhiannon is a clinic escort at the Planned Parenthood I go to."

My mother stops up short, her mouth falling open in unvarnished stupefied shock.

Rhiannon, playing it off like nothing, adds, "I also run our stitch n' bitch."

"Oh, so you're the one dragging my sister kicking and screaming to actually finish what she starts for once?" Iris says it lightly, like she means it as a harmless little jab, but it stabs through me all the same.

Nonetheless, I'm prepared to laugh it off the way I always do, but this time Rhiannon saves me the indignity.

"No dragging necessary, actually. Poppy's perfectly capable of seeing things through...*if* they're actually worth the effort."

My sister flushes. "R-right. Good. Of course!"

"She's already done mitts and booties for the bun in her oven. And now she's started on her first miniature sweater..."

Iris doesn't take long to find an excuse to get away from us after that, and our mother, predictably, chases after her.

With a pang of guilt, I follow Rhiannon in the opposite direction toward the refreshments table, where pink and blue frosted Magnolia Bakery cupcakes, towers of pink and blue macarons, and even matching twin crystal bowls of pink and blue punch, await.

Rhiannon shamelessly loads up her plate, ignoring the side-eyes of my sister's rich guests.

"So I take it your sister's been sitting pretty on that pedestal of hers for a while, huh?"

"Wh-what? What makes you say *that*?" I'm lucky I'm too afraid to eat in front of these people, or else I'd probably have choked on whatever I was chewing just then.

Rhiannon scoffs. "The way she dishes it out, but she can't take it?" She stuffs a macaron into her mouth in one angry bite. Continues as she chews, "Sure she acts all bubbly and sweet, but then she goes straight for the low blow on you! Giggling the whole damn time, no less!"

"That's not—"

"But sure, as soon as I call her out on her bullshit, serve her a spoonful of her own syrupy poison, she runs off like a damsel with your mother in tow!"

"She didn't mean it to be mean. I'm sure she didn't! I doubt she knows—"

"Okay, fine. Maybe she didn't know...before. But she knows *now*. And a better person would take this opportunity to actually apologize and make amends, not turn around and act like the victim! I'm just saying. Princess Iris needs a reality check!"

Someone nearby, overhearing, casts a horrified look at us over her shoulder.

I steer Rhiannon away from the table, hissing, "Lower your voice!"

"What, now you're suddenly on their side?" Rhiannon

practically digs her heels in as I push her to a less crowded corner of my parents' living room. "Against yourself, no less?"

I tighten my hands into fists, struggling for a response. "No, but—"

But what? Shouldn't I feel good that Rhiannon is defending me so fiercely? Aren't I the one who's spent the last few months of our relationship constantly complaining about how they treat me? Why do I suddenly feel so damn conflicted?

Rhiannon either doesn't notice or doesn't care about my inner struggle, barrelling forward with her speech regardless. "I get it, Poppy. The whole world tells you that no matter how they treat you, you have to put your family first, above everything, even yourself. But that's not true!"

The longer she speaks, though, the more she takes notice of my reaction. The way I'm practically squirming in visceral discomfort at her display.

"I just…know you deserve better than this, dammit!" With that last-ditch justification, she swallows thickly. "But now's not the time or the place for this conversation, is it?"

I look around us, where my sister and mother's guests are all milling around, studiously *not* looking at us. "Y'think?"

She slumps guiltily. "And here I am, playing the white knight, coming to your defense without even considering whether that's what you want or need from me right now." With a sorry smile, she sweeps a strand of my hair behind my ear. "I'm sorry, Poppy. I completely overstepped. Can you forgive me?"

"Your heart, as always, was in the right place," I relent.

"But do you think maybe we can go the rest of the party without making unnecessary trouble? I accept your presence here is gonna rock this boat automatically, but that doesn't mean we have to turn this whole shindig into an episode of *Maury*."

"Aw, and here I was hoping instead of cutting a cake or whatever, we'd be tearing into a paternity test results envelope!" She laughs at her own joke, then notices the crowd of scandalized stares all around us. "Uh, not that the results would be in question, obviously!"

I sigh and shake my head. "Nice save."

The people around us, rolling their eyes, all return to their conversations.

Once again, Rhiannon has narrowly avoided crisis by managing to smooth things over.

For now.

Chapter Twenty-Four

This isn't that hard. I've done it a thousand times before.

Sort of.

More or less.

Rhiannon in tow, I circulate my sister's party, shaking hands and making small talk.

Or trying to, at least. Mostly, I just get grilled.

About my pregnancy. About Rhiannon.

A thousand probing questions.

"So it's true? You're expecting, too?"

"And you…know who the father is, I hope?"

"You look…different. Your face is rounder."

"Have you gained weight?"

"'Eating for two' is just an expression you know!"

"You're lucky your sister doesn't mind sharing the spotlight!"

"So how far along are *you*?"

"And Rhiannon, you're Poppy's…friend?"

"Poppy's…p…artner?"

"That's a pretty big commitment, are you sure you know what you're getting into, little lady?"

"Especially with this one! Where was it you were working again, Poppy?"

"And how's the health insurance there?"

"You're not expecting your parents to foot the hospital bill, are you now?"

"So Rhiannon, does this make you the baby's daddy?"

"So I suppose you two are hoping for a girl? I imagine any son you had would grow up confused…"

"Really, now. I know of plenty of lesbian couples raising children together!"

It's all so invasive, so presumptuous, I'd almost prefer to run a gauntlet of strangers fondling my pregnant belly.

But I weather it all. Smile and nod and answer their questions without sarcasm or venom.

Refusing to ruin my sister's special day by making a scene.

Rhiannon, for her part, doesn't say much at all.

If you don't have anything nice to say…

She just grimace/smiles her way across the party, her grip on my hand periodically tightening as an outlet for her suppressed rage.

When we've finally made the rounds, I lead her out into a nearby empty hallway to decompress. Not that I couldn't use some space away, myself, but Rhiannon?

She looks ragged. Exhausted. Which, considering the nature of her volunteer work, says a lot.

"Bet you're wishing for that big pink umbrella right now, huh?" I try to joke, but Rhiannon rounds on me with a cornered snarl.

"I'm *wishing* to be around people who aren't such blatant fucking assholes!" She seethes.

"Really, I'm not that bothered…"

"Good for you, Poppy! Because I *am* bothered! I'm bothered a lot!"

"Didn't we just decide you weren't going to get all offended on my behalf without my permission?"

"Offended on your behalf? I'm offended on my *own* behalf! Do you even hear half of what these people are saying to us right now? Or are you just immune to it after being exposed your whole life?"

Shit. Talk about completely neglecting to consider how everything today might affect her. I was so caught up in my own hurt feelings, I straight up forgot that she was on the receiving end of it, too.

She half paces away from me. Turns around abruptly and comes back again.

"You know what, I need some air. You coming?"

Just then, Iris strides in looking flustered, with a decorative cake knife in one hand. "Oh Poppy! There you are! We're just about to cut the cake! You ready?"

I look to Rhiannon, already halfway through the foyer.

Look to my sister, who's obviously anxious to return to her party…with her little sister at her side.

The front door slams.

★ ★ ★

The cake cutting is further delayed by the disappearance of my mother, who—rather unlike herself—has managed to choose the world's worst moment to go AWOL from the party she's hosting.

"I'm so sorry, everyone, I swear my mother was just here…" Iris, standing next to her three-tier cake at the head of the room, does her best to put her buckets of charm to use, but even she looks awkward as more time passes. "I'd go ahead and cut this amazing Insta-worthy cake without her, but she was just so excited for the big pink or blue reveal!" She smiles and laughs, but I can almost hear her inner voice: *This whole circus was her damn idea and now she's not even here, leaving me standing around like an idiot.*

Or at least, that's what I'd be thinking if it were me. Iris has never seemed quite as put out by our mother's expectations as I always was.

Maybe because she actually managed to meet them the majority of the time.

As they always do when it comes to Iris, resentment and empathy get all mixed up, curdling like that time I put milk in Rhiannon's raspberry tea.

She shifts from foot to foot, smile growing more and more strained, and I imagine she's split between trying to look calm when she wants to explode, and trying to hold that ribbon-wrapped cake knife in a such a way that it won't inadvertently look like a weapon in all those identical *Still waiting to find out what it will be!* photos her guests are taking.

It's unbearable.

And as for me, I once again find myself torn between my family and Rhiannon.

Split between loyalty to my sister, who needs me here for support especially now that things have turned tense, and my growing anxiety that every moment wasted standing around here is another moment I could be patching things up with Rhiannon outside.

If she's still here at all, that is.

I rub my temples, feeling the first rumblings of what will probably be a *massive* stress headache.

The room feels too small, too close, too crowded.

All these people I don't even like, who don't even like me.

My sister, having to share the spotlight.

My mother, having to pretend to be happy for me even as I embarrass her.

Rhiannon, who couldn't stand another moment of any of it.

Who stopped just short of practically begging me to leave with her.

Nobody wants me here. I don't want to *be* here.

A wave of dizziness hits me head-on and I realize I'm about to have a panic attack.

I spin in place, looking for an opening to escape through, but there are party guests surrounding me on all sides.

I try to push through them, but find myself listing into them and rebounding away again, instead.

"Rhiannon…" I mutter, unable to manage a more eloquent explanation or apology. "Fresh air…"

Clutching my forehead, I feel a slick of cold sweat, my bangs plastered down to my face.

My heart thrums in my chest, fast and shallow and *wrong*. *I'm going to die. I need to get out of here. I'm dying already.*

"Excuse me, excuse..."

"Poppy? Are you okay?"

I turn, but with all these white floating blobs in the way, I can't make out the face of whoever called after me. *Rhiannon?*

No, my sister. She's chased after me through the crowd, has her hand clasped around my shoulder in concern.

"Somebody get our mother!" she shouts in a hoarse voice. I've never heard her so...ill-composed before. Worried. No, scared.

"Mom?" I call out, mirroring the panic in her voice. My voice sounds so thin and small, like the child I'll always be.

Chapter Twenty-Five

I wake up in hospital, an IV in my hand and my mother by my side.

As soon as I see her, I flinch, and I realize it's because I'm genuinely expecting her to lecture me for ruining Iris's big gender reveal.

But then I notice the look of concern on her face, the smudges of mascara under her eyes, the fact that she's wearing the same rumpled outfit as she was at the party.

She's actually worried about me.

"Oh Poppy, thank God!" She clutches my hand tightly. "I *knew* you couldn't be getting an appropriate standard of care at some sliding-scale clinic!"

Theeeere we go.

I sigh and collapse back into my pillow. "What happened?"

"You have pre-eclampsia. Not surprising, considering your weight and your lifestyle." I flinch again, too wrung out and exhausted to do anything other than weather her words. "Don't they check your urine for protein during whatever passes for prenatal appointments at that place?"

"Planned Parenthood, you mean? Believe it or not, I have a pee test every time I'm there. You make it sound like I'm going to some roadside snake oil salesman..."

"Well, compared to your *sister's* ob-gyn..."

"The one who oversaw her multiple miscarriages, you mean?"

My mother recoils as if I've slapped her, and I regret my words immediately.

"S-sorry," I manage to say.

"You've had a stressful ordeal. I'm sure you're not quite in your right mind just yet."

More like backed into a corner like a helpless, hissing animal.

Pre-eclampsia. I've read all about it in all the usual "fear-mongering, but make it upbeat" pregnancy books. One of the biggest, baddest freak pregnancy complications, nobody's quite sure why it happens, although I'm sure there's a long line of doctors just salivating at the possibility of blaming it on my weight.

It can happen to anyone, anytime, often with little to no advance warning.

High blood pressure. Seizures and stroke. Organ failure. Miscarriage and stillbirth. Maternal death.

I can't bluff my way out of this one.

"So what now?" I ask miserably.

"Well, the only surefire treatment is to deliver the baby, but you're not far enough along yet for that." My mother's expression suddenly seems...triumphant? "Which leaves no other alternatives but close observation and bed rest until you are."

The threatening tone she uses when she mentions bed rest is not at all reassuring, but I try not to let it get to me.

Outwardly, at least.

"Bed rest," I repeat, but with all the false confidence I can muster. "Okay. I can handle that."

My groggy mind immediately goes to work, problem solving.

I have lots of knitting to work on in bed, lots of novels and Netflix to catch up on to occupy my time, at least. My combined sick time and long-term disability coverage through my work should be enough to keep me afloat money-wise... I think? I might need to consult Tracy's expertise on that one. She's worked there longer, after all. I can order my meals from a gig economy delivery driver. As for cleaning and laundry and driving me to my undoubtedly more frequent prenatal appointments, I'm sure *someone* can stop by and help?

Just...maybe not Rhiannon, considering everything that's gone down between us.

Or Jake.

Or my sister.

My mother raises her eyebrows. "Bed rest, Poppy. Maybe *now* you'll stop being so knee-jerk resistant to the idea of moving home with your family?"

I hate that she's not wrong. If ever there were a time

to lean on my family—even if it means submitting to my mother's control—now would be that time.

"You must be loving this."

"Poppy!" I can't tell if my mother is genuinely hurt by my cruelty, or just offended by my disobedience. Which makes it really hard to determine whether I should feel guilty or justified.

Both at once turns out to be a heady combination.

"What! It's true, isn't it?" I tighten my fists around my blankets. "I didn't need you before, but now I'm in a position where you think I do. You can wait on me hand and foot like I'm a helpless little girl, and all the while you can guilt trip me and decide what I eat and control who's allowed to visit and transfer my prenatal care to a doctor you approve of, probably one of your personal friends, so you can influence them, too..." I take a deep breath. "And then after I deliver the baby, when I'm free to leave, I won't. Because you're counting on me playing the role of the lazy millennial who'd rather just stick with the comfort of the status quo versus trying to move out while I've got a newborn to care for. And the longer I stay, the less likely I'll be to leave, is that it?"

My mother, who has shown remarkable restraint in listening to all of this in quiet, simmering rage, finally takes her turn to speak. "What kind of diabolical super villain do you take me for, Poppy? Do you even hear yourself? These are the rants of a paranoid schizophrenic!"

I let out a hysterical laugh. "Gaslighting! Why am I not surprised?"

My mother sets her jaw. Stands. Doesn't meet my eyes.

"A lesser woman would tell you 'Have things your way' and retract any offer of future help." Her voice is soft and measured, a portrait of perfect motherhood. Unfairly tested, but still patient. Like a saint. "But I'm not that woman. Your desperation for unearned, premature independence has you lashing out, saying hurtful things."

I want to fight back, argue my case, but interrupting her now would only prove her point.

"I understand, even if I think it's shortsighted and foolish. So I'll walk away. I'll be the bigger person and let you try to do this on your own. Let the fledgling leave the nest. And when you're ready to admit defeat, my door will still be open. Because I'm your mother, and that's what mothers do. One day, you'll realize that, too."

A couple of days and one massive hospital bill later, I make my "triumphant" return to my apartment.

I should be proud of myself for successfully turning my mother away and enforcing my boundaries at last, but mostly I feel like shit.

I'm wearing the wrinkled dress from Iris's party, returned to me in a sketchy plastic bag when I was discharged. There's a load of dirty dishes in the sink that have gone moldy during my unexpected absence. The floor is an eruption of clean and dirty laundry, mixed together just enough that even the clean stuff probably stinks. My knitting lies abandoned on the couch right where I left it, still plagued by the dropped stitch I was waiting on Rhiannon to help me fix.

And I'm supposed to be on bed rest.

I hobble over to my bed, strip naked, select the nearest Schrödinger's musty floor shirt to wear, and climb in.

At least all alone nobody has to see me like this.

Then the front door buzzer for my apartment rings.

Of course.

I consider ignoring it at first, but considering all the help I'm going to need over the coming weeks, that seems a little counterproductive.

Just as long as it's not my mother, right and ready to break out the big *I told you so* because I couldn't last twelve hours without her.

With trepidation, I answer: "Who is it?"

The intercom crackles and spits out: "It's Grace!"

"And Louise!"

"And Mary!"

"And uh, me. I'm assuming you know who I am," Damian's baritone finishes.

Ungrateful piece of shit that I am, all I'm hearing is *But no Rhiannon.*

"Poppy?"

I try to summon up a tone that makes me sound a little less like the Before in a depression med commercial.

Side effects may include selfish and self-centered behavior and attitudes, pushing away everyone who loves you, living in filth, and the overwhelming need to just fucking give up entirely.

"S-sorry! Come in!"

I have just enough time to pull on a pair of maternity leggings before there's a knock at my door. In they come, the entirety of my stitch n' bitch minus one, crowding my tiny apartment to the point of claustrophobia.

Before any one of us even says hello, Mary barks out, "Grace, laundry. Damian, dishes. Louise—"

"Wait, hold on, what's going on? What are you guys doing here?" I look around me in panicked shame.

Louise takes my hands in hers with an earnest look. "We came to bring you some more knitting!"

"But that clearly isn't the priority now," Mary announces.

Is that disgust in her voice, or am I projecting?

"It's not *that* bad," I protest.

Who do they think they are, barging in here and trying to take over like this?

"There's no cat litter smell, so you're a step ahead of me, at least," Louise comforts me...or tries to, anyway.

Grace, with an honest to God pair of my dirty panties in her hands, pauses in her chore to lecture kindly: "It's okay to ask for help, Poppy. Rhiannon told us your situation."

"She did what?" I shriek. "What situation?"

"The pre-eclampsia. Taisha's mom had it. Nearly died, too. Taisha had to be delivered three weeks early." Damian clamps his lips shut, backtracking: "Not that you should be worried! They're both totally fine now. Another win for modern medicine!"

Grace and Louise both rush to my side.

"You'll be just fine," Grace assures me.

"I bet you even carry baby to term!" Louise coos.

But it's not the pre-eclampsia that's got me quaking.

It's the fact that Rhiannon *knew*!

Bad enough that she hadn't called for days after we lost track of each other at the party, but to do it knowing I was sick and had been hospitalized?

It feels like a stab to my heart.

"I should lie down," I say.

"Yes, yes you should. Come on, I'll help you to your bed." Grace takes me by the elbow, but I shake her off.

"No!" In my small, crowded apartment, my distressed shout seems ten times louder than I intended it to be.

Hearing it, they all...stop. Just stop.

It's so silent I can hear the slosh of water in the sink as Damian meekly sets down the dish he was washing.

I stare down at my feet, voice raw, but as close to calm as I can manage. "I don't need any help, okay? I need you all to leave."

"But we haven't even showed you the presents we knitted for you!" Louise reaches into her cat bag desperately. "As soon as we heard you were in hospital, we got right to work. I made you some slippers, and Mary made you—"

My calm act goes right out the window. "Slippers?! Don't you think that if I needed slippers I would just order some online or something? Amazon could have slippers at my door delivered by bike courier in two fucking hours!"

Louise flinches, but doesn't buckle. If anything, her voice gets even more cheerful. "Of course, but you know what knitters always say! You can't buy 'hand-knit with love' at a store!" She holds out the slippers to me in offering. Practically shoves them at me.

"Is 'hand-knit with love' going to pay this hospital bill? Is 'hand-knit with love' going to make sure this baby isn't born too early to breathe on their own? If you actually wanted to be helpful, you would..." I look around me, seeing them all frozen in place and staring at me with hurt in their eyes. Stopped right where they stood mid-apartment takeover.

Picking up my laundry. Washing my dishes. Cleaning out my fridge.

A humiliating uninvited intrusion, maybe, but an undeniably helpful one.

Damian does the disappointed father head shake.

All the righteous anger leaves me at once.

I drop onto the edge of my bed in exhausted defeat. "I'm putting the 'bitch' in 'stitch n' bitch' right now, aren't I?"

Louise raises a correcting finger. "Actually, the 'bitch' in 'stitch n' bitch' refers to the act of bitching, as in complaining and gossiping. The verb, not the noun."

Grace puts her hands on Louise's shoulders protectively. "Pretty sure she knows that, Louise."

Mary crosses her arms. "Pretty sure what she means to do is apologize."

"I'm sorry," I say, and even though I mean it, the timing makes it sound utterly forced. "It's just… Rhiannon…"

The explanation dies before it even starts. Just because I'm angry with Rhiannon, feeling betrayed and abandoned, doesn't mean I should be taking it out on them. Rhiannon and the stitch n' bitch may be one and the same in my mind, but that doesn't mean it's actually true.

But just the start of that sentence is enough to get people's backs up.

"What about her?" Grace challenges me head on. "Rhiannon and I were able to set aside *our* awkward situation for the sake of the group, so why can't you?"

Louise nods along, still clinging to her slippers. "Right!

Me and Mary, too. There was that time she tried to give me a card for that 'hoarding specialist' headshrink, just because I have a bigger stash of yarn than her..."

"It's more than yarn and you know it, Louise," Mary snaps.

"Okay, okay..." Damian steps in, putting out his hands.

Now it's Grace's turn to lash out. "Don't you pull that 'I'm the man here so I better keep the little ladies in check' shit with us, Damian! I swear, crafty men think they should be the kings of every group they grace with their presence."

"Give me a break." Damian's voice is the practiced calm of a man who knows that even the slightest expression of anger, justified or not, is a permanent mark against him. "It's you who puts me on a pedestal just for being a guy. Fawning over me like a man crocheting is as remarkable as a dog walking on its hind legs."

I watch helplessly as they turn on each other.

Because of me.

"You guys, stop!" I cry. "Just stop it, okay! Don't you see what's happening here? You had something so pure and so special, and then I came along and...and...poisoned it! Brought all my drama and bullshit to the group along with my project." Possessed by sudden conviction, I stand up and march over to the couch, to my half-knit baby cardigan and its dropped stitch. My most ambitious project to date. "Well not anymore! I quit the group!" I grab the cardigan up and yank it straight off the needles.

"Poppy, no!" someone shouts in genuine horror.

Like my knitting is a fucking hostage I've taken, or something.

In stubborn defiance, I take hold of both sides and *pull*.

Pull, until all my painstaking rows of stitches unravel into an unholy tangle, something as messy and confused as I feel. "You can tell Rhiannon—Miss Perfect, Miss Boundaries, Miss Above All This Drama—she can have the group to herself again! I quit!"

Nobody begs me to change my mind.

They all just leave.

Chapter Twenty-Six

Less than an hour later, Rhiannon arrives. Grace probably
called her from the damn hallway outside my door.

"Let me in," she tells me over the intercom, her voice
ice cold and in no mood to argue.

I'm in no mood, either. I let her into the building without a word.

She knocks on my door, which is exactly what I'd expect her to do.

Boundaries, she calls it. I call it keeping people at arm's
length, forcing them to remain a stranger whether either
of you wants more than that or not.

"It's unlocked," I call from my place in my bed, blankets yanked up to my nose. I roll so my back is facing the
door. So I don't have to look at her.

I hear her dusting her hands on her jeans. "So I see you're well on your way to being the disaster child your mother says you are."

Despite my intentions, I can't resist rising to that bait. I roll to face her furiously.

"And what do *you* know about what my mother says about me? What do you know about our relationship? About any of this?"

"Only what she told me herself." Rhiannon tucks her hands into her pockets.

I sit up, unable to mask my surprise. "She...talked to you?"

"At your sister's party. Yeah." The party she didn't want to go to in the first place. She doesn't say it aloud, but I can hear it in her voice.

"What did she say, exactly?"

"The same stuff she's probably been telling you your whole adult life, I imagine. That you've bit off more than you can chew. That you're making decisions without fully considering the consequences. That you know you're in too deep but you're too proud to admit it." Rhiannon pauses, adds, "That you need help, but that you'll refuse to *let* anyone help you until it's too late."

Out of the corner of my eye, I catch sight of my half-washed dishes, water gone cold... Right where Damian left them.

The shame and despair nearly swallow me whole. "And you believed her? What she said about me?"

"Of course I didn't. She's full of fucking shit." I almost laugh at that, but when Rhiannon doesn't even crack a smile, the sound dies in my throat. "It's all a transparent attempt to justify her sick, twisted need to infantilize and control you."

Sick? Twisted?

"That's still my mom you're talking about," I bite out, suddenly on the defensive. "She's an overbearing C–U–N–T but she still loves me and has my best interests at heart."

"Your best interests, huh? And did she have your best interests at heart when she very sincerely advised me to break up with you, that this whole bisexuality thing is just some belated rebellious phase, and that once that baby comes and you get some perspective, you'll go back to being—and I quote—'my normal girl again'?"

"She said that?"

"Yeah, she did. And don't try pretending you don't believe me, because I know you do. She may not have said it where you could hear, but you damn well know it's something she *would* say."

I can't argue with that logic, but that doesn't mean I'm going to give in. "Well, maybe she's right. She was right about me not being able to do this on my own. And she was right about the fact that when push came to shove, there would be nobody I could actually depend on." I will every word into a dagger, pointed right at Rhiannon's armored heart. "Nobody but *her*. And huh, look at that! Jake flakes on my ultrasound and when I leave the clinic, there she is. I wind up in the hospital with pre-eclampsia, and it's her at my bedside when I wake up!"

"I thought we went over that!" Rhiannon protests. "I

thought you understood why I needed to keep my distance."

"Oh, we went over it, all right. Over and over! But at some point you need to acknowledge there's 'taking it slow' and then there's 'spinning our wheels, going *nowhere*'."

"Just because we're not going at the speed you'd like doesn't mean we're going nowhere, Poppy."

"Then maybe it's time for both of us to admit we're just too far apart on this. Because I get it, Rhiannon. You don't want me depending on you. You want me to have realistic expectations about where our relationship is going and not get my hopes up. For my own good, you keep saying. To save me from disappointment." I swallow hard. "But it's not, is it? You're so fucking mature and self-aware. Why can't you just fucking admit it's you who doesn't want to get too close to me? *You* who wants to protect *yourself,* because if you actually made the decision to be with me for real, then you'd have to actually face the big scary feelings you have for me and the baby you wish I wasn't having."

Rhiannon's guarded expression closes off entirely. "I would never. Ever. Tell you what you should have done with your pregnancy, Poppy. Ever."

Tears well up in my eyes. But are they for myself, or her?

"But you're right. I did keep my distance for selfish reasons as well. I was afraid of getting too involved, too close, only to have my heart broken worse than ever before. To lose not only a girlfriend, but a *family*."

Me. Her. My unborn child.

A family.

I hold my belly. "Rhiannon…"

"Your mother may not have been right about who you are or what you're capable of, Poppy, but she is right about *some*thing. You and I *should* break up." She turns from me. Her hands clench and unclench into fists. Not out of anger…at me *or* my mother. But because they're shaking with emotion, and she doesn't want to let it show. "And *you* should move back home. It's the safest place for you now, at least until the baby comes." She walks to the door, reaches for the doorknob, pauses. Looks over her shoulder at me with a heartbroken look. "Be with your family, Poppy, such as they are, because they're all you've got."

She walks out.

The door closes behind her, but all I hear is her echoing words:

All you've got.

Right. Because I certainly don't have Rhiannon now.

I don't think I ever did.

Chapter Twenty-Seven

My phone is ringing.

And as if a phone call wasn't enough, the caller ID says it's Grace on the other end.

I groan and roll over in bed, briefly considering letting it go to voicemail. I feel awful about how that last disastrous unofficial meeting with the stitch n' bitch went, and with everything else going on I'm not sure I'm emotionally stable enough to face up to it all.

On the other hand, if I really feel awful, if I'm really sorry, then the adult thing to do—the only *right* thing to do—would be to answer for it by answering Grace's call.

So I pick up.

"Hey," I say tentatively.

"Hey," Grace repeats, sounding about as awkward and

awful as I feel. "I'm sorry for calling you out of the blue like this—"

"Don't be." I sit up in bed, combing a hand through my oily hair.

"You just weren't answering any texts so I just wanted to make sure you were all right."

"I'm…" I consider my answer a moment. "Fine."

And I am. Technically.

I have food to eat and a roof over my head. I'm safe, and provided for, and with nothing more to do or worry about than keeping my baby safe inside me for as long as possible.

That's the definition of "fine", right?

"That's good," Grace replies, not sounding remotely comforted. "I was—we were—worried, you know, since you haven't been coming to stitch n' bitch."

"I can't," I say.

"That's why I was calling, actually. We all talked it over and even though things went, um, the way they did, we all agree you're still welcome to come." She sounds unsure, almost sorry, to be offering me the undeserved gift of her forgiveness.

"It's not that. I mean, don't get me wrong, it's sweet of you to call and it means a lot you guys are willing to give me another chance but I…can't." I look around me, at this room that is somehow twice as big as my apartment, yet it feels infinitely smaller. "Because I moved back home to Long Island."

"…Oh." Grace takes a couple careful breaths as she gathers her thoughts. "That makes sense."

"Didn't Rhiannon tell you?" I ask with a wince. She

hasn't been avoiding the stitch n' bitch, has she? Because that wouldn't be fair.

"All she said was you two broke up. I didn't pry."

Even now that I'm her ex, Rhiannon respects me so much she'd pass up her right to vent about me to her closest friends. I swallow a lump in my throat. *How the hell did I screw up so bad to let go of a woman like her?*

But this conversation isn't about Rhiannon. It's about Grace and the stitch n' bitch, and their magnanimous generosity in reaching out to me.

"I'm sorry, Grace. I owe you and the rest of the stitch n' bitch a serious apology for how I acted before." As unstable and unmoored as I've been feeling ever since I moved home, in this one thing I feel completely sure. "I'd just received some shitty news and wasn't remotely handling it, but that didn't give me the right to treat the rest of you that way. Especially not when you were just trying to help."

"We shouldn't have barged in on you like that, especially without asking if that was what you needed."

"That's the thing, I think it *was* what I needed. To know I had friends looking out for me. To know I didn't have to do this all alone."

"And you do, Poppy. One hundred percent. Sure your outburst hurt our feelings, although not as bad as watching you tearing apart that sweater hurt our sensibilities as knitters, but that doesn't mean we're not still in your corner. We're family, Poppy. We're not going to abandon you just because you acted like a bitch that one time."

I feel myself smiling weakly. "I really did act like a total bitch."

"Oh my God, truthfully? You really did. And I would know."

"You? A bitch? *Never.* I don't believe it."

"Believe it! Just ask the guy who didn't move his bag off the last empty seat on the subway last week after I'd just finished working a twelve hour shift."

"Is it still being a bitch if the other person deserves it?" I wonder aloud, and now we're both laughing.

It's the lightest and least trapped I've felt in the weeks since I returned to my parents' house and my mother's control.

"I'm serious though, Poppy. Long Island or no, whether you can make it to meetings every week or even at all, whether you and Rhi are together or not, your stitch n' bitch are *here* for you. Whatever you need. Late night gelato craving, someone to go with you to interview doulas, advice on how to do cable cast on…whatever!"

"Thank you," I murmur sincerely.

It's a cathartic point to end things on, but it seems Grace isn't finished with me yet. "And while we're on the topic of mending bridges you thought you'd burned, I wouldn't write Rhiannon off just yet, either. She may be tight-lipped about your breakup, but I know her well enough by now to know when she is *pining.*"

"I don't know," I mumble, suddenly feeling vulnerable again. "She seemed pretty confident about it at the time."

"Of course she did. You don't get to be a career clinic escort without some serious steel in your spine and certainty in your beliefs. But that doesn't mean she can't still be wrong about shit."

"You think we were wrong to break up?" *Why am I even asking her? I don't want to know!* "On second thought, please don't answer that."

"Oh, I wasn't going to. I'm aware I usually have an opinion on ev-er-y-thing, but even I know my limitations." Grace releases a brief but unrestrained peal of self-deprecating laughter. "I'm just saying, Rhiannon might act like she's immune, but she's as much of a fickle, impulsive mess emotionally as the rest of us mortals. She can make mistakes, too. Even when she's really, really sure at the time that she's right."

"Or maybe she really is right? Maybe she thought our situation through logically and came to the only sensible conclusion, which is that I come with way too much baggage?"

"Maybe. Or maybe when she was seventeen years old her nana was diagnosed with stage four cancer literally out of the blue and died before she could even process the news, and ever since then she's been unable to trust anything good or seemingly stable in her life to last."

"She never told me it happened when she was that young," I whisper.

"Of course not. She wouldn't want to burden anybody else with that heavy shit. Rhiannon's a caretaker. Has been ever since she took over full time care of her siblings after her grandmother's diagnosis."

To be seventeen and dealing with that grief and holding it together for your brother and sister who depend on you, all while your parents just keep grinding away to keep the lights on. No wonder she seemed so torn over how much

I was growing to need her. No wonder she refused to let herself get too close.

"She'll probably stop speaking to me for telling you this, and in her defense I'm definitely overstepping, but dammit, you deserve to know this isn't all about *your* baggage. It's about hers, too. And who knows, maybe if Nana were alive and kicking Rhi still would have decided she wasn't ready to commit to a girlfriend and a baby. But I can't sit here and listen to you talking about Rhi's unassailable 'logic' as if it's a foregone conclusion that any *sensible* person would see you're pregnant and decide a relationship with you isn't possible, or worse, worth it."

"I don't know what to say," I admit. I suppose after Jake doing his disappearing act, Mom acting the martyr, and Rhiannon waving the white flag on our relationship, some part of me believed I *was* asking too much by wanting people to be a part of my life now that I had a baby on the way.

"Don't say anything," Grace replies matter-of-factly. "…At least not until I fess up to Rhiannon about my blabber mouth personally. I don't regret telling you what I did, but she still deserves to hear it from me first."

I heave a pessimistic sigh. "I don't think there's any risk of that. What the hell would I even tell her? 'After hearing about your dead nana I no longer believe you were in your right mind when you dumped me'?"

"Well, no, because when you put it like that you sound like some gaslighting nightmare." Grace sniffs in derision. "But you could always give her the opportunity to change her mind."

Invite her back, gently, genuinely, without bitterness or

artifice, the same way Grace had invited me back to stitch n' bitch at the start of this conversation.

"Hell, you wouldn't even need to bring up her dead nana!" Grace adds on cheerfully.

"I wasn't planning on it, but that doesn't mean you shouldn't still come clean with Rhiannon about telling me."

"I know, I know." Underneath Grace's petulant tone, I can tell our conversation has lifted a weight off her shoulders. "I should probably hang up and do that now, before I lose my nerve. Wish me luck?"

"You don't need it. Rhiannon loves you. She won't throw you out."

"She wouldn't throw you out, either, Poppy. And neither will I."

That lump in my throat is back, and my eyes burn with unshed tears. "Thank you, Grace. F–for this. For everything. I mean it."

Grace's voice is a little pitchy when she replies, "Prove it by calling me once in a while."

"Long distance from Long Island," I remind her.

By the time I hang up, my tears have begun to fall.

But I'm smiling.

The weeks on bed rest pass in drips and spurts. Some days I sleep ten hours then nap four more, losing so much time I can't tell if it's Monday or Thursday. Some days I count the minutes like hours.

I don't call Rhiannon.

I just can't open myself up to being hurt again like that, not now when everything is so precarious.

What a hypocrite I'd been, shaming her for being afraid to get too close to me.

The truth is, we're both afraid, and for good reason.

But despite being too much of a coward to follow the word of Grace's advice, I do try to follow the spirit of it.

To believe people are here for me, want to support me, aren't looking for an excuse to throw me away.

We're family. We're not going to abandon you just because you acted like a bitch.

So I don't call Rhiannon, but I do text Iris.

An unassuming *How have you been?* later, and there's a nervous little rap on my bedroom door.

"Come in," I say, without asking who it is. My workaholic father won't be home for hours, and it can't possibly be my mother, who never knocks.

Sure enough, Iris spills into my room, although I have to admit I don't recognize her at first. Her normally sleek blond hair is frizzy with dark roots showing, her chin is red and shiny with hormonal acne, and she's wearing maternity leggings hiked right up to her bra-less boobs.

"Don't say anything," she scolds instantly, like she actually expects me—of all people—to criticize her dishevelled appearance.

Part of me wants to tease her about "her pregnancy glow", but I hold my tongue. We've barely spoken since the day of her gender reveal, and I'm not exactly sure where we stand.

Iris clearly doesn't share my insecurity. She pulls back my blankets and piles into my bed without so much as a *by your leave.*

I only mind a little.

After the recent frank conversations I've had with Grace and less successfully Rhiannon, I'm expecting Iris to also want to hash things out between us, but no.

"I've been on maternity leave for like four days and I have to ask. What do you even *do* all day?" she asks.

As if I'm the lifelong expert on laziness to her productive overachiever.

How about you use that big lawyer brain of yours and puzzle it out? I think to myself, annoyed, but aloud I reply, "Pretty much what we're doing now? I sleep, I read, I watch Netflix…"

I've even started knitting again, but I'm not about to tell Iris that. I'm way too tender to weather any more snide comments, even if I think the chance of her making them is pretty low after Rhiannon called her out.

I want to talk to her about that, about everything, but that's just not how things are done in our family. We keep calm and carry on, even if it usually ends in me forgiving things nobody's apologized for.

Well, at least this time we're even. Iris can skip apologizing for making fun of my hobby, and I can skip apologizing for upstaging her and ruining her big day. Of course, I couldn't exactly help having pre-eclampsia. Her being a condescending bitch, on the other hand, was all her.

Anyway.

Maybe *this* time pretending nothing happened will actually make it like nothing did.

"You want to watch a rom-com?" I ask her, trying my best to make it so.

"Sure, as long as there's no pregnancy subplot."

Well, that's one thing we can agree on, at least. I pull out my laptop and open it up, balancing it on our bellies.

But before it even boots up, my door swings wide open and our mother swans in. "Iris! I thought I heard your voice!"

"Hi, Mom." Iris sits up abruptly, knocking my laptop off-kilter.

So much for the fragile peace the two of us had just begun to build.

"Maybe *you* can convince your sister that being on bed rest is no excuse to skip childbirth classes."

I sigh. Is there any point telling either of them that I've been reading up on this for months and I'd really rather not endure the experience of going to some upper-crust Lamaze class unaccompanied?

No, of course not. Because, once more with feeling, that's not how things are done in our family.

"How about instead of convincing her, I offer to go along with her? You know, as a sister bonding activity?" I can't tell if Iris says it because she wants to appease my mother by playing peacekeeper as always, or because she wants to protect—if not quite stand up for—*me*.

Iris bats her eyelashes at me, and even with the acne I'm reminded of the fact that she's still my poised, perfectly accommodating princess of a sister.

And I can't stay mad at her.

Week 34: Your baby is the size of a cantaloupe!
I picture my body as an overripe fruit ready to be cracked

open, and inside it, my baby, slimy and nestled among the seeds.

Thirty-four weeks pregnant.

Thanks to a course of steroids and pure, dumb luck, I've reached the point where my baby has a ninety-nine percent chance of surviving outside the womb if I go into labor early.

Not that I'm planning on it happening or anything.

I wish I could be excited, but mostly I just feel huge and tired and trapped, with a guillotine hanging over my neck. The housekeeper does my laundry. A nutritionist plans my meals, which my father flawlessly executes. Iris keeps me company: the two of us crammed into my childhood bed with our big baby bellies balancing a laptop playing Netflix. My mother fluffs my pillows and drives me to my weekly prenatal appointments with my new ob-gyn who luckily isn't a piece of shit despite his association with my mother, so there's that.

It's all…very peaceful. Civil, and sensible, and safe.

And oh so fragile.

The saying is "walking on eggshells", but it's more like… never letting yourself talk above a whisper because you're afraid that even the slightest rise in volume might as well be shouting and trigger the looming avalanche that threatens to bury everyone.

Or wake the ominous nameless *thing* that slumbers in every corner of this uneasy house.

I can't decide if it's an indifferent force of nature or malevolent monster I'm dealing with here.

My mother plays her part by being almost too polite

and conscientious, like a perfect party host. I play mine by being obedient.

Seen and not heard, the "normal little girl" my mother wanted me to be once more.

It's surprisingly easy to just give up. Soul crushing, but easy.

Entropy is always easy.

Which is precisely what my mother is counting on when she spontaneously announces:

"Poppy, I think you should move back home with us. Properly."

I look up from my phone, more shocked than I probably should be. "What?"

"I think you should move back home with your father and I. You'll need help caring for the little one when he comes, and space for a proper nursery. And then when he gets older, I can be a full-time grandma and you can go back to school. Give him the life he deserves!"

Of course this was the end game. Of course it was! Bring me home, make me comfortable, get me to the point where even if I wanted to leave, it would just be so much easier not to…

And then once I was there, take back control of my life. But now it's not just my life, but my baby's, too. A whole new generation to control.

"I just think that you're obviously going to be staying here long term anyway, so why waste money paying rent for an apartment you don't intend on returning to? And don't worry about your lease, your father and I will have no trouble releasing you from any obligation."

I stare at her, unable to even speak.

Not sure what I'd even say.

"This pregnancy has to have opened your eyes to the realities of your life. How ill-prepared you are for major changes. How much help you still need. How inherently unstable your situation is."

"You know what, Mother?" The words start coming without my even meaning them to. "It *has* opened my eyes. It's opened my eyes to how much you want to hold me back, and how little you think of me. How little you've made me think of myself."

"I don't want to hold you back, I—"

"No, you had your chance to talk, and now you're going to listen. You're going to listen, or I'm going to end this conversation here and now. Those are my terms. You say I'm 'ill-prepared' for major life changes, but whether I was prepared or not, I've handled them all anyway. I went to Planned Parenthood. I walked through a wall of protesters. I decided to go through with my pregnancy and planned for a future with a baby in it.

"Yes, I need help, but so does everybody! And that's okay! It's okay to ask for help, and need help, and lean on other people, especially in your time of need! That's why we have friends. People we can count on, who can count on us, too!

"You want to talk about my unstable situation? I'm in the middle of a seismic shift! Who could be stable in the middle of this? But I have an apartment I can pay the rent on. I have a job with insurance. I have quality medical care and friends who come by to clean my apartment when I get unexpectedly put on bed rest."

Friends I scorned and sent away.

"I may not have a college education, but I also don't have a college debt load! And neither did my girlfriend, who—let's face it—even if she *did* get a degree, would probably still be working at the same cafe for the same wage, but now with more than half those wages going to student loans!

"The life I'm bringing this baby into might not look like much to you, but considering the context of the world we live in—the actual world, not the fantasy rich baby boomer dreamland you call home—I think I'm actually doing just fine!"

Better than fine, if I'm honest. Other than my train wreck of a relationship with my mother, I've got it pretty good.

"For fuck's sake, when I realized I needed to become more of a competent adult for my baby's sake, the main change I made was to learn to knit! Not because I was too stupid to know what my priorities should be, but because everything I could do to be ready for this, I'd already done!

"Because finally learning to knit was literally all there was left for me to do!"

Learning to knit, and by extension, proving to myself that if the thing was worthwhile, if I really *wanted* it, then yes, I could follow through.

And I did. I have the little knit booties and mitts and slightly lopsided but still perfectly serviceable hats to prove it.

Would have had a sweater, too, if I hadn't gotten in my own way. And speaking of which...

"And do you know what the worst part is? It's the fact that this whole time, I never gave myself credit. Not for any of it. Not for my job or my apartment or my bravery or my growth as a person or how much more consistent my tension is in stockinette now.

"Nope, I just kept getting down on myself for the qualities I didn't have, the accomplishments I hadn't made, all the arbitrary endless boxes I couldn't tick. All from a checklist you made, that I had no part in forming and never even agreed to!

"It's like all those crash diets you put me on, ever since I was a kid. Unrealistic expectations and self-hatred and trying to force myself to be a hundred and twenty pounds just to please you when the life I have at the weight I am is *just freaking fine.*"

I burst into a laugh that walks a tightrope between hysterical, bone deep grief and unbridled fucking joy.

"I am just. Freaking! Fine! The size of my body is fine. The way I choose to feed myself is fine. The life path I've made for myself is fine. My apartment is fine. My sexuality—girlfriend or not—is fine. The choices I've made regarding my body, this pregnancy…all fine!

"The only thing wrong with any of it, is how shitty *you* made me feel about it!

"And sure, I still have insecurities about how good of a mother I'll be to this baby. Who wouldn't? But at least I'll know better than to be the goddamn origin story of my own child's perpetual inferiority complex!"

My mother's carefully composed face, so stoic and perfect and dignified, has gone a mottled red. "You…you…"

Tears well up in the corners of her eyes, and for a brief moment, I actually believe she's ashamed and sorry. That I've finally gotten through to her. "You have no right to speak to me this way, Poppy! I raised you, I gave you every opportunity, I clothed you and fed you and paid for your schooling. And now, in your time of need, I took you in!"

"Parenthood isn't a loan you cash in on, Mother. Just because you fulfilled your obligations as my parent— technically—doesn't mean I owe you control over my life and my feelings and my dignity in return. But if that's the way you feel, then fine. I'll leave. Break this sick contract you think we have between us. Which shouldn't be a prob- lem, since you did say you and dad would have no trouble releasing me from any obligations…"

"It's all well and good to turn my words on me and make a petulant little stand, Poppy, but you've still got weeks of bed rest ahead of you. And a baby on the way at the end of it all. If you walk out of here now, you best not be expect- ing me to drive you to the hospital when you're in labor!"

"You know what? At this point I'd rather depend on my flake baby daddy than you. At least his half-assed support doesn't come with a hundred pages of fine print stipula- tions!"

"Or we could go with the third option." The unexpected third voice has my mother and I rounding on the door like a whole news crew has just walked in on our fight. But it's not a news crew, it's Iris. "Poppy, I'd be happy to drive you to the hospital when the time comes. And you're wel- come to stay with me in the meantime, as well. It seems our mother needs some solitary reflection time to learn to be a better mother if she has any desire to ever be a grandma. To either of our babies."

"Iris, you can't be serious!"

"I'm certainly not practicing my stand-up, Mother. Come on, Poppy. It's past time for your big sister to finally step up."

Iris takes me calmly by the hand and leads me away.

We leave our mother gaping, speechless, in our wake.

Chapter Twenty-Eight

By that evening, I'm officially moved out of my old bed-room and into Iris's guest room. Not that there was much *to* move—one suitcase of maternity clothes, my laptop, and my knitting is about the extent of it—but that doesn't stop Iris and I from rewarding ourselves with a tub of ice cream once we're done.

And what a reward it is, because unlike me, Iris keeps her freezer stocked with the good stuff.

Or at least, *I* think it's good.

Iris on the other hand just prods at the tub listlessly, sig-nificantly less enthused than you'd expect a pregnant lady eating twelve dollar ice cream to be.

Whatever's eating at her, it's definitely putting a damper on her eating ice cream. She sets down her spoon with a sigh, covering my hand with her own.

"I owe you an apology, Poppy. A seriously overdue apology."

The sincerity in her eyes has me suddenly *deeply* interested in where the next richest deposit of cookie dough might be.

"Pff, yeah right." I flap my spoon at her. I'm so used to pretending everything's fine and downplaying my feelings, I don't know how to do anything else. "You've already taken my broke ass under your roof and caused World War Three with our dictator of a mother on my behalf. I think we're good."

"No, we're not." Iris's voice trembles with reined-in emotion. Even in this moment, she clings to her sense of propriety and self-control. She really is like my mother, in some ways.

And in others, not at all. Because my mother has never admitted she was wrong. Which Iris is apparently insisting on doing. "I may have done the right thing today… finally, but I could have done more, sooner. I could have stuck up for you."

All those times Iris silently watched Mom berate me, consoling me afterwards that "She's only hard on us because she cares," even when Mom never seemed to be as hard on Iris as she was on me. Would it have killed her to just once to take my side?

Not that it would have made a difference. It may have even made things worse, knowing my mother. To have not one but two daughters refusing to behave? Who knows how far she'd go to regain her sense of control. "We were kids, Iris. You can't hold yourself responsible for how she raised me. Us."

"Key word there, sis: 'were'. We *were* kids. We're adults now. And I have my own house and career and everything. I have no excuse for taking as long as I did to use that in your defense."

My throat thickens.

"Well, like you said. You did the right thing today. That means something. But I appreciate the apology, all the same. In fact, I think I owe you an apology, too."

"You do?"

"Mom was constantly putting you on a pedestal, pitting us against one another, and it made me…resent you." I'm reminded of the year Mom put me on my first diet. I'd just hit puberty but failed to slim down the way Iris had at the same age. Eating my four ounces of skinless chicken breast and cup of steamed vegetables, it was hard to miss the fact that Iris never had to measure *her* food. Harder still not to hold it against her, while simultaneously wishing I could *be* her.

But when the two of us crossed paths in the school cafeteria at lunch, my one meal of the day outside our mother's control, Iris never commented on what she saw on my tray. Not to shame me, as she'd seen our mother and half our classmates do a million times. Not even to gently, helpfully remind me of what I was supposed to be eating.

And she *never* reported back to Mom, even when I dared to sneak an entire plate of French fries.

But the sense of shame and inferiority hung over me as if she had.

It was all such a mindfuck, it's no surprise it took me this long to make sense of any of it. But I think I finally have. "It was *Mom's* boot on my neck. But I acted as if it were yours."

"I never wanted that for you, Poppy. Or for us." Iris chews her bottom lip, eyes shining, so distraught she can't even look at me. "To be honest, when I heard you were pregnant, too, I almost felt guilty for not having another miscarriage because I knew our mother was going to use me to make you miserable. And she did. God!"

Well, that's it. I can't stop myself crying now.

"Please don't, Iris." I lurch forward, pushing the tub of ice cream that stands between us out of my way so forcefully that it and both spoons hit the floor. I grab my sister tightly by both hands. "Please don't feel guilty. You've gone through so much. You deserve to have this baby. To make a family. To be happy. You deserve to be a mother. Because you're going to be great at it. You're going to be amazing."

Iris gasps and hiccups, and two big fat tears roll down her cheeks.

"So will you, Poppy! So will you!"

Correction: two big fat tears accompanied by one genuine ugly-cry snot bubble in her left nostril.

I look at it, and she sees me looking at it, and I worry she's about to become humiliated by her own humanity, but instead she lets out a sobbing guffaw of a laugh that ends in a perfectly executed stick-the-landing snort.

She may have a designer hospital gown and an expensive birth photographer to turn the agony of childbirth into black and white art, but to me, she'll always be as ugly and imperfect as she is in this moment.

Imperfect just like me.

Week 38: your baby is as big as a

Oh, who the fuck gives a single shit about what fruit best approximates my baby in size?

It may as well be a watermelon—no, an oversized durian covered in fucking jagged spines—because that's what the hell it feels like coming out of me right now!

I brace myself against the nearest wall and grit my teeth.

"Breathe through the pain, Poppy. Like we practiced." Iris's voice is calm and measured and gentle and fucking infuriating beyond all belief.

My first instinct is to reply with something along the lines of *fuck your breathing exercises, actually*, but that's just the pain talking, and as the wave of the contraction washes away, what comes out instead is the slightly less visceral but still satisfyingly snarky, "I am going…to make you eat those words next month, you know that, right?"

Iris ignores my threat, high-mindedly focusing on the task at hand, instead. "I assume since you're speaking full sentences, then that's time?"

I nod, and she taps the button on her phone's irritatingly cutesy contraction stopwatch app.

Oh, to be young and innocent again, blissfully unaware of the fact that childbirth-specific phone apps were a thing. Needed to be a thing.

Counting down to my impending agony like the digital counter of a time bomb, except *pink!*

"That's six minutes apart," she reports. "And if it's all the same to you, I'd really prefer if you didn't spend this entire process actively reminding me that I have all this to look forward to? Well, except for when your beautiful healthy baby makes her debut. Then you can definitely lay it on super thick." She rubs my lower back with a warm smile.

As resentful as I felt just a second ago, I'm nothing but thankful for her now.

And once I stop trembling from the aftershocks of the pain, she gently asks, "Do you want to try walking again?"

Walking. Rocking in a chair. Straddling a birthing ball. Under the stream of a shower. On the damn toilet, even. All the time-honored ways of weathering the protracted pains of labor. Gentle and natural and—holiest of all— drug free.

Me, I'd prefer to cuss my way through it, the way swearing at the top of your lungs supposedly alleviates the pain of a stubbed toe.

But even at the peak of the contraction, the height of that pain, a part of me refuses to let go. Even with my mother banned from my birth, I still feel her presence.

Don't make a scene. Don't be difficult. Make yourself small and pleasant and unobjectionable.

Taking me by the arm, Iris walks me in a slow circuit of her open plan main floor. I can't help but feel guilty in advance that I might sully her gleaming hardwood with my various…fluids. But Iris is unfazed, steady for the both of us in more ways than one.

On the second loop of her kitchen island, I come to an abrupt halt.

Iris has her stopwatch out and at the ready before my fingernails get the chance to dig into her arm.

"Time?" I ask, my last coherent thought before the building pain swallows me up entirely.

"Five minutes twenty seconds." Her voice takes on an edge of anxiety. "Is it too soon to take you to the hospital? My childbirth guide says—"

I bend double, clutching my tensing belly with the hand not currently clinging to my sister for dear life.

"Ffffffffffffffuck your childbirth guide." No filter this time. We're in the shit now.

"Fuck my childbirth guide," Iris agrees. "As soon as this contraction passes, I'll grab your hospital bag, and we're out of here."

"Okay," I say, those two syllables taking every ounce of control and focus I have. "Okay."

"Before we go, though… Is there anyone you want me to call?"

Rhiannon, my mind supplies instantly. *No. I can't.* But that doesn't mean I'm alone.

"Grace. But don't call her for me. Let me talk to her." I reach out with trembling hands for my phone.

"Are you sure?" Iris asks. "Because I really don't mind passing on a message."

"I have to say this myself."

Iris hands me my phone. "I'll go get your bag then."

As soon as she's out of the room, I call Grace.

She answers on the first ring.

"Poppy, hey! What's up? Is it the baby?!"

I breathe through the mounting pain.

"It's the baby. It's cuh-*oming!*" My strained voice rises into a shriek.

The contraction builds, worse than any that came before it.

"What hospital are you in? Do you want me to come?"

The pain crashes over me, washing away everything but my basest instincts.

"Rhiannon," I announce on a groan. This time, the pain is too intense to feel ashamed of asking. To second-guess myself or question what I want or agonize over whether I have the right to ask.

"That's my girl! I'll see what I can do for you, okay? Now put someone else on so they can tell me what hospital you're delivering in."

Iris, harried, has returned with my bag and her husband in tow.

"It's for you," I say, handing the phone over. The contraction subsides, leaving me so exhausted I can barely stand. I turn to her husband, saying, simply, "I have to go now."

It's time.

Chapter Twenty-Nine

Iris's husband, who's done a very good job of making himself scarce thus far today, has appeared in the nick of time to drive us to the hospital.

Which frees up Iris to sit in the back seat with me, where she's best positioned to squeeze my hand and rub my back and murmur soothingly as required.

And as soon as we've arrived at our destination, he makes himself scarce all over again.

Which is kind of too bad for him, because Iris could be teaching a masterclass right now on how to be the world's best birthing coach.

She checks me in at admitting, stays close by while I have my cervix prodded and examined, fetches me cups of ice chips, talks me through my intensifying pain until I tell her to just shut up now, please.

"Do you want something for pain?" a nurse asks me at one point, and even though I know Iris has read enough new age childbirth books to have a definite opinion on the matter, she doesn't breathe a word of it now. Not even when I'm in too much pain to speak at first.

Of all the life defining, watershed moments a walk through the fire experience like childbirth can precipitate...

For me, it's this:

The space to answer for myself.

And after taking my time to consider my options, weighing the pros and cons, choosing the words, all of it without any pressure to reply on a certain timeline, I answer, "Not yet. I want to try and do this."

The nurse nods. "Of course. You let me know if the situation changes."

Really? Just like that? I almost can't believe it. Someone asked me a question, waited (silently, without offering strongly worded suggestions) while I took my time to answer, and then respected the answer I gave?

I'd pinch myself, if not for the fact that an up and coming contraction is giving me all the pain I could possibly need to confirm I'm awake.

"Ohh," I moan, squeezing my eyes shut, and immediately wish I'd have asked for the strongest painkillers they had.

I can change my mind. I can change my mind at any time. I'm in charge. I'm in—

The pain comes and goes, like cresting waves that build and fall and rise again even higher. A storm in the open ocean is the perfect metaphor for it, actually, because it's terrifying and inescapable and the most intense thing I've ever experienced.

And I'm lost inside it.

The only way out is through, I repeat to myself like a grizzled old sea captain, leaning into the image.

The only way out is through.

After hours, my body decides to push, quite without my knowledge or permission. I drop down into a squat right there in the hospital hallway, for the first time in my life completely unheeding of how I must look, what people must be thinking.

Right now, there's only me and my body, and the job we have to do together.

"Poppy?" Iris asks, her tone so light and airy she must be shitting bricks levels of terrified. "Poppy?"

I can't answer. Not in words, at least.

Turns out, I don't need to.

"Nurse!" Iris calls, and someone in scrubs—I don't even register their face—comes hustling over from the desk.

"Was that a push, Poppy? Is baby coming?" the nurse asks and I nod. "Okay. As soon as you're ready, I want you to stand up and I'll walk you back to your room and get you checked over, then we can call the doctor."

Blah, blah, blah. Cervix. Crowning. My feet in stirrups and my brain awash in pain, it all goes by in a blur. How can I be simultaneously so profoundly connected to my body's every sensation and yet completely dissociated from everything happening to me?

"You're almost there," Iris coaches me. "Not long now!"

I must have asked for pain meds at some point, because the next time I scream, it's muffled by a mask.

Which doesn't seem to be doing shit, but at least it gives me something to focus on other than the sensation of being torn apart from the inside.

"You're doing great, Poppy. You can do this!"

I can't do this.

I can't possibly do this. There's no way I can do this.

"Make it stop, I change my mind! I can't do this! I can't! I don't want to do this!"

I only realize I've been saying it all aloud when Iris hushes me and strokes my hair.

"Yes you can. We're all here for you."

We?

In a haze of pain, I look over and see Rhiannon standing over me. Iris, on the other side of the bed, is holding my hand in both of hers. It's Rhiannon's cool palm on my forehead.

"Rhiannon?"

"You called. I came." Rhiannon smiles and shrugs, like her being here is no bigger deal than if she'd come to bring me a coffee at work. "Iris said I could come in, but is that still what you want? Because I can go."

I reach up and grab her hand, crushing it with my own. "Don't you dare!"

"Heard," Rhiannon says, like I've heard her respond to her other baristas a hundred times. "Now stop being so fucking negative and down on yourself and see this through!"

See this through. Finish what you start. You're the only one who can do this and now you're the only one left standing in your way.

"Next contraction is about to hit. Grit your teeth and try not to scream this time. No point wasting energy." Rhiannon's no-nonsense direction might have pissed me off, coming from someone else, but it's her, and no matter what else has happened between us, I trust her to point me in the right direction.

Everything she's saying, she's saying for my benefit. For me, above all others.

She's here for me.

So I grit my teeth and clamp my lips shut, breathing in sharp puffs through my nose. Gripping Iris in one hand and Rhiannon in the other, I push until I hear a scream.

Not my scream.

My baby's.

Chapter Thirty

Post-birth hormones are a hell of a drug.

If I tore, if I had to be stitched up, if I delivered my slimy afterbirth, if I took a shit on the delivery table in front of God and everybody, I wouldn't even know it.

A tiny, red-faced little human, hair still damp from my body, lies nestled on my bare chest, the weight of him the most perfect and natural sensation I've ever felt.

"Hello," I say softly, at last. The same tiny, innocuous word a different Poppy once whispered to that very first ultrasound image all those months ago. "Little stranger, hello."

I reach out, and my baby reaches back, wrapping his tiny, surprisingly strong fist around my finger.

We hold each other tight.

"Will I give you some time alone?" Rhiannon asks with a nervous, conflicted smile.

"You can stay," I reply without even having to think it over. "If you want to. Stay."

I know I should feel insecure about what she chooses to do next, but there's simply no room in my heart for that feeling right now.

There'd be no need for it anyway, as it turns out.

Rhiannon doesn't even hesitate: she pulls a chair up to my bedside and drops right down into it.

"Little stranger," she says to herself, echoing my words, and stares down at my baby admiringly.

"You should probably name him," Iris prompts gently.

The three of us all stare down at our little stranger, brimming with limitless possibility and potential.

"Jake," I say dreamily.

Rhiannon visibly pales in barely hidden horror and my serious face breaks out in a mischievous grin.

"...Just kidding."

"You're lucky you're holding a baby, or I'd hit you right now." Rhiannon mock glowers.

I look down at my baby again, contemplating. I swear I wrote a whole list at one point, but now that the moment's here, do you think I'd remember a single line of it?

"Oliver," I say, struck by sudden inspiration. It just *fits*.

"Oliver," Rhiannon and Iris repeat, and by the contented satisfaction in their voices I can tell they agree.

Oliver. My little stranger.

We've got our whole lives to get to know one another, and I can't wait.

★ ★ ★

Iris was a champ to stay with me for my entire labor, all while eight months pregnant herself, but as much as she obviously wants to stay and dote on Oliver, the hours have caught up with her. Her feet are swollen and her posture has gone as limp as her unwashed hair. It's past time for her to take a break.

"You sure you'll be okay?" she asks, and I flap a hand at her.

"Yes, yes. Rhi's here, not to mention an entire team of nurses. You go home with your husband. Have a hot bath, have a sleep. Olly will still be here when you get back."

Which is still kind of unreal, to be honest. I mean, logically I know I'm his mother and that kind of thing is forever, but a part of me still feels like he's going to go back somehow.

But no, he's mine.

He's mine, and I'm his, and what a privilege I've been given to have the chance to do right by him, to nurture and grow this bond between us for the rest of our lives.

With one last kiss to her nephew's head, Iris and her husband take their leave.

Now it's just the three of us. Me, Oliver and Rhiannon.

Just the three of us. I wonder what shape that's going to take?

"So…" I say, feeling suddenly awkward.

"So…" Rhiannon says right back. She looks down at Oliver, and I can tell it's only because he provides her a convenient out not to look at me.

You just gave birth in front of her, for Christ's sake. Surely you can let yourself be vulnerable for her now.

"So I called for you, huh?"

There. Cards on the table.

"Yeah. You called Grace, then asked for me."

I vaguely remember that, yes.

I cover my face with my hand, embarrassed.

"And you came? As soon as you heard? Just like that?" My chest squeezes, my heart caught mid-beat by the enormity of it all.

"Well, not *quite*. When I actually got to the hospital I wasn't sure whether I should let myself into your room or knock or what." She looks down at her hands bashfully. "And to be honest I was genuinely scared that you'd changed your mind. But then Iris poked her head out the door and told me how you were in there *right now* screaming 'I don't care anymore, I want Rhiannon!' clear as day, so that kind of answered that question."

"I called and you came," I murmur in wonder, still stuck on that bit. "Even after everything?"

"Honestly, even after everything, even before Grace actually called me, I'd already made up my mind." Rhiannon clears her throat, leg jiggling. "I had a lot of time to think things over, these last few weeks. Well, less think things over and more give myself a stern talking-to for being such a coward."

"I don't think you're a coward."

"That's very adult and reasonable of you." Rhiannon lets out a dry laugh. "No doubt influenced by a *certain conversation* with Grace? But you'll excuse me if I hold myself to a slightly higher standard. I *was* a coward. I was afraid of getting too close only to lose you, afraid what we had wouldn't last, and because of it I ran hot and cold when what you needed was for me to just be *consistent*, no matter what that ultimately looked like."

"You're not wrong. Not that I didn't appreciate having you there, but I probably would have worked things out for myself if you'd made the decision to stay hands-off and stuck to it."

"But instead I pulled a Jake on you, acting invested one second then ghosting you the next."

"Maybe, but it's not like it was all you. You were pretty clear you didn't want to get too involved in my pregnancy, but I just kept trying to recruit you anyway. You could have said no, but I could have made it easier by not asking unless you volunteered." I was just so scared and overwhelmed and unsure of myself, unsure of my ability to handle any of this. Those fears seem so small and insignificant now compared to the enormity of the responsibility currently sleeping away on top of me.

"Let's set the record straight here and now then, Poppy. This is me, volunteering. You called, and I came. Because as afraid as I am, I'd rather live with that fear of uncertainty than give up on the chance to be with you." She cups the back of Oliver's impossibly small head. "Whatever you need, I'm here. For as long as I'm here, I'm *here*."

She stares into my eyes, and I stare back into hers. Oliver stirs and snuffles, and we both instinctively reach to give his soft, bare back a comforting pat.

Oliver's back rises and falls as he breathes, and Rhiannon moves to cover my hand with her own, the three of us falling into the rhythm of this precious new life.

Wordlessly, Rhiannon cups my cheek with her other hand, turning my face to her own. I tilt my chin up with a contended smile and, Oliver cradled safe between us, held at the center of our embrace, we kiss.

"I love you, Poppy," Rhiannon confesses against my mouth, saying it aloud at last. "You, and Olly."

Even if she's never actually said it before now, part of me always knew it was how she felt through it all. I may never have known where I stood with her, but her love for me was never in doubt.

And neither was mine.

In this tender, vulnerable moment, I'm finally free to announce myself.

"I love you, too."

Chapter Thirty-One

Oliver is two days old, and all going well, if my blood pressure cooperates, today is the day I get to take him home.

We get to take him home.

I watch from my comfy spot on the bed as Rhiannon disposes of *yet another* wet diaper and does up the snaps of his onesie. "There you go, you little bundle of bodily functions. And just in time, too!"

Rhiannon hefts Oliver up to her shoulder as someone pulls back the curtain around my bed.

"Hello!" Louise's jolly voice calls out.

"Shh! Hospital, remember?" Mary scolds her with a hiss.

"Am I okay to come in? Is she decent?" Damian asks from behind the curtain.

I pull my backwards hospital gown tighter around my

front in a poor attempt to disguise my engorged breasts. "I'm fine if you are."

After our only partially resolved fight, you'd think I'd feel more awkward, but in fact I'm overjoyed to see them all.

My stitch n' bitch, back together again. They fill the small partitioned space around my bed, surrounding me with noise and life and love.

Except… "Where's Grace?"

"I'm here, too! Just a sec! These three are so baby crazy they forgot we brought gifts! Left me holding the bag…" Grace elbows her way in, a giant, bulging gift bag hanging from her arm.

"You didn't have to bring anything." My protest gets lost in all the noise and excitement.

"Oh, give him here, give him here! Come to Auntie!" Mary takes Oliver from Rhiannon with a delighted coo. "And don't worry, Mama, I washed my hands. Twice!"

"It's fine. I trust you not to bring him the gift of his first cold. In point of fact, I wasn't expecting gifts of any sort." I reiterate myself uselessly. "You already threw me a shower, remember?"

Louise clucks, too entranced with Oliver to look my way even as she corrects me. "Yes, but those were *baby* gifts."

"Exactly! These are gifts for *you*!" Grace dumps the gift bag into my lap. "Go on, open it!"

Post-natal bath salts. A clip-on booklight. ("For all your late nights," Damian intones, more than a little ominously.) A gift card to a nearby coffee shop.

"This is so sweet, you guys, thanks!"

"There's more," Mary says, handing Oliver to Louise, who has been making grabby hands for several minutes now.

I dig underneath a layer of tissue paper to find several balls of unquestionably expensive yarn and even a set of interchangeable circulars.

"Time for you to up your knitting game," Grace tells me. "Advance to the next skill level. You're ready."

My heart squeezes.

Rhiannon points to the circular set. "I can teach you to knit in the round with those."

"And I'll teach you magic loop," Louise interrupts, "Since Rhiannon—"

"Is *still* never learning magic loop." Rhiannon finishes Louise's sentence with supreme, unbending stubbornness. Then she looks at me and her expression, and her tone, softens. "That is…if you want to come back to the group, Poppy."

"I've said it before and I'll say it again. We really would love to have you back," Grace says.

"It's not the same without you," Mary agrees.

I squirm, a little uncomfortable with all the sincerity. "Really? I find that kind of hard to believe. It's not like I've been a part of the group even half as long as any of you…"

"Maybe not, but that doesn't mean you don't belong." Louise speaks with the conviction of someone who knows exactly how it feels to be left out…and how life-changing it can be to finally be invited in and included.

"I still save you a seat every week," Damian says without artifice, the simplicity of the gesture speaking for itself.

"Even after how I acted?" I finally say. "Because I was a grade A ass to you all when all you were doing was trying to help."

"You were, but luckily we knitters are well versed in the value of tinking back even the most egregious of mistakes," Mary says. "No matter how far back we have to go, or how long it takes."

"Tinking is knitting backwards!" Louise explains helpfully.

"And to that end, we've got one last gift for you," Grace says. "I hope you don't mind, I kinda stole it from your apartment when we...left."

"When I kicked you out," I admit humbly.

Grace reaches into her omnipresent knitting bag, pulling out not her latest WIP in indie dyed silk merino, but a project knitted from familiar baby acrylic.

My sweater. The one I tore apart in front of them all in a fit of despair.

Whole again and back on the needles.

"Th...thank you. I don't know what to say." My throat feels thick just to look at it.

"Don't thank me. I just grabbed it. Rhiannon is the one who fixed it."

I look to Rhiannon, overcome, and she just smiles.

"It took some work, but I managed to get it back to where you left off," Rhiannon says. "The tension might be a little off between my stitches and yours once you take back over, but you deserve to finish it yourself."

Finish it myself. Me, Poppy, finishing what I started. Helped, supported, but ultimately responsible for my own follow-through. For binding off my own stitches and weaving in my own ends.

To the casual observer, it's just a misshapen baby sweater, seven-eighths finished.

To me—no, to *us*, to me and Rhiannon and the rest of our stitch n' bitch—it's an expression of trust and faith. A labor of love we've all had some hand in.

Just like the son I birthed and now we all share.

More than a stitch n' bitch, somewhere along the line we became a family.

Chapter Thirty-Two

Oliver is being such a fussy little expletive redacted lately I almost didn't want to come out, but now that I'm here at the coffee shop with the rest of the stitch n' bitch, I'm glad I did.

Partly because it gives me an excuse to brush my hair and put on a bra. Partly because it's nice to have some adult company; Rhiannon stops by my place as much as she can in between shifts at the cafe and Planned Parenthood, but that still leaves me a lot of hours alone with a screaming diaper machine that only smiles at me when he's farting.

Mostly I'm glad because it means the *both* of us can pass Oliver off for a blissful, hands free couple of hours.

"Oh, look at you! You're wearing the sweater Mummy knitted for you!" Right on cue, Mary takes Oliver under the arms, lifting him overhead to show him off.

"Not for long, by the looks of him. Kid's growing like a weed!" Damian snatches Oliver from Mary and gives him a tender squish.

Louise rises to her feet, clinking her mug. "Attention, everyone! We have an official Finished Object on our hands!"

I groan and cover my face as a coffee shop full of bewildered, confused patrons applauds me nonetheless.

The sweater's recipient has just turned one month old, and I've finally finished. Woven in the ends and sewed on the buttons and everything.

Much as Rhiannon warned, there was a definite difference between my tension and hers when all was said and done.

Much as Grace consoled me, it "blocked out"—mostly.

But much as Damian predicted, Oliver doesn't care in the slightest.

"So what's next for you, Poppy?" Grace asks, fussing with a loose stitch at Oliver's pudgy wrist.

"Something for yourself, I hope," Mary says archly.

"After the week she's had? Poppy deserves nothing less than the sweet, soft caress of a baby alpaca sweater." Rhiannon drapes an arm around my shoulders and gives me a protective squeeze.

The others lean forward, ready and willing to lend a supportive ear, if that's what I need.

Maybe it is.

"Where to start? Well, Iris had her baby. I went to the hospital, of course. My mother was there, ready and raring to lay on the guilt trip. It was like she'd been rehearsing for the moment!" Just the thought of it opens a pit in my stomach.

Rhiannon rubs my back. "Yeah, but so had you, babe. And you totally stood your ground!"

"That's what I like to hear!" Damian cheers.

"And so?" Mary prompts.

"How'd it go?" Grace asks.

"I laid down the law. I told her we weren't doing this when Iris needed us to be there for her." I ball my hands into fists, remembering how good it felt to stand up to my mother and assert myself. Not that I hadn't done it before, but that had been after being pushed to the breaking point. I'd been upset, furious, screaming. This time I'd been calm and measured and clear, with Rhiannon by my side. "And then I told her the same thing I told Jake."

Jake, who'd shown up about a week after Oliver's birth with a slightly pitiful olive branch in the form of a Star Wars onesie.

You already had him? I thought you weren't even due yet!

Points to him for actually remembering my due date, I guess, but it was going to take more than a Star Wars onesie to make up for the rest of it.

"I told her I was willing to give her a second chance, but that I wasn't going to be compromising my boundaries anymore, and if she wants to be a part of my and Oliver's life, I need to see evidence of actual change in her attitude and behavior. Not perfection, but progress."

Not perfection, but progress. A phrase I borrowed from my new philosophy for knitting, repeated to myself every time

I knit when I was supposed to purl, or picked up a stitch from places unknown, or skipped a line of pattern.

It's how I stuck with it and finished my first sweater.

And you best believe I texted a smug picture of it to Iris as soon as it was done.

Good for you, baby sis. Happy to be proved wrong. Now when are you knitting one for me?

"So anyway, long story short, it looks like I'm not ready to put away the baby acrylic just yet. Iris wants a sweater for her kid to match his cousin's."

"'His cousin'? Iris had a boy, then?" Grace asks.

"Yep." I chuckle. "But here's a funny story: the inside of her big gender reveal cake was actually pink when she got around to cutting it. A thousand pink onesies later, out comes... Edward."

Rhiannon joins in on my laughter. "Gender essentialism aside, it turns out just because an ultrasound tech doesn't see a penis doesn't necessarily mean there is a vagina."

"Our mom was having a veritable fit about how they didn't have anything *reeeeeeeeady* for a baby boy, and Iris just says 'fuck it' and puts him in the cutesiest pinkest sleeper she had. I'm so proud." I mime wiping away a tear of joy.

Suddenly, Grace seems to remember the original point of our conversation. "So Iris wants a sweater, too? Did you start it yet? Let's see it!"

I hold it up proudly for them all to inspect. I'm about three inches in and already ten times happier with it than my first effort.

"Did you cast this on yourself? Your edge is so neat!" Mary says.

"And look at your tension! So consistent!" Louise adds.

Damian leans in. "And I love the color."

"Acrylic?" Grace asks, doing her level best to keep the judgment out of her voice, bless.

I puff up my chest and smile smugly at her. "Acrylic and superwash wool *blend*."

Grace cheers. "Your first foray into the world of snob yarn! I'll convert you yet!"

"I still can't believe you're knitting *another* baby sweater," Rhiannon says.

I scoff. "Says the woman who knits nothing but socks."

"I'm just saying, give yourself a break and just buy her one. Iris will understand!"

"Ah, but a very wise woman once told me, you can't buy 'hand-knit with love' from a store." I smile at Louise and she preens.

"True, true." Rhiannon nods along. "Which is why I took pity on you and made you this."

Rhiannon reaches into her knitting bag and pulls out the world's fluffiest infinity scarf, draping it around my neck like a hug.

"But this isn't socks!" I exclaim, snuggling into it. It smells like her. "When the hell did you have time to make this?"

"Literally every moment we've been apart. Obsessively. Like a woman possessed. I figured I didn't have much alone time left to get it done before we go full U-Haul lesbian and move in together." Rhiannon laughs, and I realize...

she just brought up the possibility of us moving in together without the slightest hint of hesitation or doubt or fearfulness at the enormity of the commitment. "So you like it, then?" she asks, and her voice is a little reedy like she's maybe realizing the same thing herself.

"I love it," I tell her. "And I love the woman who made it."

Rhiannon and the rest of the stitch n' bitch taught me how to knit, but they taught me something else, too.

They taught me knitting is love.

Every stitch is love. The time we share in the craft, needles in hand, is love. Each skill passed down, each tip and trick, is love. Each finished object, gifted or donated or worn with pride, is love.

And the lesson of knitting is something I live out every day, with Rhiannon and Oliver and my sister and my found family, too.

Love isn't just something you feel, it's something you craft.

Stitch by stitch.

★ ★ ★ ★ ★

Acknowledgments

Thank you to my editor, Ronan Sadler, and the rest of the team here at Carina Adores for their hard work and expertise; to my beta readers, Cathy Pegau and James Hale for their guidance and cheerleading; and to my weekend writing date partner, Sheldon L'Henaff, who was sitting across from me at Remedy Café with his many immaculate drafting notebooks on the day I finally wrote THE END.

Thank you, as well, to everyone who kindly answered my call to share their experiences with abortion services and the American healthcare system when I first started plotting this book way back in 2015.

And last but not least, thank you especially to J, who when we were sixteen told me about her abortion and became the first person in my life to give a human face to this routine, very necessary procedure. You honored me with your honesty that day, and I hope I've done you justice.

*A man who's been moving his whole life
finally finds a reason to stay put.*

*Charlie Matheson has spent his life taking care of things.
Rye Janssen has spent his life breaking things.
But when they renovate an old house together,
they might just find something neither of them has had before:
a home, and someone to share it with.*

Keep reading for an excerpt from Best Laid Plans *by Roan Parrish*

Chapter One

Rye

After sixteen hours of driving and a miracle that prevented his car from dying, Rye Janssen was exhausted and slap-happy, but hopeful.

Around hour three, his cat, Marmot, had realized she could squeeze between the headrest and Rye's neck and bat at his hair as he drove. By hour nine, Rye had consumed so much gas station coffee he was practically vibrating and Marmot had exhausted herself and curled up on the dashboard, snoozing in the sun.

As the road spooled out behind him and before him, Rye felt like he could breathe for the first time in years. He used to love Seattle. As a child, the city had felt like a world of possibility. When had it become claustrophobic?

His car stereo had broken ages ago, so Rye hummed to himself. Then he sang, loud, belting words he hadn't thought of in years, letting the wind rushing by his open windows snatch the sound away.

When Marmot crawled onto his lap and looked up at him with her alien eyes, he realized he was crying. Marmot licked at his chin and he smiled.

"Best decision I ever made, pulling you out of that oil can," he told her fondly.

And it was.

Rye only hoped the decision he was currently making turned out anywhere near as well.

When Rye had gotten the call three days before, informing him that he'd inherited a house from a grandfather he'd never met, Rye assumed it was some kind of scam. He hung up, irritated it hadn't been someone calling about one of the many job applications he had submitted. But after several more hours of phone tag and internet research, eventually Rye believed it.

He had inherited a house in some town he'd never heard of in Wyoming, a state he wasn't absolutely positive he could point to on a map.

In the end, the decision was surprisingly simple. Rye was broke. He'd been crashing with different groups of friends every week since he and his housemates had been evicted two months before. It had been his third eviction, and this time there were no more places to scrape together first, last, and security for.

Throw in the fact that he was pretty much out of cat-friendly couches when he wore out his welcome on this one, and suddenly a house of his own sounded pretty damn appealing. Maybe he didn't know anyone there; maybe he had to google map it; but at least he'd have a roof over his head.

So Rye had packed his few belongings into his untrustworthy Beretta, grabbed Marmot, and hit the road as the sun set over the bay.

When he arrived at the address the lawyer had given him in Garnet Run, Wyoming, Rye thought he'd been punked. Hoped he *had* been, because if this was what he'd just left Seattle for, Rye was utterly screwed.

The house stood in a wind-blasted field surrounded on two sides by woods, with nothing around but a horror movie scarecrow clinging to its post and a pack of chipmunks that seemed intent on taking over the world. Were there tornadoes in Wyoming? Because it looked like one had hit the house.

Rye crept cautiously in the open front door, hoping the roof wasn't about to cave in. Marmot sniffed delicately, sneezed, hissed at her own sneeze, then scampered off to explore.

The interior appeared to be held together by spiderwebs, dust, and a few rusty nails that looked like they'd originated in the Lincoln administration. The walls sagged, the ceiling sagged; the whole damn house looked like it was being pulled straight down to hell by some central sinkhole beneath it. To the right was a narrow staircase, presumably to the second floor, but Rye would be goddamned if he was setting one foot on that obvious death trap.

A doorway beyond that led into a small kitchen, and through that another door led outside, where a porch even saggier than the house drooped. From the back of the house, far away, Rye could see the peak of one solitary rooftop. Had he moved to some kind of ghost town?

He walked a little ways away (because, seriously, the house—god, *his* house—looked like it could collapse at any second) and sank into a crouch, hand clasped across his mouth to keep in the sound of his panicked breathing.

"Fuck, fuck, fuck, fuck, fuck!" He squeezed his eyes shut. "What did I do?"

He was a thousand miles from the only place he'd ever lived. No one knew where he was except the friends he'd been crashing with and some lawyer he'd never met. What little money he had wouldn't last more than a week if he spent it on a hotel, and he didn't even know where a grocery store was. The house would clearly make an excellent playground for Marmot, but Rye would rather sleep in a cozy open grave.

A *hush* came through the grass and Marmot jumped onto his shoulder and butted his head. Her orange tail flicked his back like a windshield wiper.

"Mrew?" Her tiny voice matched her small form but not her fierceness.

"It'll be okay," he assured her. "I'll figure something out."

Rye stood slowly so he wouldn't displace Marmot and did what he'd learned to do over years of evictions, challenging roommates, getting fired, getting robbed, and getting dumped. He looked at the situation and chose to acknowledge all the dimensions of it.

Dimensions (as he thought of them) weren't positive or negative. They were simply the truth of how he felt about things.

"It smells good here, hmm? Fresh air and trees and shit," Rye said firmly, eyes searching the landscape.

Marmot purred against his neck.

"And we've got all this space to ourselves. I bet we could yell and no one would care." The sinister implications of that hung in the air, and Rye acknowledged them too. "I could walk around naked whenever I want. Once it gets warmer, anyway. And, hey, we could barbecue outside. I'll just, like, learn how to make a fire. And barbecue."

Marmot perked up at that.

"Yeah, I'll make you chicken. Or... I dunno...wild birds? Maybe you'll catch a bird and...well, then you'd probably just eat it raw. Gross, dude. Still, we can make s'mores. And...and..."

Rye wracked his brain for more dimensions.

He couldn't stay in a hotel. He wasn't about to go back to Seattle, where nothing awaited him but no job and the search for another couch to crash on. This property and the crumbling ruin on it were all he had.

"Marmot," Rye said. "We're gonna figure out how to build a house."

Rye unrolled his sleeping bag in the corner of the living room that looked in least imminent danger of collapse.

Marmot curled inside the sleeping bag with him, her tiny weight a great comfort.

Then Rye did what anyone who'd spent their whole life figuring shit out for themselves would do: he went on YouTube and looked up *how to build a house.*

The results were overwhelming, and mainly featured teams of very strong-looking men hoisting walls in groups of seven or eight, so Rye refined his search.

How to fix a house that's falling down alone.

Not good.

How to fix a house that's been abandoned alone.

Very not good.

How to fix a hell site that's clearly been blasted by an otherworldly curse. Alone.

Interesting ghost hunter videos that he bookmarked for later perusal, but not useful.

Rye sighed. He didn't want to waste his phone battery but panic was starting to creep in again, so he put on Riven's first album and let himself listen to his favorite three tracks to distract himself enough to go to sleep.

Theo Decker's voice sank into him, honey warm and sharp as a razor. The album was years old, but it soothed him every time. Now, it helped drown out the terrifying sounds that Rye assumed were nature.

They definitely *weren't* the creepy scarecrow becoming animate in the moonlight and hunting for prey. They certainly were *not* wolves or bears or whateverthefuck terrifying animals lived in Wyoming coming to eat him and Marmot. And they absolutely, one hundred percent, *weren't* a mob of torch-wielding villagers coming to spit the clueless city boy and roast him over their ravenous flames. Nope.

"Everything's fine. It's just nature," Rye told Marmot, whose sleeping purrs indicated that she wasn't the one who required reassurance.

Theo Decker sang, and Rye fixed his whole attention on the music, squeezed his eyes closed tight against the darkness, pulled the sleeping bag over his ears, and tried to sleep in the crumbling house that was now his only home.

Chapter Two

Charlie

In the thin light of dawn, Charlie Matheson woke up gasping. The dream was an old, familiar haunt of meat and bones and loss, and he shook it loose like a spiderweb. It didn't do any good to linger on dreams, good or bad.

Instead, he ran. Out his kitchen door and through woods springing to life after winter's long spell. Up and up the rock-strewn path to the promontory, Lake Linea still half-frozen far below. Up here, the air was thin, and Charlie's temples pounded with exertion. Up here, he was a dot, blasted to nothingness by immensity.

Not responsible for anything or anyone.

But as the sun crested the trees, Charlie couldn't afford

to be nothing anymore. He *was* responsible for things, so he made himself head for home.

Inside the kitchen door sat Jane, waiting impatiently for her breakfast. Her black and gray fur was ruffled like she'd just writhed herself awake, but the tufts at the tips of her ears stood straight up as always. She meowed at him, a sound like tearing metal, and he bent to offer her his hand. She twined herself around his ankles instead, rumbling a purr of welcome and demand.

"Hi, baby," he cooed to the huge cat, and scratched between her tufty ears.

A drop of sweat dripped off his nose and landed on her paw. She looked up at him as if he'd defiled her.

"Sorry, I'm sorry," he soothed, and Jane, placated, jumped onto the counter so she was at kissing height.

Charlie had never let anyone else see him do this. He couldn't be sure, but he'd always imagined that the sight of a very large man exchanging nose bumps and whisker kisses with a very large cat might be cause for amusement. And Charlie and Jane took the ritual seriously.

Even on the counter, Jane had to go up on her back legs and Charlie had to bend down. They locked eyes, Jane's glittering green to Charlie's placid hazel, and Jane ever so slowly bumped Charlie's nose with her own—a tiny, cool press, her luminous eyes so close to his own that Charlie imagined he might follow the rivers of color inside her. He slow-blinked once, and she slow-blinked back to him. Then she brushed her whiskers over his beard and he kissed the top of her furry head, right between her ears.

Ritual completed, Jane yipped—a sound very similar to her metal-tearing meow, but shorter and more demanding—and Charlie poured her food.

"I'm gonna take a shower and then get to the store," he told her.

She crunched her breakfast.

"I saw a hawk out at the promontory," he told her.

She crunched her breakfast.

"I'm gonna put you on a leash someday and take you out there with me," he told her.

She crunched her breakfast.

"Okay, maybe I'll just take you to the store and you can be a shop cat and get pet by strangers," he told her.

Her meow of protest rang through the house and Charlie smiled as he stepped into the shower.

Matheson's Hardware and Lumber opened at eight, and Charlie arrived by 7:30 to make sure things were in order. There was always something: the register was out of receipt tape; 12d nails had found their way into the 16d nail bin; the key-cutting machine was out of blanks; someone had spilled coffee in aisle three.

Charlie walked the store, plucking this screw out of that bin, straightening coils of wire, and sometimes just running his fingers over the shelves he'd installed and the inventory he'd ordered. He knew every inch of this place, and there was a comfort to its predictability, even if it sometimes smothered him.

Marie arrived as he was turning on the lights, carrying her blue camping thermos of coffee. She high-fived him, tied on her apron, and shooed him out from behind the cash wrap. She never spoke until a customer entered, saving every iota of energy for the day's interactions.

He'd known Marie for ten years and she was the best manager he'd ever had. Also his best friend. Fine, his only friend. Marie didn't lie and she didn't sugarcoat—mainly because she didn't say much. But when she did, it was considered, concise, and final.

Charlie spent the first few hours of business squeezed into the desk in his tiny office at the back of the shop. It had been a closet when his father ran the store, and Charlie's broad shoulders barely cleared the walls. His father had done all his bookkeeping at home on the kitchen table—perhaps why, when Charlie took over the business, the books had been a hopeless mess.

He processed orders and filed receipts, answered a few emails and returned some calls. This part of the job wasn't something he enjoyed, but it had to be done and he was the only one to do it.

When Marie took her lunch break, Charlie went into the store to do what he liked more: helping customers find the right tools for their projects. He listened carefully to what they wanted to achieve, then walked with them, gathering the things they'd need and explaining different ways they might proceed. He loved problem-solving; the more arcane the project, the better he liked it.

He was just walking Bill Duff through replacing his garbage disposal when he heard a clanking and scraping sound from outside.

Through the glass front door, Charlie saw an ominously smoking car grind to a halt in the parking lot. It looked like it had originally been a late-eighties two-door Chevy Beretta but had since been Frankensteined of multiple vehicles' pieces, many of them different colors and some of them clinging desperately together, helped only by electrical tape and grime.

Charlie winced, fingers itching to put the car together properly—or, perhaps more practically, drive it to the junkyard and put it out of its misery.

Marie was bagging Bill Duff's purchases when the door burst open. In stepped a man Charlie'd never seen before.

He certainly would have remembered.

Long, dark hair fell messily over his shoulders. He was slim and angular, with a slinky walk that made him look like he was made of hips and shoulders. The cuffs and collar of his long-sleeved T-shirt were worn rough and the knees of his jeans blown out. He looked like ten miles of dirt road.

Charlie raised a hand at the newcomer.

"Welcome to Matheson's. I'm Charlie. Can I help you find anything?"

The man's light, kohl-lined eyes darted around, as if Charlie might be talking to someone else, then, looking confused, said, "Uh. No."

He hurried off down aisle one and Charlie let him alone. Some people didn't want help or attention while they shopped, and Charlie was just glad of a new customer—and a young one at that. Business was okay, but with each passing year overnight shipping and Amazon ate further into his profit margin, particularly with customers under forty.

The stranger walked up and down the aisles, muttering inaudibly, swearing audibly, and consulting his phone every minute or so, as if the answers he wouldn't accept from Charlie lay there.

After the better part of half an hour, he approached the register, arms full, though there were baskets and small carts available.

"Find everything okay?" Charlie asked as the man dumped his purchases on the counter.

"Uh, sure."

He sounded distracted and was glaring at the items he'd chosen.

"You need any help with…" Charlie gestured at the hardware equivalent to marshmallows, cheese, and spaghetti before him.

The man raised a dramatic dark eyebrow but didn't say anything. His eyes, Charlie could see now, were gray, and his skin was pale, as if he were a black-and-white image in a color world.

That pale glare lanced him, and he looked away, ringing and bagging things up.

The man swiped his credit card like he was ripping something in half and had to do it again when the machine didn't get a read. He glared at it.

When Charlie handed him his bags he couldn't help needling the man a little.

"Need any help getting things out to your car?" he asked, as he'd ask anyone.

The man glared down at the bags he was holding, then up at Charlie.

"No," he said, like the word was his favorite one and, in

his mouth, capable of expressing every feeling and thought he had.

"Okay, then," Charlie said, purposefully cheery. "Have a good one."

The man narrowed his eyes like there was a barb hidden in the words he simply hadn't found yet.

"Uh-huh," he said, and wrinkled his nose suspiciously, backing out the door.

"Who was that?" Marie asked. Charlie turned to see her lurking in the doorway from the back room.

"I don't know," Charlie said.

But he was damn sure gonna find out.

The glarer was back the next day, bursting through the door in a palpable huff. Marie elbowed Charlie subtly—as subtly as a pointy bone to the ribs can be administered, anyway.

"Welcome back," Charlie said. "Help you find anything?"

The man shook his head, glaring, and walked to the back of the store. After that, Charlie didn't see him for long enough that he got concerned and went to make sure he hadn't impaled himself on an awl or stumbled into the band saw.

When he turned the corner on aisle six, though, Charlie didn't see any carnage. What he saw was the man's back, messy hair tumbling around his shoulders, and his phone screen as he watched a YouTube video that appeared to be about framing in a wall.

Charlie snuck back to the cash wrap without the man seeing him. He helped another customer, sent Marie to cut the wood for Ms. Mackenzie's decking order, and organized an endcap of gardening tools, seeds from the local seed company Kiss Me Kale, fertilizer, and seed starting soil. He was adding hose nozzles to the display when the man walked to the front of the store with a pack of common nails, a hammer, an axe, sandpaper, and two flashlights, even though he'd bought one the day before.

"Do you sell wood?" he asked. "Like, cut wood?"

Charlie nodded. "Yup, any dimensions, cut to any length you want. We don't have everything in stock, but I can get it for you. What do you need?"

"Um, I'm not sure yet."

"Okay. Well, just let me know, and we'll take care of you."

The man nodded, eyes narrowed, and piled his purchases on the counter.

Everything in Charlie wanted to make sure the man had used an axe before and knew how to do so safely. Every year vacationers chopped off bits of themselves thinking that chopping wood meant whaling on a stump they found in the woods. But given how this guy had responded to a simple friendly greeting, Charlie doubted he'd take well to being questioned.

This time when the man left the store, his shoulders were a little lower than before.

Two days later the man arrived just as Charlie opened the store. His hair was messier than ever, and his clothes even more rumpled. There were dark circles under his eyes, and instead of a glare, his face was fixed in a nostril-flared pinch.

"Morning," Charlie drawled.

"Hey, um, can I get that wood?"

"Sure. Tell me what you need and I'll see if we have it or if I need to order it."

The man took out a faded, spiral bound notepad from his back pocket. "I need, uh, 2x4s. About nine feet each."

There were unspoken question marks after each statement.

"And how many of them do you need?"

"Oh, uh." The man squinted, as if picturing the project. "Ten. No, twenty… Uh, yeah, twenty."

"Twenty 2x4s at nine feet each?" The man nodded. "No problem. I can cut those for you right now."

"Okay, cool."

Charlie cut the boards quickly, forcing himself not to ask the questions he so badly wanted to. This guy obviously didn't know what he was doing, and Charlie yearned to get involved.

When he went back out front, Marie was ringing the man up. For the first time, Charlie took a moment to watch him. He was a bundle of energy, fidgeting and biting his lip as he waited. But the longer Marie went without speaking to him, the more he relaxed. His shoulders dropped and his chin lifted, and Charlie saw his nostrils flare as he took a deep breath.

Charlie also saw that he was beautiful. Utterly, heart-stoppingly beautiful. Without the glare, his light eyes framed by dark lashes were tempestuous and deep; his cheekbones and chin were delicately pointed; his nose was strong and straight. And his mouth—cruelly bitten red— was a luscious pout, painted more brightly than the rest of his coloring.

He was wearing jeans and a long-sleeved T-shirt, as he had been the last two times he'd come in, and the lines of tattoos snaked out of his cuffs and collar. Today he also wore a gray bandanna tied around his neck as if to pull over his mouth and nose, and Charlie wondered what DIY abomination the man was attempting that would require such a thing.

"Hey, Charlie," Marie called, jerking him out of his reverie. "Are we sold out of those blue plastic tarps?"

"Yeah. But we'll be getting more in next week."

At least they would be now.

The man shook his head.

"'S fine," he muttered.

"Depending on what you want it for," Charlie ventured, "I have one in the back. It has a small tear in the corner and some paint splatter, but you're welcome to borrow it."

"Oh, um. Okay," the man said. "Yeah, thanks."

Charlie got the tarp and loaded the cut wood onto a cart. He wheeled it to the parking lot, where it was immediately clear that it wouldn't fit in the death trap parked there.

The man came outside, purchases in hand, and Charlie said, "I'll follow you with this in my truck, all right?"

"Oh, it'll fit," the man said.

Charlie raised a doubtful eyebrow as the guy tried to shove one of the 2x4s diagonally through the passenger door and between the seats. It didn't fit.

"I can just drive with the door open," the man said, biting his lip. "No one's ever around here anyway."

He jammed another 2x4 in the same way. All twenty were obviously not going to fit. After he shoved in three more, he kicked at the ground, nostrils flaring, and crossed his arms.

"I can make another trip…"

"Three more trips," Charlie corrected. The man glared. "Why don't you just let me follow you in the truck?"

The guy was either incapable of gracefully accepting help or he was worried about Charlie knowing where he lived. As a big guy, Charlie knew quite well that sometimes people equated *large* with *menacing*.

"Or Marie can follow you?"

But the man just rolled his eyes, so Charlie didn't think it was fear. After kicking at the ground again, he sighed, "Fine." Then, as if it were physically painful for him to utter, "Thanks."

Charlie hadn't heard a more grudging *Thanks* since his younger brother, Jack, had broken his leg the year before and needed Charlie's help around the house.

"No problem," Charlie said easily, a spark of satisfaction flaring inside him that he got to intercede on behalf of this total disaster.

"Marie," he called in the door, "I'm gonna drive this wood to— What's your name?" he asked the man.

"Rye."

"—to Rye's house. I have my cell."

She raised an eyebrow that said *Can't wait to hear how that goes*, and saluted. Charlie loaded the wood into his truck, taking the 2x4s that Rye had put in his car out so the passenger door could close.

"I'll follow you," he said.

Rye's nostrils flared again but he just nodded. The car started after two attempts and Rye set off down the road, car clanking and coughing exhaust. Charlie let a bit of distance grow between them so he didn't have to breathe it in and enjoyed the clear, sunny day.

The window of Rye's car rolled down and Rye stuck his arm out, elbow resting on the door, fingers trailing through the air. The wind whipped strands of his hair out the window too, where it flapped like dark wings.

He turned left on Lennox, right on Oakcrest, and then swung onto Owl Creek Road. It was the route Charlie took to his brother's house. He decided he'd text Jack later and invite him and his boyfriend Simon over for dinner next week. Simon liked a lot of notice for social plans; it eased his anxiety if he had time to mentally prepare.

Rye slowed at the turnoff just before Jack's. Crow Lane was a long dirt path through the trees that terminated in a clearing and a house. A house that looked like the before shot in a home renovation show where a home was saved from demolition.

Had Rye bought the place to fix up? To flip? Certainly not, when he clearly had no experience with construction.

Rye got out of his car swearing at it, shoved his hands in his pockets, and glared at Charlie.

"My brother lives about a half mile south of you," Charlie told him, nodding in that direction.

Rye nodded. He started pulling the lumber out of the

truck and carrying it to the dilapidated house. Charlie followed him, dropping his own armload beside Rye's, on the front stoop.

"Did you buy this place?" Charlie asked, when no explanation seemed forthcoming.

"Inherited it," Rye said.

Charlie's stomach clenched. Had Jack's neighbor been Rye's parent?

"Oh, I'm sorry for your loss," Charlie said haltingly.

Rye waved him away.

"I didn't even know him. My grandfather. I dunno why he left it to me. No one else to leave it to, I guess?"

And he walked past Charlie to get another load of wood from the truck.

"Are you going to live here once it's fixed up?" Charlie asked.

"That's the plan."

"Where are you staying until then?"

Rye raised an eyebrow. "You ask a lotta questions for a total stranger out in the middle of the woods."

Charlie raised his hands, palms out.

"Sorry. Didn't mean to pry. Just, we don't get that many new people moving to town. I was curious."

"Well, I'm not gonna murder your brother in his sleep or anything, if that's what you're worried about."

"I am *now*," Charlie muttered.

For the first time, Rye's mouth quirked into a smile, revealing sharp, slightly overlapping teeth and a dimple.

A mew came from behind Rye.

"I better..." He gestured to the house and the lumber.

"Sure."

"Thanks. For the tarp and the help."

Charlie knew he should just nod and leave but he couldn't help himself.

"This looks like quite the job. Do you have people helping you? Experience in demo and construction? Because if you want—"

"Either you've got a mad hero complex or you're bossy as hell, man," Rye said.

Charlie drew himself up to his full height, which wasn't insignificant.

"Who says it isn't both?" he said. "I'm Charlie, by the way. Charlie Matheson." Then he winked and walked back to the truck.

He only let his eyes flick toward Rye for an instant as he threw the truck into gear, but he thought the man was smiling.

Don't miss Best Laid Plans *by Roan Parrish,*
out now from Carina Adores!

www.CarinaPress.com

Discover another great contemporary romance from Carina Adores.

Charlie Matheson has spent his life taking care of things. When his parents died two days before his eighteenth birthday, he took care of his younger brother, even though that meant putting his own dreams on hold. He took care of his father's hardware store, building it into something known several towns over. He took care of the cat he found in the woods...so now he has a cat.

When a stranger with epic tattoos and a glare to match starts coming into Matheson's Hardware, buying things seemingly at random and lugging them off in a car so beat-up Charlie feels bad for it, his instinct is to help. When the man comes in for the fifth time in a week, Charlie can't resist intervening...

Best Laid Plans by Roan Parrish is available now!

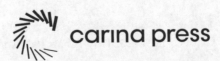

CarinaPress.com

CARRPBLP0421TR

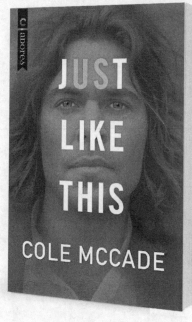